The English Patterns You Got to Know

高中生要懂，你也一定要知道！

破解英文常考句型

想要快速讀懂文章，
請先掌握英文關鍵句型！

前言 PREFACE

學好英文關鍵句型，閱讀寫作沒在怕！

常有同學抱怨，考試時英文題目其實都看得懂，但因為閱讀速度太慢，所以總是來不及寫完。也有很多同學提到，寫作或是翻譯常常不知從何下筆，等到時間快到了，還有一半沒有寫完。

其中的原因到底是什麼呢？原來是因為大部分人在準備英文科時只專注在文法和單字上，而較少去了解一般句子的結構，對句型不夠熟悉的結果使得在考試中光是閱讀、理解就占用了太多時間。反之，讀者若能熟記英文中的常用句型，便能加快閱讀速度，並有助於寫出結構清楚且正確的短文。

有鑑於此，鴻漸文化特邀英文權威大師張翔老師及各大英語學習機構王牌講師易敬能老師共同編撰本書，蒐錄歷年學測、指考以及各大英文考試出現頻率最高的英文句型精華，搭配與主題密切相關的經典題目與解析。只要熟讀本書，便能在各大考試中，一舉提高克漏字選填、閱讀測驗、中翻英、英文作文四大類型題目的作答速度與準確度。

本書自企劃之初，即以貼近考生的需求為考量，在市面上眾多的句型書中，唯有這本，最適合想在短時間內補強重要觀念，達成考試目標的你。

【本書特色】

(1) 貼心為讀者排出4週共28天的讀書進度，一天一個主題，內容完整而有系統，幫助考生及一般英語學習者善用寶貴的時間做最有效的學習。

(2) 每個句型均搭配簡明易懂的觀念透析及豐富例句，重要文法貫串其中，無論是作為考前總複習，或是平時作獨立單元查閱之用，本書都是最佳選擇。

(3) 有別於坊間的句型書，本書捨棄題海作戰，每個句型附上5題以內的關鍵練習題。因為寫得完，當然願意寫，讓你輕輕鬆鬆打下堅強實力。

(4) 超值附錄高分寫作妙用句，讓你寫作不卡關，自信迎戰各種主題的英文作文；另附句型背誦卡，隨身好攜帶，通勤、零碎時間也能即時複習。

學習英文不能強記背誦，28天的英文句型課，絕對是一場精彩絕倫的豐盛饗宴，讓您滿載而歸，英文功力更深厚一層。這是一本適合英語考前衝刺的教戰手冊，帶您輕鬆突破句型文法學習瓶頸，謹獻給孜孜不倦的讀者們，希望本書能在您奮力苦戰的英語學習路上，助您一臂之力，奪得佳績，並在準備考試的過程中，學到「真正的英語」！

鴻漸文化 謹識

USER'S GUIDE

使用說明

1 超高效句型速記

帶讀者在30秒到1分鐘內快速瀏覽句型公式及精選例句，學習效率NO.1！

令某人……的是

to one's + 心理名詞

- To no one's surprise, it has enjoyed similar popularity.【學測】
  毫不令人意外的是，它受到同樣的歡迎。

2 觀念提點與豐富例句

名師提點句型重點，搭配豐富例句與補充，適合想要補強文法觀念的讀者。

1. 定冠詞 the 可和某些形容詞組成名詞詞組，用來表示具有該特徵的「一群人」，此時「the + 形容詞」為複數名詞，使用複數動詞。常見用法包括：

the deaf 聾人	the dead 死者	the blind 盲者
the young 年輕人	the weak 弱者	the old 老人
the strong 強者	the sick 病患	the wounded 傷患
the killed 被殺者	the injured 受傷者	the living 活著的人
the unemployed 失業族群	the oppressing 壓迫者	the oppressed 被壓迫者

- The disabled used to be confined to very few places.
  （以往身心障礙人士被侷限在少數地方。）

3 本書使用英文縮寫與符號對照表

S 主詞	V 動詞	VR 原形動詞	V-ed 動詞過去式	V-ing 現在分詞	Vp.p. 過去分詞
N 名詞	O 受詞	OC 受詞補語	adj. 形容詞	adv. 副詞	( )括號內 字詞可省略

4 獨家！陷阱題直擊

陷阱題總是害你與高分失之交臂？本書特別收錄考生容易誤選的題目，提醒你一定要小心！

陷阱題直擊

1. The good ________ the enemy of the best.
（自滿是精益求精的敵人。）
(A) are
(B) is
(C) will be
(D) has been

1. 本題 the good 為抽象名詞，表達「良好」的概念，並非指一群人，因此動詞應為單數，而非複數。又因本句在敘述一般性事實，故使用現在簡單式。

答案：(B) is

5 題題附解，自修不求人

練習題皆附上中文翻譯與詳細解說，就像請了英文家教一樣！

Level One

實力養成

1. 傑夫昨天面試遲到了。令他鬆一口氣的是，面試官沒有生氣。
中翻英：________

2. 儘管吉米認真工作，令他遺憾的是，他還是被裁員了。
中翻英：________

3. Zoe was bitten by a dog. ________, the pet owner did not apologize at all.
(A) For her anger (B) To her angrily
(C) With her anger (D) To her anger

4. ________, they decided to marry on the spur of the moment.
(A) For our surprising (B) On our surprise
(C) To our surprise (D) In our surprise

5. Winnie came across her old friend on the street. ________, she couldn't recall his name.
(A) Much to her embarrassment (B) To her much embarrassment
(C) To embarrass her (D) In her embarrassment

答案

1. Jeff was late for his interview yesterday. To his relief, the interviewer did not get upset.
2. Although Jimmy worked very hard, to his regret, he was still laid off.
3. (D) To her anger
柔依被狗咬。令她生氣的是，狗主人完全沒道歉。
解析 anger 是 angry 的名詞。(A) for 表示目的，但本句為「令她非常生氣的是……」，因此不選；(B) To her angrily 應該要改成 To her anger；(C) With her anger 表示「伴隨著她的怒氣」，與語意不合。

Day 01 Day 02 Day 03 Day 04 Day 05 Day 06 Day 07

25

6 為您規劃好完整讀書進度

本書將92組常考句型分為4大篇，每篇再依文法主題訂出7天進度，讀者只要按部就班研讀，即能打造出堅強英文實力。

USER'S GUIDE

使用說明

7
超值附錄第一發「高分寫作必備句型」

提供寫作最常用到的轉折詞與妙用句型，從此下筆腦筋不打結，輕鬆寫出邏輯清楚的英文作文！

Appendix 附錄 高分寫作必備句型

斷定

As far as + S + be + concerned, S + V	就……而言，……
Certainly, S + V	當然，……
For whatever reasons, S + V	無論如何，……
Granted that + S + V	假定……；就算……
Generally speaking, S + V	一般而言，……
I am convinced that...	我相信……
Indeed, S + V, but S + V	沒錯，……，但是……
It is generally agreed that...	一般認為，……
It is widely / generally believed that...	一般認為，……
It is (high) time for + 名詞 + to VR	該是……的時候
Naturally, S + V	當然，……
Needless to say, S + V	不需說，……
Of course, S + V	當然，……
There was no exception that...	毫無例外，……
名詞 + is no exception	……也不例外
There is no denying that...	不可否認，……
There is no doubt that...	無疑地，……
To be sure, S + V	誠然，……
Undoubtedly, S + V	無疑地，……

248

8
超值附錄第二發「句型背誦卡」

將全書句型製作成小巧好握的小卡片，讀者可自行剪下，隨身攜帶、隨時記憶。

Smart Cards 句型背誦卡

the + 單數名詞

表全體或抽象概念

- The polar bear is a bear native largely within the Arctic Circle and its surrounding seas and land masses.
  北極熊是遍布於北極圈及周圍海域和土地的本土熊類。
- The average visitor to the Middle East finds camels fascinating.
  一般前往中東的遊客都深深地為駱駝著迷。

1

the + adj.

形容詞作名詞（集合用法）

- The rich are not always happier than the poor.
  富人未必都比窮人幸福。
- The homeless are a diverse group facing many difficulties.
  街友是一群面臨著許多困境的多元化族群。

2

①名詞 + 現在分詞 / 過去分詞
②形容詞 + 現在分詞 / 過去分詞
③副詞 + 現在分詞 / 過去分詞
④形容詞 + 單數名詞-ed
⑤數量 + 單數名詞

複合形容詞

- Wedding planning is very time-consuming.
  籌備婚禮非常耗時。
- Smart phones are now in widespread use.
  智慧型手機目前被廣泛使用。
- He is a kind-hearted old man.
  他是一個好心的老人。

3

so + adj. / adv. + as to + VR
so + adj. / adv. + that + 子句
such + a + (adj.) + N + that + 子句

如此……以致於……

- Sam was so lazy as to enrage his supervisor.
  山姆懶散到使他上司發怒了。
- Jason ran so fast that no one could catch up with him.
  傑森跑得很快，以致於沒有人可以追得上他。
- He is such an honest man that everybody trusts him.
  他很誠實，以致於（所以）大家都相信他。

4

adj. / adv. + enough + to VR

足夠去……

- It is warm enough to swim.
  天氣夠溫暖可以去游泳了。
- Does he sing well enough to attend the *American Idol* show?
  他唱歌有好到可以參加《美國偶像》嗎？

5

to one's + 心理名詞

令某人……的是

- To no one's surprise, it has enjoyed similar popularity.【學測】
  毫不令人意外的是，它受到同樣的歡迎。
- I ordered a dress online, but, much to my disappointment, it was not as beautiful as it looked on the website.
  我網購了一件洋裝，但令我非常失望的是，它並沒有網站上看起來這麼漂亮。

6

Contents

目錄

Level Three 實力篇 129

Level Four 進階篇 197

Level One

基礎篇1

The English Patterns You Got to Know

Day 1 名詞句型

Day 2 形容詞句型

Day 3 介系詞句型

Day 4 對等連接詞句型

Day 5 代名詞句型

Day 6 助動詞句型

Day 7 關係詞句型

DAY 01 名詞句型

句型速記 1 表全體或抽象概念

the + 單數名詞

- The polar bear is a bear native largely within the Arctic Circle and its surrounding seas and land masses.
  北極熊是遍布於北極圈及周圍海域和土地的本土熊類。
- The average visitor to the Middle East finds camels fascinating.
  一般前往中東的遊客都深深地為駱駝著迷。

1. the + 單數名詞
= a + 單數名詞
= 複數名詞
「定冠詞 the + 單數可數名詞」可表示全體。此用法等於「不定冠詞 a + 單數可數名詞」，也等於複數可數名詞。

- The dog is a useful animal.
  = A dog is a useful animal.
  = Dogs are useful animals
  （狗是一種有用的動物。）
- The scallop lies on the floor of the ocean in shallow to fairly deep water.
  = A scallop lies on the floor of the ocean in shallow to fairly deep water.
  = Scallops lie on the floor of the ocean in shallow to fairly deep water.
  （扇貝遍布於從淺海到深海的海底。）

2. 有些「the + 單數可數名詞」可以表示該名詞本身的特色、能力或性質。

- What is learned in the cradle is carried to the grave.
  （幼年所學，終生不忘。）

⇨cradle 是「搖籃」，加上定冠詞後，可解釋為「幼年」的意思；而 grave 是「墳墓」，加上定冠詞後，可表示「死亡」的意思。

1. 恐怖分子對美國的攻擊極具新聞性。

中翻英：________________________________

2. 鋼琴是透過鍵盤彈奏的樂器。

中翻英：________________________________

3. If you hold them by the stalk, the pear ________ thickest at the bottom, while the apple ________ thickest in the middle.
(A) is ; is (B) are ; are
(C) will be ; will be (D) would be ; would be

4. From an environmental perspective, the shark ________ endangered animals for years.
(A) is (B) are (C) has been (D) have been

答案

1. The terrorist attack on the United States is highly newsworthy.

2. The piano is a musical instrument played by means of a keyboard.

3. (A) is ; is
如果握住果柄，梨子在底部最厚，但蘋果卻是中間部位最厚。
解析 此句在闡述事實，時態應為現在簡單式。此外，the pear 雖表整體，但屬單數，因此答案為(A) is ; is。

4. (C) has been
就環境的觀點而言，鯊魚已經瀕臨絕種好幾年了。
解析 本句有關鍵字 for years，表示從過去持續到現在的狀態，時態應為現在完成式。另外，the shark 的動詞應用單數，答案為(C) has been。

形容詞作名詞（集合用法）

the + adj.

- The rich are not always happier than the poor.
  富人未必都比窮人幸福。
- The homeless are a diverse group facing many difficulties.
  街友是一群面臨著許多困境的多元化族群。

觀念透析

1. 定冠詞 the 可和某些形容詞組成名詞詞組，用來表示具有該特徵的「一群人」，此時「the + 形容詞」為複數名詞，使用複數動詞。常見用法包括：

the deaf　聾人	the dead　死者	the blind　盲者
the young　年輕人	the weak　弱者	the old　老人
the strong　強者	the sick　病患	the wounded　傷患
the killed　被殺者	the injured　受傷者	the living　活著的人
the unemployed　失業族群	the oppressing　壓迫者	the oppressed　被壓迫者

- The disabled used to be confined to very few places.
  （以往身心障礙人士被侷限在少數地方。）
- The sick sometimes feel desperate.
  （病人有時會感到絕望。）

2. 當「the + 形容詞」指的是某個人或是一個抽象概念時，則屬於單數名詞，應使用單數動詞。

- Is the accused guilty?
  （該名被告有罪嗎？）
- The unknown is often feared.
  （未知的事物經常令人恐懼。）

Day 01 Day 02 Day 03 Day 04 Day 05 Day 06 Day 07

1. The good ________ the enemy of the best.
（自滿是精益求精的敵人。）
(A) are
(B) is
(C) will be
(D) has been

1. 本題 the good 為抽象名詞，表達「良好」的概念，並非指一群人，因此動詞應為單數，而非複數。又因本句在敘述一般性事實，故使用現在簡單式。

答案：(B) is

1. 一般人認為受壓迫人士通常為工人，而壓迫者為資本家。

中翻英：____

2. 弱者是信念薄弱（weak in faith）的人。

中翻英：____

3. Some of the living want to believe that the dead ________ still with them so that they feel less lonely.

(A) have been　　(B) is
(C) has been　　(D) are

4. If you compare two people at the same age—one employed, one unemployed, the unemployed one ________ typically much less happy.

(A) are　　(B) is
(C) has been　　(D) have been

5. The deaf ________ with each other by using body language.
(A) communicate (B) communicates
(C) communicative (D) communication

1. It is considered that the oppressed are usually workers and the oppressing are usually capitalists.

2. The weak are those who are weak in faith.

3. (D) are
有些生者想要相信死者們常圍繞身旁，如此才不覺得太過寂寞。
解析 the dead 指「死去的人們」，表複數。另外，題目中「Some of the living want to believe...」使用現在簡單式表示一般性事實，依照語意，子句時態使用現在簡單式。

4. (B) is
若比較兩個同年紀的人，一位有工作，一位失業，則失業者必定較不快樂。
解析 本題 the unemployed 後面接 one 當作代名詞，所以應為單數，(A) are 以及(D) have been 為錯誤選項。又因為句中有 typically（典型地）表示「失業者較不快樂」為一般性的事實，時態上採用現在簡單式。

5. (A) communicate
聾人以肢體語言彼此溝通。
解析 the deaf 指「聾人」，為複數名詞，因此要用複數動詞。

MEMO

DAY 02 形容詞句型

句型速記 1 複合形容詞

①名詞 + 現在分詞 / 過去分詞
②形容詞 + 現在分詞 / 過去分詞
③副詞 + 現在分詞 / 過去分詞
④形容詞 + 單數名詞-ed
⑤數量 + 單數名詞

- Wedding planning is very time-consuming.
  籌備婚禮非常耗時。
- Smart phones are now in widespread use.
  智慧型手機目前被廣泛使用。
- He is a kind-hearted old man.
  他是一個好心的老人。

複合形容詞為兩個以上獨立的字所組成的形容詞，大致分為八種形式：

1. **N + V-ing**：前面的名詞為後面動詞的受詞，例如：heart-warming（窩心的）、peace-loving（愛好和平的）。當句子為主動語氣時，會使用 V-ing 現在分詞。

- It is so heartwarming that soldiers handed food to starving kids.
  （士兵們將食物親手送交飢餓的孩童一舉，真是窩心。）
  ➪「士兵們的行為溫暖人心」為主動語氣，因此使用現在分詞。

2. **N + Vp.p.**：由「be + Vp.p. + by + N」而來，例：handmade（= made by hand 手工的）。

- Amy felt heartbroken at the miserable scenes on TV news.
  （電視新聞上的悲慘畫面讓愛咪心碎了。）
  ➪此句可想成愛咪的心因為電視新聞的悲慘畫面而碎了，屬於被動語氣，因此須使用 broken 而非 breaking。

3. **adj. + V-ing**：後方的動詞為連綴動詞，前方的形容詞則是該動詞的補語，例：good-looking（美貌的＝看起來很美的）、high-sounding（誇張的＝聽起來很誇張的）。

• William talked about his life experiences with high-sounding phrases but no one believed him.
（威廉用很誇張的字眼談論他的人生經驗，但是沒人相信他。）

4. **adj. + Vp.p.**：由「be + Vp.p. + OC(adj.)」而來，此形容詞是主詞補語。例：ready-made（現成的）、clean-cut（輪廓鮮明的）。

• This ready-made suit is smart and elegant.
（這套現成西裝既時髦又優雅。）

5. **adv. + V-ing**：副詞在前，被其修飾的動詞在後，例：hard-working（認真工作的）、fast-moving（移動快速的）。

• Fast-moving cartoons like *Sponge Bob* may impair kids' focus.
（海綿寶寶這類畫面快速移動的卡通，可能會影響小孩的專注力。）

6. **adv. + Vp.p.**：由「be + Vp.p. + adv.」衍生而來，例：well-known（廣為人知的）。

• Brian leaned over, and began to direct the driver to a well-known hotel.
（布萊恩往前傾身，開始指示司機開往一家著名的旅館。）

7. **adj. + N-ed**：由「adj. + N」而來，例：gray-haired（灰髮的）、kind-hearted（仁慈的）。若是**序數**與名詞結合成形容詞時，則不用加「ed」，如：second-hand（二手的）、first-class（最高級的）。

• Sad, hungry gray-haired cats meow loudly in the alley on a rainy night.
（哀傷又飢餓的灰貓，在雨夜的巷弄中大聲地喵喵叫。）

• Groupies always get first-hand information on their idols.
（追星族總是有偶像的第一手資料。）

8. **數量 + 單數名詞**：此名詞必須為與時間、長度有關的單位，例：nine-year-old（九歲的）、three-hour（歷時三小時的）。

- A twenty-year-old tennis athlete died choking on pizza.
（一名20歲的網球選手吃披薩噎死了。）
- *Avatar* is a three-hour movie.
（阿凡達是一部三小時的電影。）

陷阱題直擊

1. The number of ________ people has jumped to its highest level since records began.
（自由業的人數已躍至有史以來的新高點。）
(A) self-employ
(B) self-employed
(C) self-employing
(D) self-employs

1. 自由業屬於自僱行業，英文應為「be employed by self」。當使用複合形容詞時，應寫成「N + Vp.p.」形式。

答案：(B) self-employed

1. 這個令人心碎的電影感動了上百萬人。

中翻英：____

2. ________ pets are cute and fluffy, which can be a problem when it comes to hygiene.
(A) Long-hairing (B) Long-haired (C) Hair-long (D) Long-hair

3. The ________ streets in our town encourage robbers.
(A) dim-light (B) dimly-lighting (C) dimly-lit (D) dim-lit

4. That ________ man is actually philanthropic（仁慈的）.
(A) ugly-looked (B) looked-ugly (C) looking-ugly (D) ugly-looking

5. Ang Lee was able to attract the money necessary to make other ________ films, inclusive of *Eat Drink Man Woman* and *The Ice Storm*.
(A) award-winning (B) award-won
(C) winning-award (D) won-award

答案

1. This heart-breaking movie touched / moved millions of people.

2. (B) Long-haired
長毛寵物又可愛又毛茸茸的，有可能會造成衛生問題。
解析 長毛的名詞 long hair 若當形容詞，應把名詞加上 ed，變成「adj. + N-ed」，答案為(B) Long-haired。

3. (C) dimly-lit
本鎮昏暗的街道讓搶匪有可趁之機。
解析 「街道昏暗」的原句應為「The streets are lit dimly」，屬被動句，改寫成複合形容詞時，應採用「adv. + Vp.p.」的形式。答案為(C) dimly-lit。

4. (D) ugly-looking
那個醜男事實上非常有慈悲心。
解析 「他長得很醜」英文應為「He looks ugly.」，改成複合形容詞時，要用「adj. + V-ing」的形式，答案為(D) ugly-looking。

5. (A) award-winning
李安得以募集到足夠的資金，好拍攝其他獲獎的影片，包括《飲食男女》及《冰風暴》。
解析 「電影獲獎」英文應為「Films win awards」，屬主動語氣，改寫成複合形容詞時，應用「N + V-ing」的形式，注意這裡的名詞須用單數，答案為(A) award-winning。

句型速記 2 如此……以致於……

so + adj. / adv. + as to + VR

so + adj. / adv. + that + 子句

such + a + (adj.) + N + that + 子句

- Sam was so lazy as to enrage his supervisor.
  山姆懶散到使他上司發怒了。
- Jason ran so fast that no one could catch up with him.
  傑森跑得很快，以致於沒有人可以追得上他。
- He is such an honest man that everybody trusts him.
  他很誠實，以致於（所以）大家都相信他。

1. **so + adj. / adv. + as to + VR**：so 為副詞，後方接形容詞或副詞來加強語氣，並且用「as to + 原形動詞」來表示結果。
   - Kate spoke so loudly as to be heard by everyone.
     （凱特講話這麼大聲，所有人都聽到了。）

2. **so + adj. / adv. + that + 子句**：so 為副詞，後接形容詞或副詞來加強語氣，並且用「that + 子句」表示結果。
   - Sam just fell out of love. He was so sad that he was not in the mood to eat.
     （山姆剛結束一段戀情。他難過到吃不下飯。）

3. **such + a + (adj.) + N + that + 子句**：本句型與「so + adj. + that + 子句」的差別在於，such 為形容詞，後面必須接名詞，並與「that + 子句」搭配，來表示「如此……以致於……」。
   - It is such an uncommon meteor shower that none of us will miss it.
     （這場流星雨太罕見，我們都不想錯過。）

陷阱題直擊

1. We took off our shoes ________ avoid scratching the newly finished floors.
（我們趕緊脫鞋，避免刮到新鋪好的地板。）
(A) so immediate as to
(B) immediate so as to
(C) so immediately as to
(D) immediately so as to

1. 本句中「...avoid scratching the newly finished floors」表「目的」（為了不要刮到新鋪好的地板），而非「如此……以致於……」所表達的「後果」。因此不該用「be so + adj. / adv. + as to + VR」句型，而是用 so as to（＝in order to）來表達目的。動詞片語 took off 則應該要用副詞來修飾。

答案：(D) immediately so as to

1. iPads are ________ a novel innovation for music and videos these years ________ they have become popular among young people.
(A) so ; that (B) such ; that
(C) so ; as to (D) enough ; that

2. Lee is able to build ________ cross-cultural influence that he is popular across many countries.
(A) so huge (B) such huge a
(C) such a huge (D) too huge a

3. John had tried so hard ________
(A) that parents are proud of.
(B) send an e-mail message to his wife.
(C) that he won the girl's heart in the end.
(D) if you had found out the truth?

1. (B) such；that

iPad 是這幾年很新穎的音樂及影視創新，因此在年輕族群間很受歡迎。

解析 a novel innovation 是名詞，所以要用 such 來修飾，而非 so。又因「they have become popular among young people」是子句，必須用 that 來連接，答案為(B) such ; that。

2. (C) such a huge

李先生能夠建立龐大的跨文化影響力，以致於他受到國際間的歡迎。

解析 本題與第一題的觀念相同。a cross-cultural influence 是名詞，所以要用 such 來修飾，而非 so。

3. (C) that he won the girl's heart in the end.

約翰非常努力，因此最後獲得了女孩的芳心。

解析 本題解題有兩個關鍵。第一，「John had tried so hard」使用過去完成式，判斷本題有兩個先後發生的過去動作，先發生的動作用過去完成式，後發生者用過去簡單式；第二，句中用 so 來加強語氣，可判斷後半段表示目的或結果，只有(C) that he won the girl's heart in the end 才符合。

足夠去……

adj. / adv. + enough + to VR

- It is warm enough to swim.
  天氣夠溫暖可以去游泳了。
- Does he sing well enough to attend the *American Idol* show?
  他唱歌有好到可以參加《美國偶像》嗎？

1. enough 如果當副詞修飾形容詞或副詞時，必須放在形容詞或副詞後面，並可接不定詞來表示「足以去……」，例如：

- He prayed that, despite fear, his son could be brave enough to face himself.
  （他祈禱兒子儘管害怕，仍能勇敢地面對自己。）

2. enough 也可以放在名詞前面，「enough + N + to VR」指「有足夠的……可以……」。

- I've earned enough money to buy a house.
  （我已賺到足夠的錢可以買房子。）

1. 那男孩跑得不夠快，沒有趕上火車。(enough)

中翻英：______________________________

2. The man was ________ survive the plane crash; almost all of the passengers died.
(A) enough lucky to　　(B) lucky enough that
(C) such lucky that　　(D) lucky enough to

1. The boy didn't run fast enough to catch the train.

2. (D) lucky enough to
該男性幸運地從墜機中存活，幾乎所有乘客都身亡了。

解析 enough 用以修飾形容詞時要放在其後方，進行後位修飾，變成 lucky enough。同時，survive 是動詞，必須以不定詞形式與 lucky enough 連結。答案為(D) lucky enough to。

DAY 03 介系詞句型

令某人……的是

to one's + 心理名詞

• To no one's surprise, it has enjoyed similar popularity.【學測】
毫不令人意外的是，它受到同樣的歡迎。

觀念透析

1. 「To one's + 心理名詞」用以表示「令某人……的是」。此類心理名詞包括 relief（放心）、surprise（驚訝）、pleasure（愉悅）、embarrassment（尷尬）等。可加上 much，表示「令人非常……的是」。

• I ordered a dress online, but, much to my disappointment, it was not as beautiful as it looked on the website.
（我網購了一件洋裝，但令我非常失望的是，它並沒有網站上看起來這麼漂亮。）

2. 此句型中的 to 屬於介系詞，後面接名詞，而非不定詞 to VR。注意以下的比較：

• To <u>our surprise</u> (N), she didn't burst into tears, nor did she rush out of the room.
（令我們驚訝的是，她並沒有哭出來，也沒有衝出房間。）
➩ 介系詞 to 接所有格及名詞，表「令某人……的是」。

• To <u>reduce</u> (VR) the chance of strokes, everyone should engage in regular exercise and consume a diet low in animal fat.
（為了降低中風機率，每個人都應該定期運動，並且攝取低動物性脂肪的飲食。）
➩ 不定詞表示目的。

1. 傑夫昨天面試遲到了。令他鬆一口氣的是，面試官沒有生氣。

   中翻英：______

2. 儘管吉米認真工作，令他遺憾的是，他還是被裁員了。

   中翻英：______

3. Zoe was bitten by a dog. ______ , the pet owner did not apologize at all.
   (A) For her anger (B) To her angrily
   (C) With her anger (D) To her anger

4. ______ , they decided to marry on the spur of the moment.
   (A) For our surprising (B) On our surprise
   (C) To our surprise (D) In our surprise

5. Winnie came across her old friend on the street. ______ , she couldn't recall his name.
   (A) Much to her embarrassment (B) To her much embarrassment
   (C) To embarrass her (D) In her embarrassment

答案

1. Jeff was late for his interview yesterday. To his relief, the interviewer did not get upset.
2. Although Jimmy worked very hard, to his regret, he was still laid off.
3. (D) To her anger
   柔依被狗咬。令她生氣的是，狗主人完全沒道歉。
   解析 anger 是 angry 的名詞。(A) for 表示目的，但本句為「令她非常生氣的是……」，因此不選；(B) To her angrily 應該要改成 To her anger；(C) With her anger 表示「伴隨著她的怒氣」，與語意不合。

4. (C) To our surprise
令我們大吃一驚的是，他們一時興起就決定結婚了。
解析 本句是「令我們大吃一驚的是……」，For、On 及 In 都不能表達這個意思，答案應選(C) To our surprise。

5. (A) Much to her embarrassment
薇妮在街上遇到老朋友。令她非常尷尬的是，她想不起他的名字。
解析 若想加強語氣，應該將 much 放在 to her embarrassment 前方（令她非常尷尬的是）；(B)選項的 much 位置錯誤；(C) To embarrass her 的意思是「為了要令她尷尬」，與語意不和。

表原因、理由的介系詞

for
of
with **+ N**
through

- She trembled for fear.
  她因害怕而發抖。
- Nobody ever died of laughter.
  一笑治百病。

1. for、of、with 以及 though 等介系詞後面可加上名詞，此時「介系詞 + 名詞」的組合，具備了副詞的功能，用來表示原因。

2. for 表原因，可接名詞或子句；也可表示目的，此時譯作「為了……」。
- We could hardly see for the thick mist.
  （因為有濃霧，我們幾乎看不見。）

- Kate participated in the beauty contest for the purpose of becoming a movie star.
  （凱特參加選美是為了成為一個電影明星。）

3. with 可指受外在原因而影響到心理或生理的情況，也可單純表原因。

- The little girl was shivering with cold.
  （小女孩因為寒冷而發抖。）
- With John away, we've got more room.
  （約翰不在，我們的空間寬敞了一些。）

4. through 常和 neglect、carelessness、mistake、fault 等詞連用，表示偶然或是不注意、疏忽的原因。

- He made a serious mistake through ignorance.
  （他由於無知而犯下嚴重的錯。）

5. die of 和 die from 皆表示「死於……原因」，但兩者在使用上有區別：

延伸句型：die { of + 病名、飢餓、衰老 / from + 外傷或不注意的原因

- He died of pneumonia.（他死於肺炎。）
- He died from eating too much.（他因吃的過多而死。）

陷阱題直擊

1. It was a pity that the great writer died ________ his works unfinished.
（該名偉大的作家去世時留有未完成的作品，真令人遺憾。）
(A) for　(B) with
(C) from　(D) of

1. 本題容易誤選(C)或(D)，但本句並非表示死亡的原因，而是表達死亡當時附帶的狀態。「作品未完成」為被動語態，因此句型為「with + 名詞 + 過去分詞」。

答案：(B) with

DAY 03

實力養成

1. Nathan's grandmother died ________ a heart attack.【指考】
(A) down (B) off (C) of (D) in

2. ________ the economy down and the housing prices still at record high, most people can't afford a decent house.
(A) In (B) On (C) Though (D) With

3. ________ safety's sake, please step back behind this red line when the train is approaching the platform.
(A) In (B) With (C) Though (D) For

4. Brian trembled ________ fear because he was extremely worried about the safety of his kidnapped daughter.
(A) in (B) with (C) though (D) on

答案

1. (C) of
南森的祖母死於心臟病。

解析 die down 意思為逐漸消失；die off 為相繼死去；die of 用於死於疾病；die in 意思是死於某災難或意外中。答案為(C) of。

2. (D) With
經濟低迷及房價維持在新高點，讓大多數人買不起好房子。

解析 the economy down and the housing prices still at record high（經濟低迷及房價維持在新高點）為買不起好房子的原因，介系詞 in、on、though 沒有表達原因的功能，答案為(D) With。

3. (D) For
列車接近月台時，請退後到紅線後方，以策安全。

解析 for one's sake 為常用片語，表示「為了某人／某事物（起見）、看在某人的分上」，答案為(D) For。

4. (B) with
布萊恩怕得發抖，因為他非常擔心被綁架的女兒的安全。

解析 fear（恐懼）是發抖的原因，所以本題必須選擇表「原因」的介系詞。(A) in 及(D) on 沒有表「原因」的意思，(C) though 則是表達轉折語氣，所以答案為(B) with。

隨著……

with + the V-ing of + 名詞

- With the approaching of Easter, winter departs and spring is near.
  隨著復活節的逼近，冬天遠去，春天翩然而至。
- Glass bottles became more and more popular in France with the opening of the Baccarat Factory.
  隨著巴卡拉工廠的開張，玻璃瓶在法國越來越炙手可熱。

with 有伴隨的意思，後面可接動名詞或名詞，意思是「隨著……」。

- With the returning of the king, the Middle Earth reverted to its original peace.
  （隨著王者再臨，中土回復原來的和平。）
- With the approaching of the voting day, all the candidates are being on edge and making a last-minute push to take the lead.
  （隨著大選日期的逼近，所有候選人都惶惶不安，在做最後的衝刺以取得領先。）

⇨上方例句中，動名詞 returning 和 approaching 也可用名詞 return 和 approach 代替。

1. ________, I grew tired and my mother felt frustrated.
(A) With the passing of the day　　(B) The day had passed
(C) As the day was gone by　　(D) Because the day went on

2. Jack and Rose went more and more despairing ________ the Titanic.
(A) as the swamping of
(B) with the swamping of
(C) , swamping
(D) due to the swamping of

3. ________ the global warming, the global climate has been turning fickle.
(A) Worsening
(B) To worsen
(C) With the worsening of
(D) With the worse of

答案

1. (A) With the passing of the day
隨著一天過去，我疲憊了，我媽媽也覺得很受挫。

解析 (B) The day had passed 為完整的句子，需要連接詞與另一獨立子句連結；(C)選項應改為 As the day went by；本句並沒有因果關係，因此也不能選(D)。

2. (B) with the swamping of
隨著鐵達尼號的下沉，傑克和蘿絲越來越絕望。

解析 as 作為介系詞時，沒有「隨著」的意思，因此不可選(A)；(C), swamping 屬於分詞用法，意思是「使鐵達尼號沉沒」；(D)選項的 due to 只能放在 be 動詞後方來修飾名詞，指「由於」的意思。

3. (C) With the worsening of
隨著全球暖化的惡化，全球氣候日益多變。

解析 (A) worsening the global worming 為分詞構句，意思為「全球氣候造成全球暖化」；(B) to worsen 為不定詞，表示目的；(D) with the worse of 中的 worse 當名詞時，意思為「最糟的事」。(A)、(B)、(D)選項皆與語意不合。

①除了……還有……；②除了……以外

①besides + N

②except + N

- I have a few friends besides you.
  除了你，我還有一些朋友。（我的朋友也包括你）
- Everyone will go except you.
  除了你之外，每個人都去。（去的人之中沒有你）

besides 和 except 都是介系詞，且中文翻譯都是「除了……」，但兩者意義截然不同，在此分別舉例說明：

1. **besides** 指「除了……之外，還包括……」，所以 besides 後面的受詞，也包含在所要說明的範圍內。
   - Besides historical figures, landscape painting was also common in Chinese brush painting.【指考】
     （除了歷史人物之外，山水畫在中國筆墨畫中也很常見。）
   - Besides being sweet and delicious, watermelons are a major source of vitamin B and C.
     （除了甘甜多汁外，西瓜也是維他命 B 和 C 的主要來源。）

2. **except** 指的是「除了……之外，其餘皆……」，所以 except 後面的受詞，不包含在所要說明的範圍內。
   - There will be one presidential US $1 coin for each president, except Grover Cleveland.【指考】
     （除了葛羅佛‧克里夫蘭外，每位總統都會有專屬的一元鈔票。）
   - He blames everyone and everything except himself.
     （他千怪萬怪都不怪自己。）

陷阱題直擊

1. GM foods are easier and cheaper to grow, and appear more beautiful. ________, GM foods are more resistant to warmth and cold.
（基因改造食品生長快速，成本低廉，也比較美觀。此外，基因改造食品也較能抗暖抗寒。）
(A) Moreover　(B) Except
(C) Beside　(D) In fact

2. Mike had no idea what went wrong with the whole situation until a gentleman sitting ________ him explained to him that nodding one's head in Bulgaria in fact means a negative answer.
（麥克不知道發生什麼問題，直到身旁的紳士向他解釋，在保加利亞，點頭代表否定。）
(A) besides　(B) except
(C) beside　(D) due to

1. 生長快速、成本低廉以及美觀和抗暖抗寒都是基因改造食品的優點，(A) Moreover 最能表達補充的概念。另外須注意 beside 與 besides 不同，beside 表示「在……旁邊」或「和……相比」的意思。

答案：(A) Moreover

2. 本題應該選擇介系詞連接 sitting 和 him，因此答案為 (C) beside，表示「坐在他身旁」。

答案：(C) beside

實力養成

1. Mulan used her wits to save her country and prove herself ________ the drawback of being a woman, especially in a traditional Eastern culture.
(A) despite that　(B) in spite
(C) despite　(D) except

2. I picked it up and found nothing inside ________ a crumpled letter written in a neat and beautiful handwriting.
(A) except for (B) besides
(C) on top of (D) rather than

3. No one was able to kill Achilles because, ________ one of his heels, his body couldn't be harmed.
(A) besides (B) in addition to
(C) except for (D) as well as

答案

1. (C) despite
儘管身為傳統東方文化世界中的女性，木蘭仍運用智慧拯救國家，並證明她自己。
解析 (A) despite that 應接子句，而非名詞詞組 the drawback of being a woman；(B) 應改為 in spite of；(D) except 指「除了……之外」，與語意不合。(C) despite 為介系詞，可接名詞表示「儘管」之意。

2. (A) except for
我把它撿起來，發現裡面空無一物，除了書寫整齊漂亮但皺皺的一封信。
解析 本句應為「除了……之外空無一物」，因此(B) besides 和語意相反；(C) on top of（在……之上）以及(D) rather than（而非）皆與語意不合。答案為(A) except for。

3. (C) except for
沒人能殺害阿基里斯，因為除了一邊的腳跟外，他的身體是無堅不摧。
解析 本題語意為「除了腳跟之外，都……」，(A) besides、(B) in addition to 以及(D) as well as 都有「而且」的意思，為錯誤的選項。

DAY 04 對等連接詞句型

句型速記 1　A 和 B 都……

both A and B

A as well as B

- Both Jeremy and Henry are engineers.
  傑洛米和亨利都是工程師。
- Jeremy as well as Henry is an engineer.
  傑洛米和亨利都是工程師。

觀念透析

1. both A and B 以及 A as well as B 為常見的對等連接詞，用來連接相同結構的單字、片語或子句，也就是如果 A 為名詞，B 也必須是名詞，若 A 為片語，B 也須是片語。

- Human health can also be affected by ecological disturbances, changes in food and water supplies, as well as (in) coastal flooding.【指考】
  （人類健康可能受到生態混亂、飲食來源改變以及海岸洪水的影響。）
- Europe's new measures should eventually both reduce the number of animals used in experiments and improve the way in which scientific research is conducted.【指考】
  （歐洲新的措施最後應該能夠減少實驗用動物的數目，並改善科學實驗流程。）

2. both A and B 當主詞時，動詞須用複數；A as well as B 因為強調的是前面的名詞，所以動詞要與 A 一致。

- Both he and his father are short-tempered.
  （他和他的父親脾氣都不好。）
- His children as well as his wife were invited to the party.
  （除了他太太，還邀請了他的小孩參加宴會。）

陷阱題直擊

1. The mayoress as well as her accomplices ________ behind bars next month because of corruption.
（女市長及共犯即將因貪污坐牢。）
(A) are going to go
(B) is going to go
(C) goes
(D) go

1. as well as 連接主詞時，應以 as well as 之前的 the mayoress （女市長）決定動詞為單數，其後方的 accomplices 並無影響，因此(A) are going to go 及(D) go 為錯誤選項；且題目中有時間副詞 next month，時態應為未來式，不可選(C)。

答案：(B) is going to go

1. Adele 和 Eliza 都是我最喜歡的歌手。（使用 both 作答）

中翻英：________________________________

2. Chiufen is known for its scenery ________ its history.
(A) as well as (B) but also (C) except for (D) so is

3. It is supposed that GM foods may have some negative effects ________ positive ones.
(A) as soon as (B) as long as (C) as well as (D) as possible

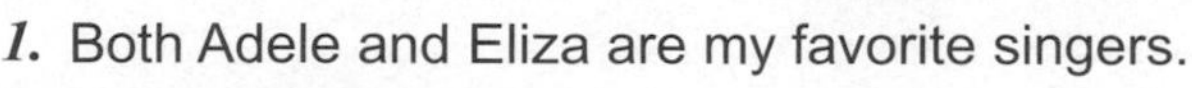

1. Both Adele and Eliza are my favorite singers.

2. (A) as well as
九份以其風景及由來聞名。

解析 scenery 和 history 皆為名詞，因此應選對等連接詞。(C) except for 為介系詞片語，由於句中並沒有 not only，所以不能選 (B) but also，(D) so is 並非連接詞，答案選(A)。

3. (C) as well as

基因改造食品也許同時帶有正面及負面效應。

解析 negative effects 和 positive ones 為結構相同的名詞，因此答案應選對等連接詞。四個選項中，只有(C) as well as 為對等連接詞。

句型速記 2 ①不是 A 而是 B；②不但 A 而且 B

①not A but B

②not only A but (also) B

- She is not my sister but my niece.
  她不是我妹妹，而是我姪女。
- Not only Jeremy but also Henry is an engineer.
  不只是傑洛米，亨利也是工程師。

觀念透析

1. not A but B 的意思為「不是 A 而是 B」，not only A but (also) B 則是「不但 A 而且 B」，其中 A、B 詞性須為相同結構的單字、片語或子句。

- It's not that I don't like your dishes, but I ate some snacks before we had dinner.
  （不是我不喜歡你做的菜，而是我在吃晚飯前吃了一些點心。）
- Grass not only creates simple depictions of the objects he is fond of in life, such as melons, vegetables, fish, and mushrooms, but also uses them as symbols for mental associations of various kinds.【指考】
  （葛斯不僅創造了他喜歡的生物的簡單描述，例如甜瓜、蔬菜、魚以及磨菇等，同時也使用它們當作各式各樣精神連結標記。）

2. not A but B 和 not only A but (also) B 作主詞時，動詞的單複數須由最靠近動詞的一方來決定。

- Not you but I am fired today. Why are you so angry?

（是我被解僱，又不是你，你生什麼氣啊？）

- Not only the children but also their dog likes eating bacon.

（不只是孩子們，他們的狗也喜歡吃培根。）

陷阱題直擊

1. Not only my parents but also my brother ________ me to be an entrepreneur now.
（現在不只我父母，我哥哥也力勸我當創業家。）
(A) is urging (B) are urging
(C) has urged (D) have urged

1. 「not only...but (also)...」連接主詞時，以接近動詞的名詞來決定動詞單複數，因此本題以 my brother 決定動詞為單數；另外本句有時間副詞 now，表示此動作為時間上的一點，不可使用現在完成式。

答案：(A) is urging

1. 這個小男孩不僅會說英語，還會說法文。

中翻英：________________________________

2. Not only her parents but also her sister ________ known all the facts.
(A) is (B) are (C) has (D) have

3. Your forgiving does not benefit him ________ .
(A) but yourself (B) instead of you
(C) rather than yourself (D) except for yourself

4. Wealth lies not in how much you have ________ you want.
(A) but how little (B) instead of how few
(C) but in how little (D) rather than in how little

5. Love is not the strong vow ________ company.
(A) but the simply (B) but the simple
(C) rather than the simply (D) rather than the simple

答案

1. This little boy can speak not only English but also French.

2. (C) has
不只是她的父母，她的姊姊也知道事實。
解析「not only...but (also)...」作主詞時，以接近動詞的名詞來決定動詞單複數，因此答案為(C) has。

3. (A) but yourself
你的寬容，不是利他，而是利己。
解析 instead of 及 rather than 意思皆為「而不是」，與語意相反。 except for（除了……之外），與語意不合。答案為(A) but yourself。

4. (C) but in how little
財富不在於財產多，而是慾望少。
解析 instead of 及 rather than 意思皆為「而不是」，與語意相反。另外，由於「not...but...」為對等連接詞片語，必須連接結構相同的兩個概念，若第一個概念為「in how much you have」，則第二個概念就必須為「in how little you want」，因此(C) but in how little 為最佳選項。

5. (B) but the simple
愛不是轟轟烈烈的誓約，而是平平淡淡的相伴。
解析 rather than 意思為「而不是」，與語意相反。另外，由於對等概念，應用 simple 來形容名詞，與 strong 對應。

3 句型速記 ①不是 A 就是 B；②既不是 A 也不是 B

①either A or B （either 兩者擇一）

②neither A nor B （neither 兩者皆非）

- Now you have two choices. Either you give up your property or you go to jail.
  現在你有兩個選擇，不是放棄財產，就是去坐牢。
- Neither Jason nor Hulk is coming to the party.
  傑森和浩克都不會出席派對。

1. either A or B 是指「不是 A 就是 B」，兩者之中擇一；neither A nor B 則是「既不是 A 也不是 B」，兩者皆非。這兩個句型中的 A 和 B 必須是對等的結構。
   - Teachers either combine volunteer work with classroom lessons or make service work a requirement.【指考】
     （教師可將義工任務與教學結合，也可規定服務工作為必要條件。）
   - He likes neither hang-gliding nor bungee jumping.
     （他既不喜歡滑翔翼，也不喜歡高空彈跳。）
2. either A or B 和 neither A nor B 皆由較靠近動詞的名詞來決定動詞的單複數。
   - Neither the kids nor their teacher was in the classroom.
     （孩子們和他們的老師都不在教室裡。）
   - Either Miss Lin or I am going to talk to you about your family issue.
     （不是林小姐就是我會跟你談談你的家庭問題。）

實力養成

1. Mark can't eat or drink in the library either.（改寫成 neither V_1 nor V_2 的句型）

   改寫句子：______________________________

2. Either Tom Riddle ________ you, Harry, ________ going to survive this brutal duel.
   (A) nor ; is (B) nor ; are (C) or ; is (D) or ; are

3. Neither the lecturer nor the students ________ the textbook well-written.
   (A) find (B) finds (C) was finding (D) were finding

4. Either Susan or her colleagues ________ to attend the shareholding's meeting.
   (A) needs (B) need (C) is needing (D) are needing

答案

1. Mark can neither eat nor drink in the library.
   馬克不能在圖書館裡吃東西或喝飲料。

2. (D) or；are
   不是湯姆瑞斗，就是哈利你會在這場殘酷的決鬥中存活下來。
   解析 Tom Riddle 以及 you 是對等的名詞，再加上句首的 Either，判斷答案必須有 or。在「either...or...」的句型中，以 or 後方的主詞，也就是靠近動詞的 you 來決定動詞單複數，答案為(D) or ; are。

3. (A) find
   講師和學生都覺得課本寫得不好。
   解析 在「neither...nor...」的句型中，以較接近動詞的主詞來決定動詞單複數，本題以 students 來決定動詞為複數。另外，由於句子並無表示過去某時間點，因此不能使用過去進行式。

4. (B) need
   蘇珊或是她同事必須出席股東會議。
   解析 本題為「either...or...」的句型，由 colleagues 決定動詞為複數。另外，need（需要）不能使用進行式，因此不能選(C)或(D)。

MEMO

DAY 05 代名詞句型

句型速記 1 前者……，後者……

the former…the latter...

= that…this…

= the one…the other…

- The generation gap between parents and their teenage children occurs when the former have different values from the latter.
  父母和青少年之間的代溝發生在前者的價值觀與後者不同的時候。
- Theory is as critical as practice, but we are apt to cherish that and despise this.
  理論與實踐一樣重要，但是我們易於珍視前者而輕視後者。
- I am raising two cats, a white one and a black one; the one is much tamer than the other.
  我養了兩隻貓，一隻黑貓，一隻白貓；一隻比另一隻溫馴多了。

1. 指示代名詞用來指出前文提過的人、事、物。常見的用法包括「the former...the latter...」、「that...this...」以及「the one...the other...」。former 指的是前者，latter 指的是後者。

- The mountain and the squirrel had a quarrel, and the former called the latter "Little Prig" .
  （高山和松鼠起了口角，前者稱後者為「小騙子」。）

2. 要注意 latter 和 later 常會混淆，latter 指的是「**兩者之間的後者**」，later 指的是「**時間上較晚出現的、後來的**」。

- If I have to choose between tea and coffee, I'd prefer the latter.
  （若要我在茶和咖啡當中做選擇，我選擇後者。）
- Some of these points will be elaborated in a later chapter.
  （這幾點將在之後的一章中作詳細闡述。）

- 除了「the former...the latter...」之外，也可選擇「the one...the other...」或是「this（= the latter 後者）...that（=the former 前者）」。
- Virtue and sin are both for you to choose while that brings happiness and this causes misery.
（善惡自取，前者致樂，後者致悲。）
- I visited London and Cambridge during the holidays. The one is truly magnificent while the other is sincerely unique.
（我在假日造訪倫敦和劍橋；一個很雄偉，另一個很別緻。）

1. 金錢與快樂皆為人所需，後者比前者更難得。

中翻英：____

2. In Olympic Games, silver medalists feel less happy than bronze medal winners, because ________ feel upset as they believe they were so close to a gold medal, while ________ believe if they were a bit more careless, they would win nothing.
(A) some ; others (B) the earlier ; the later
(C) the former ; the latter (D) the first ; the last

3. Exercise and diet are essential for our health; ________ keeps us fit while ________ provides us with nutrition.
(A) one ; other (B) this ; that
(C) one ; another (D) the former ; the latter

4. The word "record" can be used as a noun or a verb. ________ is pronounced with the stress on the first syllable while ________ on the second syllable.
(A) the one ; the other (B) this ; that
(C) one ; another (D) the former ; the later

1. Money and happiness are both essential for human beings while this (= the latter) is harder to get than that (= the former).

2. (C) the former ; the latter

在奧運中，銀牌得主比銅牌得主更不開心，因為前者相信金牌就在他們垂手可得之處，因此感到不快；而後者相信他們要是疏忽，就將空手而回。

解析 本題選指示代名詞，代替已經提過的人（銀牌和銅牌得主）。(A) some...others... 並無指示的功能；(B) the earlier...the later... 指的是時間上的先後，與語意不合；(D) the first...the last... 用於有先後順序的三者以上。答案為(C)。

3. (D) the former ; the latter

運動和節食對健康都很重要。前者讓我們體態均勻，後者提供營養。

解析 若要比較兩者，應使用「one...the other...」而非「one...other...」；在指示代名詞中，this 指的是近者（latter），that 指的是遠者（former），因此(B)應改成「that...this...」；another 為單數不定代名詞，單純指「另一個」，用於列舉項目還剩下兩個的時候。

4. (A) the one ; the other

record 這個字可當名詞或動詞用。一個重音在第一音節，另一個重音在第二音節。

解析 在兩者之中，若要指剩餘的那一個，應使用 the other 而非 other。指示代名詞中，this 指的是近者，也就是 latter，that 指的是遠者（former），因此(B)應改成「that...this...」；another 代替不特定的單數名詞，用於列舉項目尚有兩個的時候。

①一個…，另一個…；②一個…，一個…，另一個…

①one…the other... （兩者中）

②one…another…the other… （三者中）

- I have two brothers; **one** is in Taipei and **the other** is in Tainan.
  我有兩個兄弟，一個在台北，一個在台南。
- I possess three cars. **One** is a pick-up truck, **another** is a sedan and **the other** is a sports car.
  我有三輛車：一輛是小貨車，一輛是轎車，另一輛是跑車。

1. 當指稱的範圍為兩個人／事／物時，one 指兩者之中的一個，the other 則代替剩下來的另一個。

2. 當範圍為三個人／事／物時，一個用 one，另一個用 one 或是 another，第三個可用 the other。

3. 若東西的種類為三種以上，且未加以限定時，則可使用「one...another...」（一個……，另一個……）。此時不定代名詞 another 代替單數可數名詞，單純指「另一個」的意思。

- I don't like this **one**; show me **another**.
  （我不喜歡這個，給我看另一個。）

4. 它們可以當代名詞代替所指的事物，也可當形容詞修飾名詞。當作形容詞時須注意 another 接單數名詞，other 接複數名詞，the other 則可接單數或複數名詞。

- The three sisters are so much alike that you can't tell **one** from **the others**.
  （那三個姐妹如此相像，以致於你不能區別哪一個是哪一個。）⇨作代名詞。
- A substance which one person is allergic to may not be **another** person's allergen at all.【指考】
  （讓某人過敏的物質，也許根本不是另一個人的過敏原。）⇨作形容詞。

1. Poets may make use of their great imaginative power to compare one thing ________ .
(A) with another (B) to another (C) with other (D) to others

2. I tossed three pieces of clothes in your hamper. One is an overall, another is a sweatshirt and ________ is a bathrobe.
(A) others (B) the other (C) another (D) the others

3. My mom is trilingual. One language she masters is English and ________ one is Hakka.
(A) others (B) the other (C) another (D) the others

答案

1. (B) to another
詩人善用想像力來把一個事物比喻成另一個事物。

解析 本題關鍵字為想像力（imaginative power），可知語意為將某事物比喻成另一個事物，動詞為「compare sth. to sth.」。因為並無特別指定，所以應選不定代名詞單數 another 與 one thing 搭配。

2. (B) the other
我把三件衣服丟進你的洗衣籃了；一件是工作褲，一個是運動衫，最後一件是浴袍。

解析 三件衣服，第一件的代名詞為 one，第二件代名詞應為 another，最後一件應選擇(B) the other。

3. (C) another
我媽媽會三種語言。其中一個語言為英文，另一個是客家話。

解析 總共有三種語言，若只提到其中二項要使用不定單數代名詞，應選(C) another。

句型速記 3 有些……，另有些……

some...others...

- Some are for the project, and others are against it.
  有一些人支持這項計畫，另有一些人反對。

1. 「some...others...」的句型表示「有些是……，另有些是……」，可當作代名詞代替複數名詞，此時後方的動詞須用複數。
   - Some like skiing, while others (like) skating.
     （有些人喜歡滑雪，也有些人喜歡溜冰。）
2. 「some...some...」也可表達同樣的語氣。
   - Some of her money was spent on clothes. Some was spent on cosmetics.
     （她有些錢花在買衣服上，有些錢花在化妝品上。）
     ⇨ 或許還有些錢花在其他東西上。
3. 當語意為「有些是……，另有些是……」時，others 前面不加定冠詞 the。the others 則是表示「其他全部」、「其餘」的意思。
   - My room is decorated with a lot of flowers. Some are red and others are yellow.
     （我的房間裝飾著許多花，有些是紅色的，有些是黃色的。）
     ⇨ 或許還有紅、黃色以外顏色的花。
   - We have 40 students. Some passed the exam, and the others (= the rest) all failed.
     （我們有四十個學生，有些及格了，其餘的都考不及格。）
4. 若要表示三群的人、事、物，可用「some...others...still others...」的句型。

- At the swimming pool, some are swimming, others (= some) are sunbathing, and still others are drinking cocktails.
  （游泳池畔，有些人在游泳，有些人在做日光浴，還有些人在喝著雞尾酒。）

1. 盒子裡有許多皮帶。有些是我的，有些是 Mark 的。

中翻英：____

2. People's diets are different. ________ like beef, ________ like pork, and ________ like fish.
(A) Some ; others ; the others
(B) One ; another ; still another
(C) Some ; others ; still others
(D) Some ; other ; still others

3. Four pupils violated school regulations yesterday. Two were called Casey and Amber. ________ were Joanne and Lindsey.
(A) Others　(B) The other　(C) Another　(D) The others

答案

1. There are many belts in the box. Some are mine, and others are Mark's.

2. (C) Some ; others ; still others
大家的飲食各有不同。有些人喜歡牛肉，有些人喜歡豬肉，還有些人喜歡魚肉。
解析 由於飲食喜好不只三種，而且各飲食族群應為複數，因此本題應選擇(C) some... ; others... ; still others...（有些……有些……還有些……）。

3. (D) The others
昨天四位學童違反校規，其中兩位叫做凱西和安柏；另外兩位叫喬安和琳西。
解析 喬安和琳西為四人中剩下的兩個人，應選(D) The others，表示「其他全部」的意思。

的……（代替前述名詞）

that of

those of

- The price of wheat is lower than that of rice.
  小麥的價錢比米還要低。
- The igloo's walls were solid and airtight whereas those of the tepee permitted a great deal of air to enter.
  雪屋的牆壁堅硬密閉，而圓錐帳篷的（牆壁）可讓空氣大量流通。

1. 在遇到兩者相比較的情況時，若需要避免重複提及所有格，可使用代名詞 that 來代替單數名詞，those 代替複數名詞（不可用 this / these 來代替），of 為表示「所屬」的介系詞。

- A body has been found under a fallen tree in the Atlanta area that authorities say is consistent with that of a missing local woman.
  （在亞特蘭大區的一棵倒樹下發現一具屍體，相關當局表示和當地一名失蹤婦人相吻合。）

2. these 和 those 作代名詞使用的其他例子包括：

- The language women use is different from that used by men.
  （女人所用的語言和男人用的語言並不相同。）
- Teenagers in Taiwan study as hard as those in Japan.
  （台灣的青少年和日本的青少年讀書一樣認真。）

DAY 05

1. The climate here is like ________ Taipei.
(A) that of (B) those of
(C) such in (D) these in

2. Armenia's inflation rate（通貨膨脹率）is close to ________ , National Statistics Service says.
(A) EU states (B) this of EU states
(C) that of EU states (D) those of EU states

3. College students in Taiwan sleep less than ________ because the former spend more hours playing computer games or chatting online than the latter.
(A) America (B) those in America
(C) American colleges (D) them in America

4. The chimpanzee（黑猩猩）is said to have the mental capacity comparable to ________ .
(A) a five-years-old (B) that of a five-years-old
(C) a five-year-old (D) that of a five-year-old

5. The UK's benchmark borrowing costs have fallen below ________ for the first time in 15 months.
(A) the US (B) those of the US
(C) that of the US (D) this of the US

答案

1. (A) that of
這裡的氣候很像台北。
解析 由於比較基礎為兩地的「氣候」，因此必須使用單數代名詞 that 來代替「氣候」，答案為(A) that of。

2. (C) that of EU states
國家統計局表示，亞美尼亞通貨膨脹率和歐盟接近。
解析 由於 inflation rate 為單數，應用 that 來當代名詞（不可用 this）。

3. (B) those in America
台灣的大學生睡得比美國的大學生少，因為前者比後者花更多時間在玩電腦遊戲或上網和朋友聊天。
解析 連接詞連接 college students in Taiwan（台灣的大學生）和另一個與之對應的名詞（美國的大學生）。college students 為複數，可用代名詞 those 代替，答案為(B) those in America。

4. (D) that of a five-year-old
黑猩猩據說擁有相當於五歲人類的智力。
解析 在做比較時，需注意比較的主體必須一致。本題中，五歲和智力為不同主體，無法比較；要比較的是黑猩猩的智力和五歲人類的智力，因此必須使用代名詞 that。此外，當使用名詞來形成複合形容詞時，應用單數名詞。答案為(D) that of a five-year-old。

5. (B) those of the US
英國標竿借款成本 15 個月來首次低於美國。
解析 本句比較英國的 costs 和美國的 costs，因此必須使用複數代名詞 those 來代替「成本」，答案為(B) those of the US。

DAY 06 助動詞句型

大可、不妨

may / might as well + VR

- We **may as well** build reservoirs where water can be stored in case of drought.
  我們不妨建水庫來儲水，以防範乾旱。
- Being such a successful pianist, he **may as well** be proud of himself, but Pletnev is not satisfied with that.
  身為成功鋼琴家，普雷特涅夫大可以自己為傲，但他不以此自滿。

may as well 或是 might as well 意思是「沒有不做的原因」，也就是「不妨、大可」等意思。might 較 may 的語氣更為委婉。

- You **may as well** stay here and wait for another week.
  （你們不妨待在這裡再等一週。）
- He decided the only thing he had to lose was his job, so he **might as well** go all out and do the best he could.
  （他決定他唯一損失的只有他的工作，所以他大可出去放手一搏。）

1. You _________ tell us the truth now, because we'll find out sooner or later.
(A) come close to (B) catch on to
(C) opt to (D) may as well

2. I'm not sure, but if I remember it correctly, I _________ Tom in America last year.
(A) can see (B) must have seen
(C) may have seen (D) may as well see

3. We _________ clean the garage now. We've got to clean it some time and we've got nothing to do at the moment.
(A) won't (B) used to (C) can't (D) may as well

4. He hasn't showed up yet. It ________ that he is sick.
(A) might have been (B) might as well be as
(C) may well be (D) may as well be

5. I ________ kill myself as marry such a rude person like Paul.
(A) may well (B) might as well
(C) should have (D) ought to

1. (D) may as well
你現在最好還是說實話，因為我們遲早會發現事實。
解析 (A) 接近；(B) 追上；(C) 選擇；(D) 最好。

2. (B) must have seen
我不確定，但如果我記得正確的話，我也許去年在美國看過湯姆。
解析 本句中有「如果我記得正確的話」，加強了推測的肯定程度，因此情境助動詞使用 must 較適合；再者，由於本句討論的是過去的動作，因此應選擇 must have seen 來表示對過去的推測。

3. (D) may as well
我們還是清理車庫好了。我們遲早要清理，現在又沒事做。
解析 第一句以 may as well（最好還是……）表示建議，第二句表示清理的原因；(B) used to 意思為「過去總是」。

4. (C) may well be
他還沒現身，也許是因為他生病了。
解析 may / might well be 意為「很可能；儘可，有足夠理由」；(D) may as well be 意思是「大可，最好還是」，答案應選具有推測意味的(C) may well be。

5. (B) might as well
嫁給保羅這種粗人不如自殺算了。
解析 (A) 很有可能；(B) 最好還是；(C) 應該；(D) 應該。「may as well A as B」意思為「與其 B 不如 A」。

忍不住、不得不

can't (help) but + VR
= can't help + V-ing

- He cannot help but walk out of his house to check the abnormal noise from the bushes.
  他忍不住走出房子，查看灌木叢傳來的異常噪音。
- I can't help bursting out laughing every time I see him.
  我每次看到他都忍不住笑出來。

1. can't / cannot (help) but 表示「忍不住、不得不」，後面接原形動詞。
   - Jerome cannot but break up with his girl friend because he is going to emigrate to the United States.
     （因為傑洛即將移民美國，他不得不和女朋友分手。）
   - One cannot but be touched by the ending of the movie *The Bridge over Madison County*.
     （人們不由得被電影《麥迪遜之橋》的結局感動。）

2. cannot help 則直接接動名詞 V-ing（不加 but），同樣表示「忍不住、不得不」之意。
   - Gayren cannot help playing Angry Bird again and again because he is deeply fascinated with this game.
     （蓋倫忍不住一玩再玩憤怒鳥，因為他深深地著迷於這個遊戲。）

1. 我不由得想，我們為了成功而奮鬥的原因是什麼？

中翻英：____

2. We cannot but ________ at the sight of the pictures depicting the people's sufferings at the concentration camps in World War II.
(A) wince (B) evidencing
(C) annoyance (D) forcing

3. Donna ________ her career plan now that she is going to be dismissed because of her poor management.
(A) cannot help reconsider
(B) cannot but reconsidering
(C) cannot help reconsidering
(D) cannot help but reconsidering

4. After years of studying industriously, I ________ fall in love with English.
(A) make up my mind (B) cannot help but
(C) feel like (D) hit upon an idea of

5. Brian could not ________ into tears after he heard his girl friend wanted to break up with him.
(A) help himself with bursting (B) help bursting
(C) help himself out bursting (D) help to burst

答案

1. I cannot help but wonder why we strive so hard to be successful.

2. (A) wince
看到畫中所描繪人們在二次世界大戰集中營中的苦難，我們不禁倒退一步。
解析 (A)倒退；(B)顯示；(C)煩惱；(D)強迫。「cannot help but + VR」等於「cannot but + VR」，答案為(A) wince。

3. (C) cannot help reconsidering
因為唐娜即將因管理不善而被解僱，她不得不重新考慮她的生涯規劃。
解析 cannot help but + VR = cannot but + VR = cannot help (in) + V-ing（不得不），應選擇(C) cannot help reconsidering。

4. (B) cannot help but
在苦讀多年後，我不禁愛上英文。
解析 (A)下定決心；(B)不禁；(C)想要；(D)偶然想到。

5. (B) help bursting
布萊恩聽到女友提議分手後，忍不住哭了出來。
解析 「help sb. with sth.」意思為幫助某人做某事，「help sb. out」意思是「幫助……擺脫困難」，答案以(B) help bursting 較符合句意。

句型速記 3 再……也不為過

can not be too + adj. / adv.

- Winnie thinks that she cannot be too full in an all-you-can-eat restaurant.
薇妮認為在吃到飽的餐廳，吃再飽也不為過。
- One cannot be too cautious while driving at night.
夜間開車盡量小心。

1. 「cannot + V + too + adj. / adv.」意思是「再……也不為過」，或是「越……越好」。這是個反面的說法，字面上的意思是「不可能太過……」。
   - Children cannot be too nice to their parents.
   （孩子對父母再怎麼好都不為過。）
2. 除了 not 之外，也可使用 never、seldom 或是 scarcely 等具有否定意味的字眼。
延伸句型：**can + not / never/ scarcely + V + enough** 再……也不夠
   - We can never praise her enough as a heroine.
   （我們再怎樣稱讚她是女英雄，也不為過。）

1. 女人的鞋子是越多越好。(使用 can't...too... 的句型)

中翻英：________________________________

2. You ________ clear while communicating with foreigners in English.
(A) cannot be (B) cannot be too
(C) could not be so (D) do not be too

3. You ________ begin too soon. The early bird gets the worm.
(A) shall not (B) cannot (C) might not (D) must not

4. Clifford believes he can ________ have too much work.
(A) never (B) always (C) often (D) sometimes

答案

1. Women can't have too many shoes.

2. (B) cannot be too
用英文與外國人溝通時，要盡量清楚。

解析 「cannot...too...」是負負得正的用法，代表「再怎麼……也不為過」，本句的意思是「再怎樣清楚也不為過」。

3. (B) cannot
你最好趕快開始，早起的鳥兒有蟲吃。

解析 由第二句「The early bird gets the worm」可判斷第一句應指要越早越好，可以使用「cannot...too...」雙重否定句型。

4. (A) never
克里夫相信工作越多越好。

解析 除了 not 之外，也可使用 never、seldom 或是 scarcely 等具有否定意味的字，表達雙重否定。

DAY 07 關係詞句型

句型速記 1 凡是……的人

those who + are / V

people who + are / V

- Christmas is a time for us to send Christmas cards to those who live far away.
  聖誕節是讓我們寄聖誕卡給遠方的人們的時節。
- People who have to make a living on their own may envy those who can succeed in the business of their family's.
  必須自立更生的人，也許會羨慕能叱吒於家庭事業的人。

觀念透析

關係子句的先行詞是人的時候，可以選擇 that 或是 who 當關係代名詞。要注意先行詞為 those 或 people 時，只能選 who 當關係代名詞。

- Those who want to watch TV must ride the bike to switch on the TV.
  （想看電視的人必須要騎腳踏車才能打開電視。）
- People who live in glass houses shouldn't throw stones.
  （自己有缺點勿批評別人。）

陷阱題直擊

1. Winnie and Norman in the office are among the best people ________ .
（公司的薇妮和諾門，是我認識的人當中最棒的。）
(A) who I ever knew
(B) who I have ever knew
(C) that I ever knew
(D) that I have ever known.

1. 雖然先行詞是 people 或是 those 時，關係代名詞應該用 who，但是在本題當中，先行詞前面有形容詞最高級 the best，因此關係代名詞應該要用 that。

答案：(D) that I have ever known

1. People ________ in the severe recession are often told they should feel lucky to have a job.
(A) who did not lay off (B) that was not laid off
(C) who weren't laid off (D) that did not lay off

2. Vincent, after having won the election, expressed his gratitude to all the people ________ for him and ensured that he would keep his promise.
(A) who have voted (B) who voted
(C) that voted (D) that have voted

3. The last people ________ Annie wants to give her ________ money to are the bankers.
(A) who ; hard-earning (B) who ; hard-earned
(C) that ; hard-earned (D) that ; hard-earning

答案

1. (C) who weren't laid off
在嚴重經濟衰退時期未被裁員的人，常被告知他們應該慶幸有份工作。
解析 people 當先行詞時，應該用 who 當關係代名詞。本關係子句應使用被動語氣，表示「被裁員」，因此應選擇(C) who weren't laid off。

2. (C) that voted
文森在贏得選戰之後，對所有投票支持他的人表示感謝，並保證履行承諾。
解析 由於 people 前面有 all 作為修飾語，因此應選擇 that 而非 who 作關係代名詞。「投票」為過去發生的事情，應使用過去簡單式。

3. (C) that ; hard-earned
安妮最不想把努力賺來的錢給銀行家。
解析 由於 people 前面有 last 作為修飾語，因此應選擇 that 而非 who 作關係代名詞。再者，money 前面的複合形容詞，應使用「adv. + Vp.p.」的句型表示錢是「被賺的」，答案為(C) that ; hard-earned。

句型速記 2 ……之時

...when + S + V

- No one knows exactly when our history began.
  沒有人確實知道我們的歷史從什麼時候開始。
- What can the police in one country do when criminals escape to another nation?
  罪犯逃到外國時，警方能怎麼辦？

when 在文法上可接三種子句：副詞子句、名詞子句以及關係子句。

1. when 引導**副詞子句**：

when 可連接完整子句來表達動作發生的時間，屬於副詞子句；且因為該子句並非表達主要的句意，重要性低於主要子句，又稱為附屬子句。

- People seem happier and more productive when they are wearing comfortable clothes.
  （大家穿舒適衣服的時候，似乎都比較快樂，生產力也較高。）
  ⇨本句中「when they are wearing comfortable clothes」說明了「seem happier and more productive」的發生時間，為副詞子句。

2. when 引導**名詞子句**：

when 也可以引導名詞子句，做為句子的主詞或受詞。需將子句中助動詞 do / does / did 拿掉並注意動詞時態。

- Many wonder when winter finally arrived in the Lake Region.
  （很多人好奇大湖區的冬季何時降臨了。）
  ⇨本句中，「when winter finally arrived in the Lake Region」作 wonder 的受詞，屬於名詞子句。原問句中的 did 被拿掉，arrive 需要還原成過去式，變成 arrived。

3. when 引導關係子句：

when 可以接在 the day / the week / the month / the year / the time 等有關時間的先行詞後方，引導關係子句，用來修飾先行詞。此時 when 為關係副詞，等於「介系詞 (in、on、at) + which」。

- March 18th, 2005 is the day when I first saw him on the street.
  （2005 年 3 月 18 日是我第一次在街上看到他的日子。）
  ⇨ 本句中「when I first saw him on the street」是關係子句，the day 是先行詞，when 為關係副詞，等於 on which。

1. Can eye movement indicate ________ ?
(A) when are suspects lying
(B) it when suspects are lying
(C) it when are suspects lying
(D) when suspects are lying

2. A bus is a vehicle that runs twice as fast ________ after it as when you are in it.
(A) the time when are you (B) the time when you
(C) when you are (D) when are you

3. 1997 was the year ________ he was born.
(A) in which (B) at which
(C) which (D) on which

答案

1. (D) when suspects are lying
眼球運動可以暗示嫌犯何時說謊嗎？

解析 由於 indicate 為及物動詞，因此後面必須接受詞。答案因此必須選擇名詞或名詞子句。(B)和(C)的 it 為代名詞，但所指的事物並不清楚。(A)選項則是主詞動詞的順序錯誤。

2. (C) when you are

當你追公車時，公車的速度是平常你在公車上時的兩倍快。

解析 本句選擇(C) when you are 來表示時間副詞。(A)須改成 the time when you are；(B) the time when you 須改為 the time when are you；(D)須改成 when you are。

3. (A) in which

1997 是他出生的那一年。

解析 句中 the year 為表時間的先行詞，故須用關係副詞 when 或是「介系詞 + which」來引導子句。表示「在某一年」，英語習慣用介系詞 in，譬如 in 2008，所以本題選(A) in which。

……的方法、方式

the way + { that / in which } + 形容詞子句

- The way (that) they look at the world is different.
  = The way in which they look at the world is different.
  他們看這一個世界的方式不同。

要表達「……的方式」，可使用「the way (that / in which) + 形容詞子句」，此句型又通常可省略 that 和 in which。此外，現代英語中，the way 和 how 不能並存，因此「the way how...」為不正確的用法。

- Inventions, big or small in size, change the way <u>we live</u>.
  （發明，無論大小，改變了我們的生活方式。）
- The way（that / in which）<u>the courses are arranged</u> is special.
  （課程的安排方式很特別。）

1. You can't always get your own way _________ some day you will stew in your own juice.
（你不能總是為所欲為，因為來日終將自作自受。）
(A) that　　(B) in that
(C) in which　　(D) how

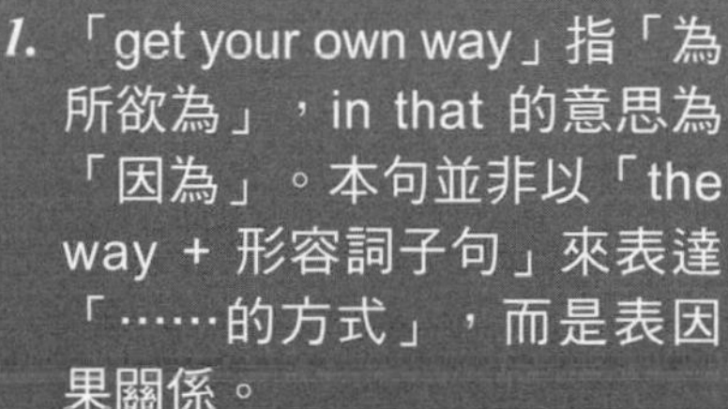
1. 「get your own way」指「為所欲為」，in that 的意思為「因為」。本句並非以「the way + 形容詞子句」來表達「……的方式」，而是表因果關係。

答案：(B) in that。

1. The difference mainly lies in the _________ a language inclusive of are listening, being a copycat and using the language.
(A) ways that children learn
(B) ways which children learn
(C) ways in that children learn
(D) ways how children learn

2. It is _________ that makes you popular or unpopular.
(A) the way that you treated others
(B) the way how you treated others
(C) the way which you treated others
(D) the way you treat others

3. Smart phones changes the way _________ people communicate with one another.
(A) with which　　(B) for which
(C) in that　　(D) in which

4. Benson is in a bad _________ he has been refusing to see a doctor.
(A) way that　　(B) way in that
(C) way in which　　(D) way how

1. (A) ways that children learn
主要差異點在於兒童語言學習方式，包括聽、模仿及使用語言的方式。

解析 關係子句在說明「方式」時，應使用「the way（that / in which）+ 形容詞子句」，本題選(A) ways that children learn。

2. (D) the way you treat others
待人的方式決定人際關係的優劣。

解析 本句用（that / in which）you treat others 修飾 the way。且本句在說明一個道理，故全句應採用現在簡單式。

3. (D) in which
智慧型手機改變人們溝通方式。

解析 溝通方式應該是 the way （in which / that） people communicate with one another，答案為(D) in which。

4. (B) way in that
班森病情嚴重，因為他拒絕看醫生。

解析 in a bad way 的意思是病情嚴重，和拒絕看醫生應為因果關係，因此應該選擇連接詞 in that。

補述用法（非限定子句）

, which + V

, who + V

- I live in New York, **which** is on the east coast of the United States.
  我住在紐約，它位於美國的東岸。
- All of the beautiful scenes were made up by John, **who** was a blind man.
  所有的美景都是身為盲人的約翰編出來的。

1. 本句型屬於關係子句中的**非限定子句**，又稱**補述用法**，目的是提供額外的資訊。關係詞 who 指的是前面提過的人，而 which 則指前面提過的事或物。

(1) 非限定子句（補述用法）：

- "People use this opportunity to vent their frustration with the situation in Tibet, which has been very strict over the last 10 years in particular," said Besten.
（巴士敦說：「大家利用這個機會來發洩西藏情勢的挫折，而西藏情勢在過去 10 年尤其緊張。」）

(2) 限定子句：

- The workers who have finished their work may leave.
（完成工作的工人便可以離開。）

在(1)的句子中，即使將「,which has been very strict over the last 10 years in particular」拿掉，也不會影響主要子句的語意。但如果將(2)的「who have finished their work」拿掉，全部的工人大概就會走光了。由此我們可以知道，當關係子句前沒有逗號時，為限定子句，它將主詞進一步訂出一個範圍來；而加了逗號的非限定子句，則為補充說明的用法。

2. 標點符號對非限定子句很重要。如果非限定子句出現在句中，子句前後必須要加逗點；如果是句尾，子句前面要加逗點。

- I found out the sender of the letter, Hannah, who was living in a nursing home.
（我找到了寄信者是漢娜，她住在療養院。）

3. 非限定子句的關係代名詞，不可以用 that，受詞關代也不可省略。

- He gave me the letter, that I read immediately. （×）
He gave me the letter, I read immediately. （×）
He gave me the letter, which I read immediately. （○）
（他把信交給我，我馬上閱讀該信。）

DAY 07

實力養成

1. Halloween ________ October 31, is one of the most unusual and fun holidays in the United States.
(A) that falls on (B) , that falls on
(C) , which falls on (D) which falls on

2. My only son ________ to France, is coming back to stay with me next week.
(A) , who emigrated (B) who emigrated
(C) , that emigrates (D) that emigrated

3. My father suddenly fell ill and passed away ________ my mother's heart and soul.
(A) which damaged (B) , which had damaged
(C) , which damaged (D) , that damaged

4. He asked God to build him a son ________ aims were set high.
(A) who (B) whose
(C) of which (D) whom

答案

1. (C) , which falls on
萬聖節，正逢 10 月 31 日，是美國最特別又好玩的節日。
解析 萬聖節是專有名詞，不需要用限定子句來限定是哪個節日。非限定子句除了子句前後要有逗號之外，也不能用 that 當作關係代名詞，因此答案為(C) , which falls on。

2. (A) , who emigrated
我移民到法國的獨子下週會搬回來跟我一起住。
解析 因為是獨子，不需使用限定子句來說明是哪一位兒子。非限定子句不可用 that 當作關係代名詞，句中 emigrate 則應該使用過去簡單式來表示過去的動作。

3. (C) , which damaged

我爸爸突然生病去世，這件事傷害了我媽的心靈。

解析 本題關係子句並不影響主要子句語意的完整，判斷應使用非限定子句，關係代名詞用 which，指爸爸去世這件事。再者，由於「生病去世」與「傷害」為同時發生，因此「傷害」應選過去簡單式 damaged，而非過去完成式 had damaged。

4. (B) whose

他希望神能幫他打造出一個目標遠大的兒子。

解析 此關係子句描述心目中理想兒子的樣子——目標遠大，因此須用限定子句。同時為了配合名詞 aim，應該選所有格(B) whose。

更……的是

what is + 比較級

- He speaks English very well; what is more, he is good at English literature.
  他英語說得很好。此外，他精通英國文學。
- The forest turned dusky; what's worse, it began to bucket down.
  森林變陰暗了，更慘的是，開始要下大雨了。

1. 「what is + 比較級」用以表示接下來的訊息值得注意，且與前面提到的事情評價一致，前方如果是優點，其所接的事情也會是優點。

- I was a lucky dog to buy the last copy of this out-of-print book. What's far better, I got it at a wonderful discount.
  （能夠買到最後一本絕版書，我真是個幸運兒；更棒的是，我還拿到很棒的折扣。）

2. 須注意「what's + 比較級」並非連接詞，所以當要連接兩個句子時，除了「what's + 比較級」外，還必須要有連接詞。

- Iris is such a skillful hairdresser and, what's more, she is never conceited.
（艾瑞絲真的是位很熟練的美髮師；更棒的是，她絕不自誇。）

3. what's more 表示接下來的訊息同等重要或更重要，隨著語意可替換為 what is better / worse / more important 等。類似的用法還有：furthermore / moreover / further / in addition / besides / additionally 等。

1. If a writer writes what readers don't understand, he fails as a writer. _________ , he causes confusion and wastes time and effort.
(A) What's better　(B) What's more
(C) What's worse　(D) Therefore

2. Fossil fuels, such as oil or coal, release harmful substances into the air when they are burned. _________ , fossil fuels will run out.【指考】
(A) Otherwise　(B) Therefore
(C) What's more　(D) In comparison

3. This grammar book is so functional that you definitely want to buy it; _________ , its price is reasonable.
(A) What's better　(B) In comparison
(C) What's worse　(D) Therefore

4. Jeremy suffered from severe injury during the car accident. _________ , his insurance company compensated him for all the consequent expenses.
(A) What's better　(B) What's more
(C) However　(D) What's worse

5. She learned everything speedily; _________ , she got promoted for her rapid mastership.
(A) nevertheless　(B) as a result
(C) what's more　(D) in comparison

1. (C) What's worse

若作家寫出讀者不懂的內容，他就不叫作家。更糟的是，他會造成混淆，也浪費時間精力。

解析 本題解題重點在了解前後文的關係，選出最佳的轉折語。由於第一句說明若作家寫出看不懂的內容，就不配稱為作家，第二句則補充更多的缺點，因此可從(B) What's more 以及(C) What's worse 中做選擇，其中「what's worse」更可強調負面的訊息。

2. (C) What's more

化石燃料，例如油或煤，在燃燒時會把有毒物質釋出到空氣中。甚者，化石燃料將會耗盡。

解析 (A)為「否則」；(B)為「因此」；(C)為「還有」；(D)為「相比之下」。本題須檢視前後文關係以選出正確答案，「化石燃料將會耗盡」為「有毒物質釋出到空氣中」之外的又一個缺點，(C) What's more 才符合句意。

3. (A) What's better

這本文法書很好用，你一定會想買。再者，它的價格很合理。

解析 價格合理為補充說明，和「好用」同屬優點，因此(A) What's better 為正確答案。

4. (C) However

傑洛米車禍受重傷，但保險公司支付所有相關費用。

解析 「受重傷」和「支付所有相關費用」兩件事為一好一壞，因此(C) However（然而）是最佳選項。

5. (B) as a result

她學習速度很快；因此因為很快上手而被升職。

解析 本題「學習速度」和「被升職」屬於因果關係，應選(B) as a result。

MEMO

Level Two

基礎篇2

The English Patterns You Got to Know

Day 1 動名詞句型

Day 2 不定詞句型

Day 3 分詞句型 I

Day 4 分詞句型 II

Day 5 特殊動詞用法 I

Day 6 特殊動詞用法 II

Day 7 表時間句型

DAY 01 動名詞句型

句型速記 1 做／喜歡／從事某運動或活動

S + go / enjoy + V-ing

S + do + (the) + V-ing

- Vivian went canoeing when she backpacked in California last year.
  薇薇安去年在加州自助旅行時，玩了獨木舟。
- Harry enjoys being a seeker in the match.
  哈利喜歡在比賽中當搜捕手。
- I do some jogging every morning.
  我每天早晨跑步。

動名詞顧名思義，是將動詞轉成名詞形態，放在主詞、受詞或補語的位置。在 do、go 和 enjoy 之後，可表示「某活動」。

- The Middle Easterner traveling abroad enjoys <u>seeing cowboys</u>.
  （出國旅遊的中東人喜歡看美國牛仔。）
- Everyone is surprised that Hank has been doing <u>the mopping</u> all by himself secretly all these years after the restaurant is closed.
  （大家都很訝異漢克這幾年來，在餐廳關門後，都偷偷地自己擦地板。）
- Another favorite spot includes Cemetery Reef, where you can go <u>snorkeling</u> right from a pretty beach.
  （另一個熱門景點是聖姆特里礁，你可以直接從美麗的海灘上直接下去浮潛。）

1. People enjoy ________ to say the nonsensical phrases regardless of sex and age.
(A) attempting (B) being attempted
(C) to attempt (D) to be attempted

2. They don't enjoy ________ for my bad attitude.
(A) around me (B) being me
(C) being around me (D) around

3. In Africa you can ________ while on safari and this way you get to do both.
(A) go to watch birds (B) go bird-watching
(C) go birds-watching (D) go to watch bird

4. Zoe is the kind of person who ________ and never listens.
(A) does all the talk (B) did all the talking
(C) did all the talk (D) does all the talking

1. (A) attempting
不論性別年齡，大家都喜歡嘗試說些荒謬的字眼。
解析 enjoy 後面只接動名詞，不接不定詞；依照語意，本題應選擇主動語氣（attempting），而非被動語氣（being attempted）。

2. (C) being around me
他們因為我態度不好，不喜歡跟我共處。
解析 enjoy 是完全及物動詞，後面需要名詞或動名詞當作受詞，因此(A) around me及(D) around 為錯誤選項。根據句意，應選擇 being around me（跟我共處），而非 being me（成為我）。

3. (B)go bird-watching
在非洲，狩獵時可以賞鳥，一舉兩得。
解析 go 後面可接動名詞，表示進行活動。另外，「名詞 + V-ing」這種複合名詞中，應使用單數名詞，所以答案為(B) go bird-watching。

4. (D) does all the talking
柔依是那種只說不聽的人。
解析 本句敘述一般性事實，且對等連接詞 and 後面的動詞是現在簡單式，因此選現在簡單式 does 而非 did。此外，表示進行活動時，應採用「do / go + V-ing」的句型，答案為(D) does all the talking。

2 句型速記 做……是沒有用的

There is no use + V-ing
= It is (of) no use + V-ing / to VR
= It is useless + to VR

- There is no use crying over spilt milk.
  = It is no use crying over spilt milk.
  = It is no use to cry over spilt milk.
  = It is useless to cry over spilt milk.
  覆水難收。

當表示「做……是沒有用的」時，有下列幾個常見的英文句型，非常好用。其中 use 是名詞，useless 是形容詞：

1. There is no use + V-ing

- There's no use stressing over something in the past, because there's not a thing you can do to change it.
  （執著過去是沒有用的，因為你無法改變任何事。）

2. It is (of) no use + V-ing = It is (of) no use + to VR

- It is of no use trying again if you have tried every means you can think of.
  = It is of no use to try again if you have tried every means you can think of.
  （如果你想得到的方式都試過了，再試也沒有用了。）

3. It is useless + to VR

- It is useless to talk about financial recovery without solving unemployment.
  （不解決失業問題，討論金融復甦是沒有用的。）

1. 擁有雄心壯志以及遠大的目標是很重要的，但想太多也無濟於事。

中翻英：Having great ambition and high goals are important, ____________

____

2. There's no use ________ . Instead, you need to find a way ________ the problem.
(A) grumbling ; solving (B) to grumble ; to solve
(C) grumbling ; to solve (D) to grumble ; solving

3. It is ________ against Nature, and whoever attempts it must suffer.
(A) no use to fight (B) no used fighting
(C) not used to fighting (D) of not use fighting

4. If you don't dream big, there ________ .
(A) has been no use of dreaming (B) is no use of dreaming
(C) is no use to dream (D) has been no use to dream

5. It is ________ me. I am not the key person.
(A) of no use to persuade (B) not use persuading
(C) of no use persuade (D) no use persuade

答案

1. but it is useless to think too much.
= but there is no use thinking too much.
= but it is (of) no use thinking too much
= but it is (of) no use to think too much.

2. (C) grumbling ; to solve
抱怨沒有用，相反的，你應該找到解決問題的方式。
解析 There is no use...（做……是沒有用的）後面接動名詞 V-ing，另外 way 當「方式」解釋時，後面的動詞使用不定詞形式。

3. (A) no use to fight
對抗大自然是沒有用的，想這麼做的人一定會吃到苦頭。
解析 (B) 應把 used 改成 use；(C) 的句型是 be used to N，意思為「現在／過去習慣於……」，與語意不合；(D) 應改為 of no use fighting。

4. (B) is no use of dreaming
夢想若不遠大，何必要做夢！
解析 本題考的是「there is no use V-ing」的句型，因此(C) is no use to dream 及(D) has been no use to dream 為錯誤選項。此句討論的是真理，應使用現在簡單式，答案為(B) is no use of dreaming。

5. (A) of no use to persuade
說服我是沒有用的，我不是關鍵人物。
解析 「做……是沒有用」的句型可以用「It is (of) no use V-ing」或是「It is (of) no use to VR」；(B) 應改為 (of) no use persuading；(C) 應改為 of no use persuading 或 of no use to persuade；(D) 應改為 no use to persuade 或 no use persuading。

在……方面沒有／沒什麼／有很大的困難

have + { no / little / much } + trouble + (in) + V-ing

- With a boy leading the way, we had little trouble in finding the old castle.
  有小男孩帶路，我們輕鬆地就找到了古城堡。
- They had much trouble tracing the footprint of the beast because of the heavy rain.
  大雨讓他們很難追蹤野獸的足跡。

1. 「在某方面有困難」可以用「have trouble (in) V-ing」來表示。在 have no / little / much trouble in V-ing（在某方面沒有／有點／沒有很大的困難）的句型中，trouble 指困境、困難，屬於不可數名詞，in 則可以省略。
   - I noticed he was having trouble walking.
     （我注意到他行走困難。）
   - She faced little trouble in convincing her executive committee to agree on her proposal.
     （她輕鬆地說服執行委員會同意她的提案。）
2. trouble 還可以替換成 difficulty 或 problem(s) 。
   - She had no problem getting along with her parents-in-law.
     （她與公婆相處毫無困難。）

1. 薇妮可以輕鬆地吃光整桌菜。(使用 has no trouble... 的句型)

   中翻英：＿＿＿＿＿＿＿＿＿＿＿＿＿＿＿＿＿＿＿＿＿＿＿＿

2. As our mother was very busy, we used to ＿＿＿＿ doing the house chores.
   (A) keep on　　(B) take turns
   (C) have trouble　　(D) take to
3. Soon you will have trouble in ＿＿＿＿ anyplaces you have visited.
   (A) find　　(B) to find
   (C) finding　　(D) being found
4. If none of the alarm clocks works for you and you still have trouble ＿＿＿＿ up in the morning, it's time you invent one that will keep shaking you until you wake up.
   (A) to wake　　(B) in waking
   (C) waken　　(D) waking

5. Because of the holiday season, those backpackers had ________ a place that they thought would be comfortable enough.
(A) no trouble in finding
(B) little trouble finding
(C) much trouble in finding
(D) many troubles to find

答案

1. Winnie has no trouble finishing a whole table of food.

2. (B) take turns
我媽媽很忙，我們以前都輪流做家事
解析 (A) keep on（繼續）；(B) take turns（輪流）；(C) have trouble（有困難）；(D) take to（開始從事）。

3. (C) finding
很快你就很難找到你去過的任何地方。
解析 「have trouble (in) V-ing」表示做某事有困難，trouble 後面有介系詞 in，因此動詞須改成動名詞，答案為(C) finding。

4. (B) in waking 和(D) waking
所有鬧鐘都不管用，你早上還是起不來，這是你該發明把你搖起床的鬧鐘的時候了。
解析 「have trouble in V-ing（做某事有困難）」的介系詞 in 可以省略，因此(B) in waking 及(D) waking 皆為正確答案。

5. (C) much trouble in finding
由於假期的關係，那些背包客無法找到他們期望中的舒適飯店。
解析 本句型中的 trouble 屬於不可數名詞，因此(D) many troubles to find 錯誤。依語意判斷，假期時要找到舒適飯店比較困難，答案選(C) much trouble in finding。

句型速記 4 值得……

① S + be + worth + V-ing

② S + be + worthy + { of N / of V-ing / to VR }

③ It is worthwhile + { V-ing / to VR }

- This book is worth reading.
  = This book is worthy of being read.
  = This book is worthy to be read.
  = It is worthwhile to read this book.
  這本書值得一讀。

1. worth 可接名詞或動名詞(V-ing)，表示「值得……」。接動名詞時，含有被動的意義。

- This museum is worth seeing. (O)
  This museum is worth being seen. (X)
  （這個博物館值得一看。）

2. worthy 後方接主動時用「of + V-ing」或「to VR」，接被動時則用「of + being + Vp.p.」或「to be Vp.p.」。

- Mr. Smith is worthy to receive such honor.
  （史密斯先生應該得到此榮譽。）
- *1995* was worthy to be elected the best film of the year.
  （電影《刺激1995》值得被選為年度最佳影片。）

3. 「It is worthwhile to VR」譯為「值得去…」，it 是形式上的主詞，指的是後方的不定詞。

1. 這部場面壯觀的電影值得一看。

 中翻英：＿＿＿＿＿＿＿＿＿＿＿＿＿＿＿＿＿＿＿＿＿＿＿＿＿＿＿＿＿＿

2. This experiment is worth ________ .
 (A) you to try (B) you try (C) your trying (D) you trying

3. Shakespeare is indeed a literary genius ________ .
 (A) worth name (B) worthy of the name
 (C) worthwhile named (D) worthy to being named

4. We believe this unique reporting approach is ________ with our TV channel.
 (A) worthy to sharing (B) worthy of shares
 (C) worthy of sharing (D) worth to shares

答案

1. The movie with magnificent / spectacular scenes { is worthy of being seen. / is worthy to be seen. }

2. (C) your trying
 這個實驗值得你試一試。
 解析 worth 當形容詞時，帶有介系詞的特性，後面可接名詞或動名詞作為其受詞，只有(C) your trying 符合名詞形式。

3. (B) worthy of the name
 莎士比亞的確是名副其實的文學天才。
 解析 worth 為形容詞，後方可接動名詞或名詞。(A) worth name 的 name 前面應加冠詞；(B) worthy of the name 為常用片語，意思為「名副其實」；worthwhile 為形容詞，必須接在名詞前或 be 動詞後；(D) worthy to being named 應改為 worthy to be named。

Day 01 Day 02 Day 03 Day 04 Day 05 Day 06 Day 07

4. (C) worthy of sharing
我們相信這個獨特的播報方式值得與我們電視台分享。

解析 worthy of 後面可接名詞或動名詞，worth 後面接動名詞，答案為(C) worthy of sharing。

阻止、防止……做某事；保護……不被……

stop / prevent / protect + O + from + V-ing

- If I can stop one's heart from breaking, I shall not live in vain.
  若我能讓人不心碎，我就沒有白活。
- It is a matter of urgency to prevent endangered animals from becoming extinct.
  防止動物瀕臨絕種是很緊急的事，我們不能再拖了。
- Many people believe that vitamin C protects people from getting colds.
  很多人相信維他命 C 讓人不感冒。

欲阻止、防止和保護某件事情時，可使用「stop / prevent / protect + O + from + V-ing」的句型。介系詞 from 帶有**去除、免掉、阻止、剝奪**等意思，後面接動名詞或名詞表示欲防止或預防的事情。

- Soldiers should protect the territory of our country (受詞(N)) from being invaded (動名詞) by enemies.
  （軍人應該保護國家領土不受敵人入侵。）

- Today more ranchers are finding other ways to protect their cows and sheep (受詞(N)) from African wild dogs (名詞) instead of killing the rare and special animals.
（今天越來越多牧場工人正在尋找其他方式來保護乳牛和羊群不受非洲野狗攻擊，而非殺掉這些稀有又特別的動物。）

1. Lucy has a leg injury that may ________ her from playing in tomorrow's game.
(A) advance (B) lest (C) prevent (D) organize

2. Unlocking the secrets of DNA ________ scientists ________ they may have the power to create life itself through the process of cloning, including human cloning.
(A) has pressed；to think (B) has led；to think
(C) has talked；into thinking (D) has protected；from thinking

3. Other Paduang legends say that it is done to protect women ________ tigers bites when they rove in the jungle.
(A) in (B) from (C) into (D) on

4. Due to the cook's effort ________, a new snack was invented.
(A) to stop a guest to complain
(B) to stop a guest's complaints
(C) stopping a guest's from complaints
(D) to stopping a guest from

5. To protect our environment ________, we should recycle and reuse, producing as little garbage as possible.
(A) for damaging (B) damages
(C) from being damages (D) from being damaged

1. (C) prevent

露西的腳傷可能讓她明天無法出賽。

解析 (A) 提前；(B) 以免；(C) 阻礙；(D) 組織。腳傷應是「阻礙」明日出賽的原因，因此選擇(C) prevent。

2. (B) has led ; to think

DNA 解密讓科學家認為他們也許擁有力量，能夠透過包括複製人的複製流程來創造生命。

解析 (A) 逼迫……認為；(B) 導致……認為；(C) 說服……認為；(D) 防止……認為。由於「解密 DNA」和「認為擁有創造生命的權利」屬於因果關係，因此應選擇(B) 導致……認為。

3. (B) from

其他巴當的傳說指出，這種做法的目的是保護女人在森林裡徘徊時，不被老虎咬傷。

解析 protect（保護）應選擇介系詞 from，來表示「免除……的傷害」，答案為(B) from。

4. (B) to stop a guest's complaints

廚師為了平息客戶的抱怨，設計出了新點心。

解析 effort（努力）後面應接不定詞，因此(C) stopping a guest's from complaints 以及(D) to stopping a guest from 為錯誤選項。(A) to stop a guest to complain 的意思是「擋下客人，並對他抱怨」，與語意不合。正確答案為(B) to stop a guest's complaints。

5. (D) from being damaged

為了保護環境不受污染，我們應該資源回收再使用，盡可能地減少垃圾的製造。

解析 防止環境不受污染，應使用「protect...from...」的片語。而「環境被污染」應使用被動語態，答案為(D) from being damaged。

DAY 02 不定詞句型

句型速記 1 要求（允許、想要、吩咐、說服）某人做某事

S + { ask / allow / (would) like / tell / persuade } + sb. + to VR

- The class was not allowed to leave until the bell rang.
  直到鐘響了班上的學生才獲准離開。

觀念透析

不定詞 to VR 帶有「命令、計畫」的含意，所以前方會搭配相關概念的動詞。

- Mother asked me to mop the floor every day.
  （媽媽要求我每天拖地。）
- The salesman persuaded us to buy his product.
  （那個推銷員說服了我們買他的產品。）

除了上述的的動詞之外，以下動詞後面也只接不定詞：

afford 負擔得起	desire 渴望	arrange 安排	help 幫助
offer 給予	decide 決定	attempt 試圖	dare 竟敢
expect 預料	learn 學習	deserve 應得	tend 趨向
appear 似乎	agree 同意	demand 要求	hope 希望
need 需要	neglect 忽視	hesitate 猶豫	fail 失敗
want 要	claim 聲稱	choose 選擇	beg 請求

實力養成

1. China ________ its citizens to hunt the panda.
(A) suffers (B) persuades (C) forbids (D) produces

2. The Internet now ________ online shoppers to purchase literally anything without actually stepping out of their houses.
(A) lets (B) admits
(C) allows (D) allowed

3. He didn't allow the children ________ in his colorful garden.
(A) play (B) played
(C) playing (D) to play

4. The chairwoman of this political party asked the spokesman ________ to that incident immediately.
(A) about not responding (B) not responding
(C) not to respond (D) not having responding

答案

1. (C) forbids
中國禁止人民捕獵熊貓。
解析 (A) 受苦；(B) 說服；(C) 禁止；(D) 製造。

2. (C) allows
網路讓網購者不出門便能購買任何東西。
解析 let（讓）後面應接原形動詞；admit（允許）後面應接動名詞 V-ing；且本句為一般性事實，時態應選現在簡單式。答案為(C) allows。

3. (D) to play
他不讓小孩在他萬紫千紅的花園裡玩耍。
解析 allow（允許）後面只接不定詞表達「命令」的意思。

4. (C) not to respond
這個政黨的女主席要求發言人不要針對這起事件立即發言。
解析 ask 作為「要求」解釋時，後面只接不定詞。「ask sb. about sth.」意思為「詢問」。

有可能、似乎

S + be likely + to VR

It is likely + that + S + V

- People without confidence are likely to be influenced by others.
  沒有信心的人很有可能會被他人影響。
- It is not likely that he should have written it.
  他不可能會寫那樣的東西。

likely 本身可當作形容詞與副詞，意思是「很可能的」。當形容詞使用時，前面可以用 very、quite 等**程度副詞**修飾，或是加 not 表示「不可能」，後面接不定詞或子句。

- Psychologists say that if children go through a disturbing event before the age of ten, they are three times as likely to suffer psychological problems as other teenagers.
  （心理學家說，若兒童在十歲前經歷不安事件，他們發生心理問題的機率是其他青少年的三倍。）
- We are not likely to see each other again.
  （我們以後不可能會重逢。）

1. 害羞的人自尊心比較低，往往比較被動。

中翻英：________________________________

2. This passage is mainly about the psychological problems children before ten ________ .

(A) are likely to suffer　　(B) like to suffer
(C) likely suffering　　(D) are likely that suffer

3. What we say here today will ________ by history, but history will remember what they did.
(A) likely forget (B) be like forgetting
(C) likely be forgotten (D) like to be forgotten

4. As awareness of the facts about dyslexia（識字困難症）increases, dyslexic individuals are less and less ________ of as stupid and more likely to have confidence in themselves and their abilities.
(A) likely to be thought (B) like to be thinking
(C) likely to think (D) like to think

1. Shy people, having low self-esteem, are more likely to be passive.

2. (A) are likely to suffer
本文討論十歲前的兒童可能會遭遇的心理問題。
解析 (B) like to suffer 意思為「喜歡忍受」，與句意不合；「children before ten are likely to suffer」為省略了關係代名詞的關係子句，用來修飾 the problem，子句中應有動詞，所以(C) likely suffering 錯誤；(D) be likely that 後面應接子句，而非動詞。

3. (C) likely be forgotten
今日言語可能被歷史遺忘，但歷史會記得所作所為。
解析 本句應用被動表示「被忘記」，(A) likely forget 以及(B) be like forgetting 為錯誤選項；「可能」為 likely（本句中作副詞使用），而非 like，因此(D) like to be forgotten 錯誤。

4. (A) likely to be thought
對識字困難症的了解越多，患者就越不會被視為愚蠢，同時越可能對自己和自身能力有信心。
解析 likely 是「有可能」，like 是「喜歡」，而「被認為」應為 be thought of。

DAY 02

句型速記 3 某人對某事的情緒

S + be + adj. + to VR

- I am glad to hear that you have been admitted to a university.
  我很高興聽到你進入大學。
- The teacher was enraged to see that the whole class was brawling.
  看到全班在吵鬧，老師很生氣。

觀念透析

不定詞可以放在表示情緒的形容詞如 glad、happy、delighted、pleased、sorry 或 angry 等後面，表示感到喜怒哀樂的原因。此時的不定詞具有副詞的功能。

- They were surprised <u>to discover</u> that the only doctor in this town was a quack.
  （他們很驚訝的發現，鎮上唯一的醫生是庸醫。）
- My mom was so delighted <u>to see</u> the return of my brother from the U.S.A.
  （我媽媽很高興看到我哥從美國回來。）

實力養成

1. Kids are ________ the ending of the fable that their teacher is telling.
   (A) desire to know　(B) desire knowing
   (C) desirous knowing　(D) desirous to know

2. That perplexed lady is ________ out any remedy to heal her husband.
   (A) anxiety to find　(B) anxious to have found
   (C) anxiety to have found　(D) anxious to find

3. That outlaw ________ the amnesty（特赦）.
(A) thrilling to know (B) thrill to know
(C) was thrilled knowing (D) was thrilled to know

4. The loving husband is extremely ________ his wife is a spy.
(A) shocking to find out (B) shocked to find out
(C) shocking finding out (D) shocked to finding out

1. (D) desirous to know
孩子們迫不及待的想知道老師所講的寓言故事的結局。

解析 本句有 be 動詞 are，不可接原形動詞，因此(A) desire to know 以及(B) desire knowing 為錯誤選項。「人+ be + 情緒形容詞 + to VR」的句型透過不定詞表達情緒的原因。

2. (D) anxious to find
茫然不知所措的女士，焦急地想找出治癒她丈夫的方法。

解析 be 動詞後面接名詞代表身分，在此與語意不合；再者，「to have Vp.p.」是用完成式來表示過去已經發生的事情，與本句「焦急地想找出」語意不合。綜上所述，判斷(D) anxious to find 為答案。

3. (D) was thrilled to know
逃犯得知特赦，心情很激動。

解析 thrill 作主動語氣時，主詞為引發激動的人、事、物；作被動語氣時，主詞為有激動感覺的人；因此(A) thrilling to know 及(B) thrill to know 為錯誤選項；同時，「人+ be + 情緒形容詞 + to VR」的句型透過不定詞表達情緒的原因，答案應選(D) was thrilled to know。

4. (B) shocked to find out
深情的丈夫發現老婆是名間諜，感到極度震驚。

解析 本句主詞為「感到震驚」的「丈夫」，主詞是人，情緒形容詞應使用過去分詞 Vp.p.，後接不定詞表示該情緒出現的原因。

DAY 03 分詞句型 I

分詞構句

V-ing / Vp.p...., S + V

• He went out of the secret chamber, holding Tim Riddle's diary in his hand.
他走出密室，手上拿著提姆瑞斗的日記。

1. 本句型介紹由**副詞子句**或是 and 連接的**對等子句**簡化而來的分詞構句，表示時間、原因、條件、讓步或附帶情況等，目的在縮短句子並增加變化性。

〔副詞子句〕+〔S + V〕
=〔分詞構句〕+〔S + V〕

• When I ran into the house, I found the sofa was on fire.
= Running into the house, I found the sofa was on fire.
（當我跑進屋子時，發現沙發著火了。）

〔S + V〕and〔對等子句〕
=〔S + V〕+〔,分詞構句〕

• He sat in front of the desk and he closed his eyes.
= He sat in front of the desk, closing his eyes.
（他坐在書桌前，闔上眼睛。）

2. 分詞構句的作法是省略副詞子句或對等子句中的連接詞和主詞，再將子句中的動詞依主動語氣或被動語氣改成現在分詞或過去分詞。

• Having written my composition, I have nothing more to do.
（我已寫完了我的作文，所以再也沒有事可做。）

• (Being) Written in simple English, the book is suitable for beginners.
（由於用簡單的英語寫成，本書適合初學者。）

3. 副詞子句改分詞構句時，若主詞與主要子句的主詞相同，為了讓句意更清楚，可保留連接詞。

- After having some hot tea, Jessica felt much warmer.
（喝了些熱茶後，潔西卡感到溫暖多了。）

4. 當分詞構句與主要子句的主詞不一樣時，必須在分詞構句前保留原子句的主詞，稱為**獨立分詞構句**。

延伸句型：**S_1 + V-ing / Vp.p., S_2 + V**

- When night came on, we started on our way home.
= Night coming on, we started on our way home.
（夜晚來臨，我們踏上歸程。）
- If weather permits, we will have a picnic tomorrow.
= Weather permitting, we will have a picnic tomorrow.
（如果天氣許可，我們明天會去野餐。）

1. ________ social insect behavior, researchers discovered a remarkable example of self-sacrifice in a species of ants found in Brazil.
(A) While studied (B) Studied
(C) While studying (D) A study on

2. Experts suggest that job seekers should dress appropriately ________ to leave a good impression on the interviewer.
(A) when interviewed (B) interviewed
(C) when interviewing (D) interviewing

3. Normally, men kneel down with a diamond ring in the hand ________ a proposal to show their sincerity
(A) when making (B) having made
(C) when have made (D) when he is making

4. ________ this regrettable story, Mr. Mandela arouses a deep sigh of contempt toward the authorities

(A) When closing up (B) Closed up
(C) A close-up on (D) When closed up

5. ________ to better your English, you undoubtedly face bottlenecks sometimes, which you need to conquer.

(A) You determined (B) Determining
(C) You determining (D) Determined

答案

1. (C) While studying

在學習群居性昆蟲的行為時，研究人員從某巴西螞蟻身上發現自我犧牲的極佳案例。

解析 本句為分詞構句句型，依照句意，研究人員「研究」群居性的昆蟲行為是主動語氣，應選擇現在分詞（V-ing）；此外，若選名詞(D) A study on，會使 researcher 和 a study 變成同位語，與語意不合。答案為(C) While studying。

2. (A) when interviewed

專家建議求職者在面試時，衣著應適當，讓面試官留下好印象。

解析 本題分詞構句的主詞為 job seekers（求職者），因此應選被動語氣 interviewed（接受面試），而非主動語氣 interviewing；此外，本分詞構句宜保留連接詞，使分詞和主要子句關係更清楚，答案為(A) when interviewed。

補充 interview 作動詞時主詞多為採訪關係中的發問者，例如面試求職者（interview the applicants ）、採訪首相（interview the Prime Minister）。

3. (A) when making

正常說來，男人求婚時手持鑽戒跪下，以表示真誠。

解析 「男人求婚」為主動語氣，應選擇現在分詞 making；同時，句中「手持鑽戒跪下」以及「求婚」兩者同時發生，不宜選擇完成式，答案為(A) when making。

4. (A) When closing up
當說完這個不幸的故事時，曼德拉先生發出一聲嘆息，表示對當局的輕蔑。

解析 本題分詞構句應選主動語氣的 closing up，而非 closed up；若選名詞，也就是(C) A close-up on，則會使 Mr. Mandela 和 close-up （特寫）變成同位語，與語意不合。

5. (D) Determined
決心努力改善英文時，無疑地有時會遇到很多需要突破的瓶頸。

解析 「下定決心」的說法為「S + be + determined」，由過去分詞作形容詞；同時，若 determined 前方加了 you，此句就變成缺乏連接詞的兩個子句，故答案應選(D) Determined。

有……（there 句型）

There is / are + S + V-ing （表主動）

There is / are + S + Vp.p. （表被動）

- There are long lines of people waiting to get into Sodagreen's concert.
  大排長龍的人們等著進去看蘇打綠的演唱會。
- There are many wild animals killed in Africa.
  非洲有許多野生動物遭到殺害。

「there + be動詞 + 名詞」後方可根據動詞的主動或被動，加上現在分詞或是過去分詞作為修飾語。

- There are not many books talking about the difficulties of an interracial relationship.
  （討論跨種族戀情問題的書不多。）

⇨本句的原句應為「There are not many books which talk about the difficulties of an interracial relationship.」，將主格關係代名詞 which 省略，並將動詞改成分詞，主動改現在分詞，被動則改為過去分詞。

- There is a little wine poured for you. Would you like to have a sip?
（倒了些酒給你，你要來一口嗎？）
- There isn't much water left in the pitcher. Can you buy some for me on your way back?
（水壺裡的水不多了，你回來時可以幫我買些水嗎？）

1. There ________ a wide variety of flowers ________ in April in Washington D.C.
(A) is ; blossoming　　(B) are ; blossoming
(C) is ; blossomed　　(D) are ; blossomed

2. ________ there any trick ________ to dismiss the Devil?
(A) Is ; telling　　(B) Are ; telling
(C) Is ; told　　(D) Are ; told

3. So far, there ________ no pictures ________ well during this trip. Maybe I am not photogenic（上相的）.
(A) are ; taken　　(B) have been ; taken
(C) are ; taking　　(C) have been ; taking

4. ________ there any custodian ________ for this orphan?
(A) Is ; assigning　　(B) Are ; assigning
(C) Is ; assigned　　(D) Are ; assigned

5. There ________ no passengers in the train ________ during that terrorist attack.
(A) were ; surviving　　(B) have been ; surviving
(C) were ; survived　　(D) have been ; survived

1. (A) is ; blossoming
奼紫嫣紅開遍四月的華府。
解析 本句主詞為 a wide variety，屬單數，因此 be 動詞該選擇 is。同時 blossom（開花）為不及物動詞，無被動型態，答案應選擇(A) is ; blossoming。

2. (C) Is ; told
有沒有驅逐撒旦的方法流傳下來？
解析 本句主詞為 trick，be 動詞該選擇 is；此外，trick 應採用被動語氣，表示「被流傳」，因此選擇 told。答案為(C) Is ; told。

3. (B) have been ; taken
這趟旅程的照片都沒照好，也許我不上相。
解析 句首 so far 表示旅程尚未結束，時態應使用現在完成式，表示「到目前為止」；此外， pictures 應採用被動語氣 taken，表示「被拍攝」。答案為(B) have been ; taken。

4. (C) Is ; assigned
這個孤兒有分派監護人了嗎？
解析 本句主詞為 custodian，be 動詞應為 is；同時，custodian（監護人）應用被動語氣 assigned，表示「被指派給孤兒」。答案為(C) Is; assigned。

5. (A) were ; surviv-ing
那次恐怖攻擊中，火車上沒有任何乘客生還。
解析 本句主詞為 passengers，be 動詞選 are；survive（倖存、生還）應採主動的說法，因此答案為(A) were; surviving。

句型速記 1　包括了……；……也被包括在內

, including + 名詞 / 代名詞
= , 名詞 / 代名詞 + included
= , inclusive of + 名詞 / 代名詞

- All on the plane were lost, including the pilot.
  = All on the plane were lost, the pilot included.
  = All on the plane were lost, inclusive of the pilot.
  機上的人全部罹難，包括機長在內。

「包含、包括」有下列三種用法：

1. 「, including + 名詞 / 代名詞」：including 為分詞作介系詞用，意思是「包括」，後面接名詞或代名詞。
   - Around two hundred crew members were being held hostage, including thirty fishermen from the Win Far 161.
     （約有200名船員被挾持，包括30名溫發161號的漁民。）

2. 「, 名詞 / 代名詞 + included」：included 是形容詞，意思是「包括在內的」或「被包括的」，放在名詞和代名詞之後做為後位修飾。
   - It was the time that Millet painted his best-known works, *The Sower* and *The Gleaners* included.
     （米勒就在此時畫出他最知名的作品，包括《播種者》以及《拾穗》。）

3. 「, inclusive of + 名詞 / 代名詞」：inclusive 是形容詞，多與 of 連用，此時用法與 induding 相同，放在名詞或代名詞前面，屬於比較正式的用法。
   - Everyone in the town was slaughtered, inclusive of women and children.
     （鎮上所有人都被屠殺了，包括婦女與小孩。）

陷阱題直擊

1. They could talk for hours on end about everything, ________ their families and jobs to their service in the military.
（他們可以連續好幾個小時談天說地——從家庭、工作到當兵都聊。）
(A) including　　(B) inclusive of
(C) from　　(D) included

1. 本題若不細看句子，可能會選(A) including 或(B) inclusive of。但句中有關鍵字 to，因此應選(C) from，表示「從……到……」。

答案：(C) from

1. In the National Museum of History, there will be 16 Millet's paintings on display, ________ the well-known *Gleaners* and *Angelus*.
(A) include　　(B) inclusive of
(C) from　　(D) included

2. Many events give the opera house a mysterious atmosphere, ________ the dead bodies and the crashing of the chandelier（吊燈）.
(A) including　　(B) both
(C) included　　(D) inclusive

3. Ang Lee was able to attract the money necessary to make other award-winning films, *Eat Drink Man Woman* and *The Ice Storm* ________.
(A) included　　(B) including
(C) which are included　　(D) inclusive of

4. To deal with the problem, we will form a committee composed of twelve members, ________ experts, scholars, and officials.
(A) included　　(B) include
(C) includes　　(D) inclusive of

1. (B) inclusive of

國立歷史博物館將展出米勒的16幅畫作，包括有名的《拾穗》及《晚禱》。

解析 本句使用「inclusive of the well-known Gleaners and Angelus」來舉例說明16幅畫作包含了哪些，逗點後面可接 including 或 inclusive of，答案為(B) inclusive of。

2. (A) including

很多事件賦予歌劇院一股神祕的氛圍，包括死屍以及水晶燈粉碎事件。

解析 本題中的「the dead bodies」以及「the crashing of the chandelier」用來舉例說明「many events」，空格應填入 including 或是 inclusive of，答案選(A) including。

3. (A) included

李安得以吸引到足夠的資金，拍攝其他得獎佳片，包括《飲食男女》以及《冰風暴》。

解析 因為 including 和 inclusive of 必須放在名詞或代名詞前面，因此本題選擇可放在名詞或代名詞後面的(A) included。

4. (D) inclusive of

為了應付這個問題，我們會組成12人委員會，成員包括專家學者以及政府官員。

解析 本題中 experts、scholars 以及 officials 是用來舉例說明 twelve members 的成員，應選擇可置於名詞前的 including 或 inclusive of，答案為(D) inclusive of。

句型速記 2 帶有……；有……的（表附帶之狀態或動作）

S + V + with + N + { 現在分詞 / 過去分詞 / 形容詞 / 副詞 / 介系詞片語 }

- She sat reading, with her cat sleeping beside her.
  她坐著讀書，她的貓睡在旁邊。
- He went angrily away without a word spoken.
  他很生氣地走開，一句話都不說。

1. 「with + 名詞 + 現在分詞 / 過去分詞 / 形容詞 / 副詞 / 介系詞片語」是用來表示「附帶狀況」或「伴隨行為」的副詞片語。with 之前可用逗點，也可以不用。

- We just need a copy of a bill, like a telephone bill, with your name and address on it.
  （我們只需要帳單副本，上面要有你的名字和地址。）

2. 要使用現在分詞或是過去分詞取決於 with 後面的動作對於名詞來說是主動或是被動。

- Taiwan surpassed both Macau and Hong Kong in 2009 and has become the country of the lowest birthrate in the world, with just one baby born per woman.
  （台灣在2009年超越澳門和香港，變成全球生育率最低的國家，每位婦女只生一個小孩。）
  ➩在本句中，小孩是「被生下來」，屬於被動，因此使用 born 來修飾 baby。

DAY 04

1. ________ an established star of TV cookery programs and a healthy diet campaigner, Jamie Oliver has wowed all generations of food lovers not only in Britain but also around the world.
(A)With (B) For (C) As (D) By

2. Although it is closely related to the brown bear, it has evolved to occupy certain ecological advantages, ________ many body characteristics ________ for cold temperatures.
(A) with ; adapting (B) with ; adapted
(C) by ; adapting (D) by ; adapted

3. These suggestions include having conversations with children, letting children express their own feelings, spending extra time ________ together and reassuring them that you love them.
(A) with they doing activities
(B) they do with activities
(C) they did with activities
(D) with them doing activities

4. In the past, most hijackings by Somali pirates were resolved peacefully, usually ________ in cash by ship owners after several months of negotiation.
(A) with ransom payments making
(B) making ransom payments
(C) with ransom payments made
(D) ransom payments making

答案

1. (C) As
身為烹飪電視節目的知名明星以及健康飲食推手，傑米奧利佛贏得英國及全球各地的歡迎。

解析 本句中的 an established star 以及 campaigner 是 Jamie Oliver 的身分，因此應選用(C) As（身為；作為）而非(A) With（伴隨）、(B)For（目地）以及(D) By（表被動）。

2. (B) with ; adapted
儘管和棕熊是近親，牠卻已進化到具備某些生態優勢，很多身體特性都已適應寒冷氣候。

解析 本題句意為「有著……的特性」，因此先排除(C) by ; adapting 及(D) by ; adapted。另外，「身體特性」經演化而適應氣候使用被動語氣，故本題答案為(B) with ; adapted。

3. (D) with them doing activities
這些建議包括與孩子談天、讓他們表達自己的感覺、陪同他們做活動以及向他們保證對他們的愛。

解析 本題解題重點在於 spend 的用法「spend + 時間 / 金錢 + (on) + V-ing」，因此(B) they do with activities 及(C) they did with activities 為錯誤選項。此外，介系詞 with 之後應該接受詞，答案為(D)。

4. (C) with ransom payments made
過去很多索馬利海盜的劫船事件都能和平解決，通常船東談判數個月之後再支付現金贖金。

解析 本題用「with ransom payments made in cash」來說明如何（以……方式）解決劫船事件。ransom payments 應使用表被動的 made 來修飾，答案為(C) with ransom payments made。

DAY 05 特殊動詞用法 I

句型速記 1 used 的用法

①物 + be used + { to + VR / for + V-ing / N }（被拿來作……之用）

②人 + { be used to / get used to } + V-ing / N（習慣於……）

③人 / 物 + used to + VR（過去常……）

- The Romans realized that glass could be used to make windows.
  羅馬人明白玻璃可以用來製作窗戶。
- I am used to having breakfast at home.
  我習慣在家吃早餐。
- Bill used to arrive at school on time but now he is late for school almost every day; his behavior is quite abnormal.
  比爾以前都準時上學，現在他幾乎每天遲到，他的行為很異常。

觀念透析

關於 used 的常見用法有三種，容易混淆。以下分別舉例說明：

1. 物 + be used + for V-ing / to VR（被拿來作……之用）：本句型用來表示主詞的**功用**，be used 在此為被動式，表示「被用」，可以接「for + 動名詞 / 名詞」，也可接不定詞。

- Bluetooth technology is not used for breaking copyright laws.
  = Bluetooth technology is not used to break copyright laws.
  （藍芽科技不是用來違反著作權法的。）

2. 人 + be / get used to + V-ing / N（習慣於……、對……習以為常）：本句型中的 used to 當形容詞用，表示**習慣的狀態**（be used to），或是**變得習慣**（get used to），後面接動名詞或名詞。

- You will soon get used to the work.
  （你很快就會習慣這項工作）

3. 人 / 物 + used to + VR（過去常……）：本句型表示過去常做的事情，強調過去常做，但是現在已經沒有持續的動作，在此當助動詞用。

- After a car accident, Debi Davis was forced to change from someone who used to be proud of her physical appearance to an amputee.
（在車禍之後，黛比戴維斯被迫從以外表為傲的人，變成截肢者。）

1. 我的叔叔過去一向只在天氣好的條件下才去爬山。

中翻英：____________________

2. I might have been angry ________ such responses.
(A) if I were not accustomed to (B) were I not used to
(C) if I had been accustomed to (D) had I not been used to

3. Now I ________ my husband's snore. I keep telling myself I am sleeping next to a lovely pig.
(A) used to (B) was used to (C) am used to (D) am used for

4. Most scholars today believe that Stonehenge was designed by ancient tribes as an astronomical calendar, ________ lunar and solar eclipses.
(A) used to predicting (B) used to predict
(C) was used to predict (D) was used to predicting

答案

1. My uncle used to go mountain-climbing on condition that the weather was good.

2. (D) had I not been used to
若不是熟悉這樣的反應，我也許會生氣。
解析 本句為與過去事實相反的假設語氣，因此 if 領導的條件子句應為過去完成式，且依句意判斷，該條件子句應為否定句，故答案選(D) had I not been used to。

3. (C) am used to

現在我習慣我老公的打鼾聲了。我不斷告訴自己，我睡在一隻可愛的豬旁邊。

解析 在名詞詞組「my husband's snore」之前，應為介系詞，因此(A) used to 為錯誤選項；依語意判斷，本題應為「現在習慣……」，因此答案為(C) am used to。

4. (B) used to predict

今天大部分的學者都相信巨石群是由古代部落所設計，當做天文曆法，用來預測月蝕及日蝕。

解析 依照句意，Stonehenge 應是「用以預測」，本句應使用「S + be + used to VR」；此外，由於主詞關係代名詞及 be 動詞可省略，因此答案為(B) (which was) used to predict。

句型速記 2 表建議、堅持、推薦、要求、命令

S + { suggest / insist / recommend / demand / order } + that + S + (should) + VR

- He suggested that I share relevant personal stories to make my point.
  他建議我分享個人相關故事，好證明我的論點。
- When it was time for the bill, he told the manager he had no money and suggested that he have him arrested.【指考】
  結帳時，他告知經理他沒錢，並建議將其逮捕。

1. 在 suggest（建議）、insist（堅持）、recommend（推薦）、demand（要求）以及 order（命令）等特殊動詞後，可接 that 引導的名詞子句，作

為此類動詞的受詞。此子句通常省略 should，而直接接原形動詞：

(1) 肯定句：Jack recommended (that) Cynthia be hired right away.
（傑克建議辛西亞馬上被錄取。）

(2) 否定句：The President insisted Sam not attend the conference.
（總裁堅持山姆不應出席會議。）

(3) 疑問句：What do you suggest he do?
（你建議他怎麼做？）

2. suggest、insist、recommend 後面若要直接接動詞，須使用 V-ing。demand 及 order 則接不定詞。

- Beth suggests going to the beach this weekend.
（貝絲提議這個週末去海邊。）
- James demanded to see the mayor.
（詹姆士要求見市長。）

陷阱題直擊

1. Yesterday my father insisted I _________ entitled to know the whole situation.
（昨天我父親堅持我有權利瞭解事情始末）。
(A) be (B) was

2. I suggest he _________ a higher degree.
（我建議他追求更高的學歷）。
(A) pursue (B) pursues

1. 即使主要子句為過去簡單式，名詞子句的動詞也仍應使用原形動詞，因此答案應選 be 而非 was。

答案：(A) be

2. 此題原句為 "I suggest (that) he (should) pursue a higher degree."，在此省略了should（可進一步省略 that），動詞應選原形動詞 pursue。注意在此類動詞後方子句中，主詞即使為第三人稱單數，仍應使用原形動詞。

答案：(A) pursue

1. 老闆要求這個案子在一週內完成。

中翻英：____.

2. 句子改寫：Mrs. Ross / her son /orders / the television / turn off / right now

____.

3. The doctor recommended that she ________ the medicine.
(A) ate (B) took (C) take (D) to take

4. These claims include requests to exchange merchandise, requests for refunds, request that work ________ . 【指考】
(A) is correct (B) to be correct
(C) is corrected (D) be corrected

答案

1. The boss demanded this case (should) be finished within a week.

2. Mrs. Ross orders her son turn off the television right now.
羅絲太太命令她的兒子馬上關掉電視。

3. (C) take

解析 recommend（建議）之後的子句，動詞應選原形動詞，因為子句中省略了助動詞 should。

4. (D) be corrected
這些要求包括要求換貨、要求退款以及作業上的修正。

解析 request（要求）同樣屬於此類動詞，句型為「A reguest the S + (should) + VR / for + N」。句中應使用被動語氣表示「要求工作能被更正」，原句為「request that work should be corrected」。

3 句型速記 只需做／只能的事就是……

all (that) + S + { have to do / can do } + is + (to) VR

- All that we have to do for a happy life is be ourselves.
  為了快樂的人生，我們所要做的就是做自己。
- You are on your maternity leave. Now all you have to do is rest and take good care of your health.
  你正在放產假，現在你只要休息和照顧自己的健康就好了。

1. 本句型中，「that + S + have to do」是關係子句，修飾代名詞 all，意思是「需要做的就是……」。be 動詞後面可以接不定詞或是省略 to 直接接原形動詞。

- To excel in English, all (that) you have to do is (to) enjoy it.
  （英文要好，你要做的只要享受它就好了。）
- All children have to do to make their parents happy is spend some time with them.
  （小孩要讓父母開心，只要多花點時間陪陪他們就好。）

2. have to do 可替換成 do / did（所做的）、can do（能做的）等動詞。

- All I did for the whole weekend was sleep and watch TV.
  （我整個週末只在睡覺和看電視。）
- Now all we can do is hold our breath and wait.
  （現在我們能做的只有屏息以待。）

1. 如果想念我，只要拿起話筒打電話給我就可以了。

中翻英：______________________________

2. 他所能為她做的只有陪在她身邊。

中翻英：____

3. All ________ Frodo has to do to end the domination of the Dark Lord Sauron is ________ the ring into the fire of Mount Doom.
(A) which ; throwing (B) that ; throw
(C) which ; throw (D) that ; throwing

4. If Jill wants to impress the parents of her boyfriend, all she needs to do is ________ them how great ________ cook.
(A) showing ; can she (B) show ; can she
(C) showing ; she can (D) show ; she can

答案

1. If you miss me, all (that) you have to do is pick up the phone and call me.
2. All (that) he can do for her is (to) keep her company.
3. (B) that ; throw
要結束黑魔王索隆的統治，佛羅多只要把戒指丟進末日山的火燄中就行了。
解析 先行詞為 all 時，關係代名詞只能選 that，又此句型中 be 動詞後只能是不定詞或原形動詞，因此答案為(B) that ; throw。
4. (D) show ; she can
若吉兒要討她男友父母的歡心，她只要向他們展現她的廚藝就可以了。
解析 若主詞為「all that + S + needs + is + (to) VR」的句型，be 動詞後面接原形動詞。此外，「how great she can cook」是間接問句，句型為「wh-疑問詞 + 主詞 + 動詞」，因此答案選(D) show ; she can。

MEMO

DAY 06 特殊動詞用法 II

1 句型速記　感官動詞（看見／聽見／注意／感覺……）

{see / watch / hear, feel / notice / ...} + O + {VR, V-ing}

- We saw the actor fall down.
  我們看見這個演員跌倒。
- I heard someone knocking loudly last night.
  我昨晚聽到有人大聲地敲門。

1. 感官動詞是指使用到人體感官的動作，包括：listen to（聽）、hear（聽見）、see（看見）、watch（觀看）、feel（感覺）、smell（聞到）、notice（注意）、perceive（察覺）等字。
2. 感官動詞後方的動詞和受詞的關係若為主動，應使用**原形動詞**或**現在分詞**，現在分詞比原形動詞更強調「正在進行」的感覺。若為**被動**，則用**過去分詞**。

   主動：

   - I could feel the whole building shake as soon as the earthquake started.
     （地震開始時，我便能感受到整座大樓在晃動。）
   - I watched this breathtaking bride, my wife-to-be, walking into the church in her elegant wedding dress.
     （我注視著這個美得令人屏息的新娘——我未來的老婆——身著雅緻的新娘禮服正走進教堂。）

   被動：

   - Penny saw the car moved yesterday.
     （潘妮昨天看到車子被移走了。）
     ⇨車子不會自己移動，因此使用過去分詞表被動語氣。

3. 若感官動詞本身為被動式，後方的原形動詞須改成不定詞，現在分詞或過去分詞則維持不變。
   - She was seen to enter the hospital.
     （她被人看見走進了醫院。）

1. People saw him ________ by a sports car.
   （大家看到他被跑車輾過去。）
   (A) be run over　(B) run over
   (C) running over　(D) to run over

1. 感官動詞的受詞與後方動詞的關係若為被動，應選擇過去分詞 Vp.p.。run 的原形動詞與過去分詞同形，因此應選擇(B) run over，表示受詞 him「被車子輾過」。

答案：(B) run over

1. 我十分鐘前聽到你媽媽在叫你。

   中翻英：________________________________

2. 大家在電視上看到消防隊員拯救小女孩，非常感動。

   中翻英：________________________________

3. Did you notice him ________ at his accomplices（共犯）?
   (A) to nod　(B) nodded
   (C) nodding　(D) to have nodded

4. The house was felt ________.
   (A) shake　(B) shook　(C) shakening　(D) to shake

5. I perceived a customer ________ in your store just now.
   (A) shoplift　(B) shoplifted
   (C) to shoplift　(D) being shoplifted

1. I heard your mother call / calling you ten minutes ago.

2. Everybody saw the firefighter rescue / rescuing the light girl and felt deeply touched.

3. (C) nodding
你注意到他對著共犯點頭嗎？
解析 感官動詞的受詞補語若為動詞，會以原形動詞或現在分詞形式出現，因此本題應選(C) nodding。

4. (D) to shake
房子在搖動。
解析 此題的感官動詞為被動式 was felt，後方動詞應選 to shake 或 shaking。(C) shakening 為錯誤拼法。

5. (A) shoplift
我看到一位客人剛剛在你店裡行竊。
解析 perceive 指「察覺、看到」，屬於感官動詞，受詞補語若為動詞，則以原形動詞或現在分詞形式出現，答案選(A) shoplift。

使……；讓……（使役動詞）

S + make / let / have + O + VR

- She makes her mother cry.
  她讓她母親哭了。
- My father would not let me take a taxi on my own.
  我爸爸不會讓我獨自搭計程車。
- That mother should have her children be quiet in public.
  那位母親應該讓她的小孩在公共場合安靜一點。

使役動詞屬於不完全及物動詞，也就是除了受詞之外，還需要加原形動詞做為受詞補語。這類型動詞表示「使、令、讓、叫」等意義，主要有 make、let、have等。下表為使役動詞句型整理：

使役動詞	受格	受格補語（主動）	受格補語（主動）
make	O	VR	Vp.p.
let		VR	be Vp.p.
have		VR	Vp.p.
get		to VR	Vp.p.

＊ get 也是使役動詞之一

主動：

- Business owners who make employees overwork should realize that overworking has a negative effect on productivity.
  （讓員工工作過度的企業主應明白，工作過度對於生產力有負面影響。）
- Please have room service send up some dessert to my room.
  （請叫客房服務送些點心到我房間。）
- Don't let anybody tell you that you can't do something.
  （別讓任何人告訴你你做不到。）
- My brother got me to do the laundry for him.
  （我哥哥叫我幫他洗衣服。）

被動：

- I won't let my son be treated in that way.
  （我不會讓我的兒子如此被對待。）
- She must have her skirt pressed.
  （她必須將裙子燙好。）
- He got his washing machine repaired this morning.
  （他今早叫人來修理他的洗衣機。）

1. Some believe that to compel left-handed children to write with their right hands may ________ them nervous and may cause stammering.
(A) let (B) cause
(C) bring (D) make

2. In order to manufacture enough monitors before the end of year, the boss made us ________ to the factory 30 minutes earlier every day.
(A) getting (B) to get
(C) get (D) will get

3. Jane used all her powers of persuasion to convince her parents to ________ abroad.【學測】
(A) make her studied (B) have her to study
(C) let her be studied (D) let her study

4. I can never make my English ________ because of my heavy accent.
(A) being understood (B) understood
(C) understand (D) understanding

5. I have quite liberal parents. They let me ________ my own decisions.
(A) being making (B) made
(C) make (D) making

答案

1. (D) make
有些人相信逼迫左撇子的兒童用右手寫字，會讓他們緊張，也許會造成口吃。
解析「makes sb. / sth.」可直接接形容詞或原形動詞，答案選(A)。若要用cause，句子須改寫為「cause them to feel nervous」；let 後面若要加形容詞，則須寫成「let them be nervous」。

2. (C) get
為了在年前生產出足夠的監視器，老闆要我們每天提早30分鐘進工廠。

解析 使役動詞 make 後面接「受詞 + 原形動詞（主動）/ Vp.p.（被動）」，答案為(C) get。

3. (D) let her study

珍恩使出十成的說服功力，要說服她爸媽讓她留學。

解析 出國讀書為主動語氣，不需使用表被動的受詞補語。因此(A) make her studied 及(C) let her be studied 為錯誤答案。此外，have 後面應接原形動詞當受格補語，而非不定詞，因此答案為(D) let her study。

4. (B) understood

因為我的濃厚的腔調，我總是無法讓別人聽懂我的英文。

解析 使役動詞 make 後面接「受詞 + 原形動詞（表主動）/ Vp.p.（表被動）」。本句直譯為「使我的英文被聽懂」，為被動的講法，應選擇過去分詞，因此答案為(B) understood。

5. (C) make

我的父母很開明，讓我自己做決定。

解析 使役動詞 let 後面接「受詞 + 原形動詞（主動）/ be Vp.p.（被動）」。本題應選原形動詞，答案為(C) make。

使保持……的狀態

S + { keep / leave } + O + OC

- They help to keep the tradition alive.
  他們協助讓傳統保存下來。
- People with mysophobia always keep their rooms tidy and spotless.
  有潔癖的人總是讓房間井然有序、一塵不染。

keep 和 leave 當「使……保持某狀態、位置、動作」解釋時，屬於不完全及物動詞，其受詞後面必須加**受詞補語**使語意完整。受詞補語可以是**形容詞**、**副詞**、**現在分詞或過去分詞**。

- Leaving the windows open can ventilate the room.
  （窗戶開著可以讓房間保持通風。）⇨ open 為形容詞作受詞補語。
- The bad weather keeps us inside the house.
  （壞天氣使我們不能出門。）⇨ inside the house 為副詞作受詞補語。
- I'm sorry to keep you waiting.
  （抱歉讓您等候。）⇨ waiting 為現在分詞作受詞補語。
- You are never detail-oriented and always keep me worried about you.
  （你從不仔細，總讓我擔心你。）⇨ worried 為過去分詞作受詞補語。

1. 保持牙齒清潔是遠離細菌的有效方法。

中翻英：______________________________

2. Leaving your work ________ when you get off work is not a good habit.
(A) to be undone (B) undone
(C) doing (D) to be doing

3. Please keep your dogs ________ at all time while you are indoors.
(A) to be leashed (B) to be leashing
(C) leashing (D) leashed

4. Leaving your workload ________ is the best means to leave your mind rested.
(A) suitable (B) suitably
(C) suitability (D) to suit

5. By keeping the cars extremely ________ with limited choices and interchangeable components, Ford was able to snap the prevailing manufacturing system .

(A) standardization　　(B) standardizing
(C) standardized　　(D) standardize

1. Keeping your teeth clean is an effective way to keep germs away.

2. (B) undone

下班時工作沒有做完不是好習慣。

解析 keep、leave 為不完全及物動詞，後面接受詞及形容詞當受詞補語。本題應選擇形容詞 undone 來修飾 work。

3. (D) leashed

在室內時，請隨時為您的狗繫上狗鍊。

解析 本題受詞為 dogs，應選過去分詞作為受詞補語，表示狗是保持在「被繫上狗鍊」的狀態，因此答案為(D) leashed。

4. (A) suitable

保持適當工作量是心靈能量充沛的最好方法。

解析 leave 當「保持」解釋時，為不完全及物動詞。本題應選擇形容詞作為受詞補語，答案為(A) suitable。

5. (C) standardized

透過汽車極度標準化，限制選擇以及零件可互換，福特得以抓住主流製造系統。

解析 keep（保持）為不完全及物動詞，必須由受詞補語來修飾受詞 car。本題句意為「使汽車標準化」，因此選由 standardize（vt.；標準化）轉化而成的過去分詞 standardized（標準化的）。

DAY 07 表時間句型

句型速記 1 在……之前，已經……

①By the time (when) S + V-ed, S + had Vp.p.

②By the time (when) S + V, S + will have Vp.p.

- By the time the President gets here, we will have stood along the road to welcome him.
  總統到了的時候，我們會已經沿路站好迎接他。
- The restaurant had already been torn down by the time they met again.
  他們重逢時，餐廳已經被拆掉了。

by the time 後面接表時間的副詞子句，表示在這個時間點，主要子句的動作正在進行或已經結束。by 表示「不晚於某個時間點」。

1. By the time when Ricky hurried into the classroom, his Chemistry teacher had started the class.
（瑞奇趕到教室時，化學老師已經開始上課了。）
⇨此句 hurry 用過去簡單式，但 start 用過去完成式，表示「開始上課」的時間（his Chemistry teacher had started the class）早於「瑞奇趕到教室」的時間（Ricky hurried into the classroom）。

2. We will have completed the road by the time you come back next year.
（等你明年回來，我們會已經把路蓋好了。）
⇨此句表示在明年回來時（副詞子句以現在簡單式代替未來式），路就會蓋好了，因此用未來完成式表示未來某時間點之前就會完成或已經發生的動作。

1. The train ________ by the time we got to the station.
(A) had gone (B) would go
(C) was going (D) has gone

2. By the time when you finish your cooking, I ________ out because of starvation.
(A) will pass (B) have passed
(C) will have passed (D) have passed

3. By the time when the economy in Taiwan ________ to boost, milk had become more and more popular in everyday life in Taiwan.
(A) is starting (B) starts
(C) started (D) had started

4. By the time when Beethoven ________ to Vienna, the city had earned itself a prestige for music.
(A) relocated (B) was relocating
(C) relocates (D) was relocated

5. By the time you finish this column, thousands of Americans ________ their comments on this Whitney Houston video.
(A) will have been posted (B) will be posted
(C) will have posted (D) will post

答案

1. (A) had gone
我們抵達車站時，火車已經開走了。
解析 副詞子句「by the time we got to the station」表示「抵達車站的時候」，主要子句的動作發生於 by the time 帶領的子句之前，應比副詞子句早一個時態，因此本題主要子句時態為過去完成式，答案選(A) had gone。

2. (C) will have passed

你煮好時，我已經餓昏了。

解析 當用時間副詞子句表達未來時間時，必須用現在式代替未來式；同時，因為要表示 I pass out 會發生在 you finish 之前，主要子句時態用未來完成式，答案選(C) will have passed。

3. (C) started

台灣經濟起飛時，牛奶在台灣的日常生活已經越來越受歡迎了。

解析 主要子句為過去完成式，同時「by the time + 子句」發生在主要子句之後，因此本題應選過去簡單式。

4. (D) was relocated

貝多芬搬到維也納時，維也納已經贏得音樂之都的美名了。

解析 由於主要子句為過去完成式，by the time 帶領的子句發生在主要子句之後，應選擇過去簡單式；此外，英文中搬家的說法，可以用 be relocated（將……重新安置）。綜上所述，本題答案為(D) was relocated。

5. (C) will have posted

等你完成這篇專欄時，數萬人也許已經看過這個惠妮休斯頓的影片了。

解析 由於「by the time + 子句」為現在簡單式，主要子句應為未來完成式，且由於主要子句的 post 應為主動語氣，答案應選(C) will have posted。

句型速記 2 自從……已經有……

It + is / has been + 時間 + since + S + 過去式

- It's a long time since I started my correspondence with Peter.
  我和彼得書信往來很久了。
- It has been a decade since Isabella dumped me.
  依莎貝拉甩了我已經10年了。

現在完成式多會配合 since 引出一個事情的起點。since 意思是「自從……起」，後面可接（過去）時間副詞或過去式子句，可放在句首或句尾。since 表示某個事件發生的起點，之後這個事件延續著，並且一直持續到現在還未停止，這就是 since 在「現在完成式」句子當中所表示的時間概念。

「It has been...since...」的句型中，主要子句用 It 表示「時間」，整句的意思為「自從……起，已經過了……（時間）」。

- It's several years since he stopped writing calligraphy.
（他已經好幾年沒寫書法了。）
- It has been two months since you got expelled from your senior high school.
（你被高中退學兩個月了。）

1. He said ________ many years since he had joined the Peace Corps.
(A) it is　(B) there have been
(C) it was　(D) there were

2. It's been several weeks since my daughter ________ with influenza.
(A) infect　(B) gets infected
(C) infected　(D) got infected

3. ________ a long time since he went into coma.
(A) There has been　(B) It was
(C) It has been　(D) There was

4. It ________ several years since the new constitutional amendment ________ effect.
(A) has been ; took　(B) is ; takes
(C) has been ; takes　(D) had been ; took

5. ________ some time since he fell head over heels for her.
(A) There has been　(B) It was
(C) It has been　(D) There was

1. (C) it was

他說他加入和平部隊已有兩年了。

解析 由於 since 子句為過去完成式，因此主要子句應為過去簡單式（主要子句通常比 since 引導的子句晚一個時態）。本題使用「It + is / has been + 時間 + since + S + 過去式」來強調時間，答案為(C) it was。

2. (D) got infected

我女兒罹患流行性感冒好幾週了。

解析 主要子句為現在完成式，因此 since 子句應為過去簡單式。且句意為「被感染」，應選擇被動語氣，答案為(D) got infected。

3. (C) It has been

他昏迷好久了。

解析 since 子句為過去簡單式，因此主要子句應為現在完成式。本句使用「It + is / has been + 時間 + since + S + 過去式」的句型來強調時間，答案為(C) It has been。

4. (A) has been ; took

新的憲法修正案生效有好幾年了。

解析 主要子句的發生不會早於 since 子句，因此(C)和(D)為錯誤選項。又本題敘述過去的事，因此(A) has been ; took 最適合。

5. (C) It has been

他迷戀上她有好一陣子了。

解析 由於 since 子句為過去簡單式，主要子句應為現在完成式，答案為(C) It has been。

當……的時候

when / while / as + S + V

- When the sun sets, the ants seal up the entrance to their nest.【學測】
  日落時，螞蟻會封住巢穴的入口。
- As I dialed Andy's cell phone number, I don't know what I would say exactly.
  當我撥安迪的手機號碼時，我不知道我到底會說什麼。

when、while 和 as 同屬副詞連接詞，帶領時間副詞子句，表達當某動作發生時，另一個動作也在進行。三者多可通用，其特性如下：

1. when 意思為「在……時刻或時期」，它可兼指「時間點」或「一段時間」，所以由 when 帶領的副詞子句中動詞既可以是持續性的動作，也可是一個發生後立即終止的動作。

- When the pop diva started to sing her love song, tens of thousands of fans flicked their lighters, waving their hands in the air, and sang along.
  （當流行天后開始唱情歌時，成千上萬的歌迷打開打火機，手向空中揮舞，跟著唱和。）
  ⇨ 本句的 start 為終止性動詞，類似的動詞包括：die、break、hit 等，都是發生即終止的動作。
- Maksim Gelman, who will face sentencing on Wednesday for the murders, says he made his first kills when he was just 18.
  （麥辛傑曼週三即將面對謀殺的判刑，他說他十八歲時第一次殺人。）
  ⇨ 本句的 was 是持續性動詞，類似的動詞包括：keep、remain、stay 等。

2. while 表示一段時間，因此可用進行式或持續性動詞：
   - "I choose the apples that are bitten up by bugs," she told me while she was replacing the apples in my basket.
     （「我選擇被蟲咬的蘋果」她在把我籃子中的蘋果換掉時這麼說。）

3. as 子句多置於句首。
   - As I hurried home, I slipped on the ice.
     （我趕著回家時，在冰上滑倒了。）

1. ________ I sat in my chair, trying to recall everyone's name, the prettiest lady I had ever seen swooped in.
   (A) During (B) As far as
   (C) As (D) since

2. Brad narrowly escaped death ________ overhead and struck his car this morning.
   (A) since a bullet flew (B) when a bullet flew
   (C) when a bullet has flown (D) as a bullet has flown

3. ________ she sang, Whitfield's voice was so powerful and soulful that everyone in the room forgot the wheelchair was even there. 【學測】
   (A) Before (B) Until
   (C) Since (D) As

4. I'll handle your marketing projects for you ________ on your business trip.
   (A) since you are (B) until you are
   (C) while you have been (D) while you are

5. Mr. Wang often takes a walk with his lovely dog in the evening ________ he takes a bath.
   (A) before (B) while
   (C) if (D) as

1. (C) As

當我坐在椅子上，想要記起所有人的名字時，我所見過最漂亮的小姐衝了進來。

解析 (A) during 為介系詞而非連接詞，因此後面不可接子句作為時間子句；(B) as far as 意思為「遠到……」，用於表達距離；(D) since 意思為「自從……以來」，用於完成式。答案為(C) As。

2. (B) when a bullet flew

一顆子彈從布萊德頭上飛過，擊中他的車，他千鈞一髮逃過死劫。

解析 依照語意，子彈飛過和逃生應為同時發生，因此(B) when a bullet flew 為正確答案。

3. (D) As

當威菲唱歌時，她的聲音是如此有力和深情，房裡每個人都忘了那裡有輪椅。

解析 依照語意判斷，時間副詞子句和主要子句動詞的發生時間應為同時；除 As 之外，Before、Until 以及 Since 皆表示兩者時間點不同。

4. (D) while you are

當你出差時，我會幫你處理你的行銷案。

解析 由於主要子句和副詞子句兩者為同時發生，因此不可選具有前後時間概念的(A) since you are 和(B) until you are 。再者，由於前後兩個子句的時間點相同，因此不應選擇現在完成式(C) while you have been。

5. (A) before

王先生經常在洗澡前，帶著他可愛的狗在傍晚時分散步。

解析 洗澡和遛狗不可能同時發生，依照語意，應選(A) before

句型速記 4 一……就……

once / as soon as + S + V

S + had no sooner + Vp.p. + than + S + V

- Once you start doing Sudoku puzzles, it's hard to stop.
  一旦開始玩數獨，就停不了手。
- A person will grow out of allergy as soon as he or she reaches adulthood.【學測】
  人成年後就會擺脫過敏了。
- Yvonne had no sooner come than she was informed of discharged from her position.
  依梵剛到就被通知被免職了。

1. 「once / as soon as」和「had no sooner + Vp.p. + than」都可以用來表示時間。其中 once 和 as soon as 的位置比較彈性，可以放在句首或句尾，口語和書面都可以用，有「立即」的含意。
   - As soon as the civil war broke out, all of the diplomats were recalled.
     （內戰一爆發，所有外交官都被召回。）
   - Once their eyes fall on these products, they are sure to be excited.
     （他們目光一落在這些產品上，他們絕對會很興奮。）
2. 「S + had no sooner + Vp.p. + than」的句型較常用在講述過去的事情。也可以將它倒裝，變成「No sooner had + S + Vp.p. + than」。
   - She had no sooner learnt that her parents had invited the minister's family over for Christmas Eve dinner than she cried.
     = No sooner had she learnt that her parents had invited the minister's family over for Christmas Eve dinner than she cried.
     （一得知父母邀請部長家人來過聖誕夜，她就哭了出來。）

1. ________ the finding of the mysterious murder case involving a number of strange signs, the French police officers immediately sent for a renowned American expert to come to their aid.
(A) As soon as (B) The moment
(C) As (D) On

2. ________ involved in bribery（受賄）, you are off the political circle for good.
(A) As soon as you (B) Once you
(C) Until you have gotten (D) Once you get

3. ________ cyclists wear a helmet, use proper hand signals, and use bicycle lanes, cycling can be a fun and healthy thing to do, even in a city.
(A) As long as (B) As well as
(C) As soon as (D) As far as

4. ________ Hareton accepts Cathy's present of a book, the vicious cycle of suffering has been broken.
(A) Once upon (B) Once
(C) As well as (D) As far as

5. ________ than we hired scooters, for they provided the most convenient way to enjoy the island.
(A) No sooner had we landed (B) As soon as we landed
(C) The moment we landed (D) After we had landed

答案

1. (D) On
由於神祕謀殺案件牽涉許多奇怪的符號，法國警方央請知名美國專家來協助。
解析 由於「the finding of the mysterious murder case involving a number of strange signs」為名詞詞組，而非名詞子句，因此本題只能選擇介系詞 on。

2. (D) Once you get

一旦涉入賄賂，就永遠離開政治圈。

解析 本句講述的是一般性事實，因此時態應採現在簡單式。「get involved in + 某事」指「涉入某事」。

3. (A) As long as

只要騎士戴安全帽、使用正確的手勢以及使用單車車道，騎單車可以是很快樂和健康的事，即使是在市區內。

解析 (A) 只要；(B) 以及；(C) 一……就……；(D) 至於。本句講述的是條件，因此選具有條件意味的連接詞(A) As long as（只要）。

4. (B) Once

一旦漢瑞頓接受凱西的書當禮物，苦難的惡性循環就此中斷。

解析 once upon 為介系詞，因此不能接子句，根據語意，本句應選擇條件子句，因此答案為(B) Once。

5. (A) No sooner had we landed

我們一落地就租摩托車，因為它們是享受島嶼最方便的方式。

解析 than 必須與比較級搭配，(A) No sooner had we landed 為正確選項。

Level Three

實力篇

The English Patterns You Got to Know

DAY 01 It句型 I

句型速記 1 對某事表達意見

It is + adj. / N + { to VR / that + S + V }

- It is hard to break with a deep-rooted habit.
  積習難改。
- It is mean that you talked to Mom that way.
  你跟媽媽那樣說話很過分。
- It is a pity that you couldn't come.
  你不能來真可惜。

1. 此句型真正的主詞為後方的不定詞片語或名詞子句，因為長度較長，所以將其放到句尾，原來的主詞位置則以 it 代替，作為虛主詞。

- It's not easy to cope with stress.
  = To cope with stress is not easy.
  （壓力不容易應付。）
- It is not necessary that they studied until 4 o'clock.
  = That they studied until 4 o'clock is not necessary.
  （他們沒必要研讀到四點鐘。）

2. 不定詞後方可接受詞使語意完整。

延伸句型：It is + adj. / N + to { Vt + O / Vi + 介系詞 + O }

- It is hard to please my grandfather.
  （我的爺爺很難取悅。）
- It is very difficult to get along with Tom.
  = Tom is difficult to get along with.
  （和湯姆相處融洽不容易。）
  ⇨ 不定詞的受詞可移至句首當主詞，原介系詞則應保留。

3. 如果要表達「對某人而言是……的」，可加入「for + 人」來表示。

延伸句型：It is + adj. + for + 人 + to VR

- It's impossible for me to surrender.
  （要我投降是不可能的。）
- It is challenging for her to hear you clearly because she has a hearing problem.
  （她很難聽清楚你說什麼，因為她有聽力障礙。）

4. important、crucial、essential、vital、necessary 等有「重要」含義的形容詞，後方子句中的動詞須用原形動詞。其句型為「It is important / crucial / essential / vital / necessary + that + S + (should) + VR」，子句中的 should 多被省略。

- It is important that every kid (should) get adequate sleep.
  （每個孩子都能有足夠的睡眠是很重要的。）
- It is crucial that every passenger be informed of our safety policy.
  （告知每位乘客我們的安全規範是很重要的。）

1. 我很難精準預見每天發生的事。

中翻英：______________________________

2. 他們要在 24 小時之內獨立完成這個案子，是不可能的。

中翻英：______________________________

3. after / be here / exciting / for us / is / It / long waiting / the / to

句子重組：______________________________

4. It is ________ a nap every noon.

(A) crucial to take　　(B) crucially takes
(C) crucial to be taken　　(D) crucially to be taken

5. It is ________ on your own medical research.
(A) feasible for you to conduct (B) feasible to conduct for you
(C) feasibly conduct (D) for you to feasibly conduct

1. It is difficult for me to foresee what will happen exactly every day.
2. It is impossible for them to finish this project in 24 hours independently.
3. It is exciting for us to be here after the long waiting.
漫長的等待之後，我們很興奮能來到這裡。
4. (A) crucial to take
每天中午小睡是很重要的。
解析 本句型以不定詞當作意義上的主詞，睡午覺（take a nap）應為主動語氣，主詞補語則應選形容詞。
5. (A) feasible for you to conduct
進行你自己的醫學研究是可行的。
解析 be 動詞後方必須接主詞補語，因此(C)與(D)為錯誤選項。此外， for you 修飾的是 feasible，應接在補語後面，答案為(A)。

認為、覺得某事……

S + { think / consider / believe / find / take } + it + adj. / N + to VR

- Do you think it wise to interfere?
你覺得干預是明智的嗎？
- I consider it bad table manners to open your mouth while eating.
我認為進食的時候打開嘴巴是不好的餐桌禮儀。

觀念透析

1. 句型中的 it 是虛受詞，指的是後方的不定詞片語。在下方例句中，我們可以視「to talk while running」為 find 真正的受詞，difficult 為受詞補語（OC）。

- I find it difficult to talk while running.

（我覺得跑步時講話很難。）

2. 除了不定詞片語，受詞補語後方也可以接名詞子句作真正的受詞。

- I think it right that children keep good hours.

（我認為孩子早睡早起是對的。）

3. 此句型的受詞補語可以為**形容詞**或**名詞**。

- My teacher considers it unforgivable to bully classmates.
（我的老師認為霸凌班上同學是不可原諒的。）
- The society thinks it a crime to take marijuana.
（這個社會認為吸食大麻是犯罪。）

4. 不定詞前方可加入「for + 人」補充句意。

- The interviewer thinks it vital for the applicant to have a passion for fashion.
（面試官認為應徵者必須擁有對流行事物的熱情。）
- My father considers it important for kids to exercise regularly.
（我父親認為小孩子規律運動很重要。）

1. 很多愛國者（patriotic men）認為國家受到攻擊時，服兵役是種光榮。

中翻英：＿＿＿＿＿＿＿＿＿＿＿＿＿＿＿＿＿＿＿＿＿＿＿＿＿＿

2. to be / take / it / granted / for / financially supported/ children / A lot of

句子重組：____

3. The new female president considers ________ a society with equal gender rights.
(A) necessary to build (B) necessarily build
(C) it necessarily build (D) it necessary to build

答案

1. Many patriotic men think it an honor to serve their country while it is under attack.

2. A lot of children take it for granted to be financially supported.
很多子女把財務支援視為理所當然。

3. (D) it necessary to build
新的女總統認為有必要建立性別平權的社會。
解析 consider 後面接的受詞為不定詞時，則使用「consider + it + OC + to VR」的句型，答案為(D) it necessary to build。

3 句型速記 似乎……

S + seem + to VR
It seems + that + S + V

- Ann seems to be afraid of snakes.
= It seems that Ann is afraid of snakes.
安好像很怕蛇。

seem（似乎、看起來）有兩種句型：

1. 第一種接不定詞：S + seem + to VR

- Some kinds of body languages seem to be universal.
（有些肢體語言放諸四海皆同。）

(1) 依語意時態的不同，可接「to have Vp.p.」，表示動作已經發生或完成：

- Venice, built on hundreds of islands, seems to have risen out of the sea.
（威尼斯，建構在數百座島嶼上，似乎從海底浮出來一樣。）

(2) seem 為連綴動詞，後方可省略 to be，**直接接形容詞或名詞**。

- Kitty seems very happy with her new job.
（凱蒂似乎對新工作很滿意。）

2. 第二種為句首使用虛主詞 it，後方接名詞子句：It + seems + that + S + V

- The stroke has left him bedridden and weak day by day. It seems (that) <u>no therapy could reverse the condition</u>.
（這場中風將他困在病榻上且使他日漸虛弱，似乎沒有療方可以逆轉病情。）

陷阱題直擊

1. Everyone seems __________ Jeremy Lin before he became famous.
（在林書豪出名前，大家似乎都低估了他。）
(A) to have underestimated
(B) to underestimate
(C) to have been underestimated
(D) to be underestimated

1. 由於空格後方有受詞 Jeremy Lin，可知 underestimate 為主動語氣。此外，由於「低估」的時間點早於「出名」，因此這裡的不定詞必需以現在完成式來表示時間點早於 became famous。

答案：(A) to have underestimated

1. 她似乎非常以她的兒子為傲。

中翻英：______________________________

2. He is a rounded-head kid who can't ________ at anything.
(A) seem winning
(B) seem that wins
(C) have seemed to win
(D) seem to win

3. ________ all the seniors in our school look forward to graduation and the day when they become freshmen in college.
(A) There seem to have
(B) It seems to be
(C) There seem to be
(D) It seems that

4. It ________ that people in different parts of the world invented umbrellas at different times.
(A) seems (B) likes
(C) looks (D) maybe

5. Joe doesn't ________ much spirit. Maybe a cold glass of beer could animate him a bit.
(A) seem to have
(B) seem to be
(C) seem that has
(D) seem to have been

1. She seems (to be) very proud of her son.

2. (D) seem to win

他是個似乎什麼都贏不了的短髮小孩。

解析 由於 seem 接不定詞或名詞子句，因此(A) seem winning 以及(B) seem that wins 不可選。根據語意，本句表達一般性事實，時態應為現在簡單式，答案為(D) seem to win。

3. (D) It seems that

似乎所有的高年級生都很期待畢業典禮，以及變成大學新鮮人的那一天。

解析 由於 seems（似乎）後方可加不定詞或名詞子句，答案為(D) It seems that。

4. (A) seems

世界上不同地方的人們似乎在不同時期發明了雨傘。

解析 「It seems that」為固定句型，後面接子句表示「似乎……」。look like 則是「看似」的意思。

5. (A) seem to have

喬似乎精神不好，也許一杯冰啤酒可以讓他振奮一點。

解析 本題(B) seem to be 和(D) seem to have been 為 be 動詞的用法，後方若接名詞，是指前方主詞等於後方名詞的情況，例：It seems to be a bad idea.（這似乎是個壞主意）。應改成 seem to have 才能搭配後面的名詞 spirit，指「沒有精神」；(C) seem that has 為錯誤的子句形式。

DAY 02 It句型 Ⅱ

句型速記 1 引述傳聞、報導、他人說法

It is said that...（據說……）

It is reported that…（報導說……）

It is believed that…（據信……）

- It is said that he is a millionaire.
  = People say that he is a millionaire.
  據說他是個百萬富翁。

此句型由 that 引導某報導、傳聞、他人看法作名詞子句，語氣上較為客觀。It 為虛主詞，代表後方子句所說的事情。said、reported、believed 等動詞皆用被動。

- It is said that <u>16 percent of American households use a cell phone exclusively for their telephone service</u>.
  （據說 16%的美國家庭只用手機來進行通話。）
- It is reported that <u>it'll take nine months for him to get back in the game</u>, but it could happen sooner, depending on the rehabilitation progress.
  （報導說他只需花九個月就能重返球場，但也可能更早，端賴復健進度而定。）
- It is believed that <u>there are more than seven thousand languages in the world</u>.
  （據說世上有超過 7 千種語言。）

1. It is said _________ before your eyes just before you die.
(A) for your life to flash　　(B) that you life has flashed
(C) that your life flashes　　(D) for your life to have flashed

2. It is reported ________ to see an ad seven times to remember it.
(A) for a customer to have
(B) for a customer to have had
(C) that a customer having
(D) that a customer has

3. ________ a lower cruising speed, that the iceberg could have been avoided.
(A) The Titanic is believed to maintain
(B) It is believed for the Titanic to have maintained
(C) It is believed that if the Titanic had maintained
(D) It is believing that if the Titanic maintained

4. It is ________ a higher life expectancy than men.
(A) saying that women enjoy
(B) saying that women have enjoyed
(C) said for women to enjoy
(D) said that women enjoy

5. ________ directed by an unknown director won the first prize in this film festival.
(A) A film is reported to be
(B) It is reported that a film has
(C) It reports for a film
(D) It is reported that a film

答案

1. (C) that your life flashes
據說死前畢生經歷會在眼前一閃而過。

解析 「It is said that」後方接名詞子句，且本句討論的是一般性事實，時態應為現在簡單式，答案為(C) that your life flashes。

2. (D) that a customer has
據報導顧客必須要看七次廣告才記得住。

解析 「It is reported that」後方接名詞子句，且使用現在簡單式表示一個客觀的事實，故答案為(D) that a customer has。

3. (C) It is believed that if the Titanic had maintained
據信若鐵達尼號航行速度慢一點，就可以避過冰山。

解析 「It is believed that」為常用句型，使用被動式，表「被眾人所相信」。此外，本題的名詞子句表示與過去事實相反的假設，時態應為過去完成式，答案為(C)。

4. (D) said that women enjoy
據說女性平均壽命比男性長。

解析 本句用「It is said that」句型，後方接名詞子句作實際意義上的主詞，答案為(D) said that women enjoy。

5. (D) It is reported that a film
據報導某位不知名的導演所執導的影片贏得了本次電影節的頭獎。

解析 本句使用「It is reported」句型，「directed by an unknown director」則是省略了 which / that was，答案為(D) It is reported that a film。

正是……；就是……（強調句）

It is + { 主詞 / 受詞 / 時間、地方副詞 / 副詞子句 } **+ that + S + V**

- It was about 600 years ago that the first clock with a face and an hour hand was made.
  就在六百年前，第一個有鐘面和時針的時鐘問世。
- It was with teamwork that we defeat the visiting team.
  正是靠著團隊合作，我們打敗了挑戰隊伍。

1. 本句型將需要強調的特定部分移到子句前面，該強調的部分可以是原句的主詞、受詞、地方、時間、原因等，除了動詞和含有「ly」的副詞外，其餘皆可放入強調位置。

- The reckless driver was responsible for the terrible accident.
  ⇨ It is the reckless driver that was responsible for the terrible accident.
  （就是這個粗心的駕駛要為這個可怕的意外負責。）⇨ 強調主詞。
- I met her on this street for the first time.
  ⇨ It was on this street that I met her for the first time.
  （我就是在這條街與她邂逅。）⇨ 強調地方。

2. 當強調的部分為人時，that 可用 主格 who 或受格 whom 代替，其他時候則一律用 that。

- It was Mary that went to Gary's home yesterday.
  = It was Mary who went to Gary's home yesterday.
  （昨天去蓋瑞家的就是瑪莉。）
- It was Professor Wang that we had lunch with.
  = It was Professor Wang whom we had lunch with.
  （和我們一起用午餐的是王教授。）

陷阱題直擊

1. It is __________ scrubbing the floor for your thoughtless behavior, not you.
（因為你粗心的行為而在刷地板的是我，不是你。）
(A) me that is (B) I that is
(C) I that am (D) me that am

1. 本題用「It is + ... + that ...」的句型來強調後方子句的主詞 I，因此子句中，動詞須與原主詞 I 一致。

答案：(C) I that am

1. It is ________ one book every month.
(A) Jessica who buy (B) Jessica that she buys
(C) Jessica who buys (D) Jessica that has bought

2. It is these three houses ________ his parents left him when they died.
(A) of (B) that (C) for (D) from

3. It was Umbridge ________ Harry write in the magic pen and had scars left on his hand.
(A) that is made (B) that was made
(C) that made (D) who was made

4. It is ________ the whole world will come to an end, according to the Maya.
(A) in 2012 that (B) in 2012 where
(C) 2012 when (D) in 2012 which

5. It may be ________ the world is torn between the rich and the poor and thus social upheaval never stops.
(A) through capitalism who (B) through capitalism for
(C) through capitalism when (D) through capitalism that

答案

1. (C) Jessica who buys
每個月買一本書的就是潔西卡。

解析 本題以「It is...that...」的句型來強調 Jessica，所以後方子句中，動詞須使用單數。且子句表達的是每個月買書的習慣，因此時態應為現在簡單式。

2. (B) that
他父母去世後，留給他的就是這三棟房子。

解析 由於 left（留下）為授與動詞，應有兩個受詞，間接受詞是 him，直接受詞就是前移的 three houses。依照「It is...that...」的句型，本題應選(B) that。

3. (C) that made
讓哈利用魔法筆寫字，在他手上留下傷疤的是恩不里居。
解析 本題使用「It is...that...」的句型。make 是使役動詞，其主動用法為「make + 受詞 + 原形動詞」，被動用法為「be made + 過去分詞」，依語意，本題應選主動用法。

4. (A) in 2012 that
根據馬雅人的說法，世界會在 **2012** 年毀滅。
解析 原句為「According to the Maya, the whole world will come to an end in 2012」，本題強調時間副詞「在2012年」，因此把 in 2012 往前移，再以 that 引導後方子句。

5. (D) through capitalism that
也許就是因為資本主義，世界被分裂成貧富兩方，因此社會動盪永不平息。
解析 本題使用「It is...that...」的句型，強調的部分是 through capitalism（由於資本主義），必須將其往前移，再以 that 引導後方的子句，答案為(D)。

花費時間

It takes + (人) + 時間 + to VR
事 take(s) + (人) + 時間
人 spend(s) + 時間 + (in) + V-ing

- It took me three days to finish my homework.
  我花了三天完成我的作業。
- The flight will take eight hours.
  航程需要八個小時。
- She spends five hours studying every day.
  她每天花五個小時讀書。

DAY 02

spend 可用在花費時間、精力或金錢上，**主詞必須是人**；take 可用來表示花費時間和精力，**主詞必須是事、物或是虛主詞 it**。

- It would take almost <u>12 years</u> to see them all.
  = To see them all would take almost <u>12 years</u>.
  （要花上快12年才能將它們全部看完。）
- Each spends <u>most of his time</u> wandering around the village, looking rather shabby. 【學測】
  （他們多數時間都在村裡游手好閒，一副邋遢的模樣。）

1. It must have ________ a century before the doctor finally came out of the ICU（加護病房）and explained to us that my father had had a stroke.
(A) cost (B) spent (C) taken (D) had

2. It ________ a lot of efforts for us to master a foreign language.
(A) costs (B) spends (C) takes (D) gets

3. Money matters a lot to me, but I would rather ________ more time ________ my parents.
(A) cost ; be (B) take ; being
(C) spend ; being with (D) spend ; with

4. It ________ him 70-plus hours to complete his latest masterpiece.
(A) costs (B) spends (C) takes (D) gets

5. To get all the way back to where he was physically before the injury ________ him a while longer
(A) will cost (B) spends
(C) will take (D) will have taken

1. (C) taken

就像是隔了一世紀，醫生才從加護病房出來，對我們解釋，我父親中風了。

解析 「花費時間」的句型，若主詞為事、物或是虛主詞 it，則應使用 take 當動詞。

2. (C) takes

我們要花很多力氣才能精通一項外國語。

解析 花費精力的句型和花費時間一樣，可使用 take 或 spend 兩個動詞，若主詞為事、物或是虛主詞 it，則應使用 take。

3. (C) spend ; being with

錢對我而言很重要，但我寧願花更多時間和父母相處。

解析 花費時間的句型中，若主詞是人，則應使用 spend 當動詞，後面接「on + N」或直接加 V-ing，說明把時間花在什麼事情上。答案為(C) spend ; being with。

4. (C) takes

他最新的傑作花了他 70 多小時。

解析 花費時間的句型，若主詞為事、物或是虛主詞 it，則應使用 take 當動詞，後接不定詞當真正的主詞。

5. (C) will take

要再花上好一陣子，他才會回復到受傷前的身體狀態。

解析 花費時間的句型，若主詞為事、物或是虛主詞 it，則應使用 take，同時接不定詞當真正的主詞。本句表示對未來的預測，因此時態採未來簡單式。

4 句型速記 花費金錢

It costs + (人) + 錢 / 代價 + to VR
物 cost(s) + (人) + 錢
人 spend(s) + 錢 + on + 物

- It cost me about $20,000 to buy the newest model of iPhone.
  最新型的 iPhone 花了我兩萬塊。
- The dress is going to cost her an arm and a leg.
  這件洋裝將會花她一大筆錢。
- My sister spent 5,000 dollars on her shoes.
  我姊姊花了五千元買下那雙鞋。

觀念透析

1. cost 多用來表示金錢上的花費，有時可用來指時間、精力及生命的**損失**或**代價**，主詞必須為事、物，或虛主詞 it；spend 則表示在某事物上的花費，主詞是人。

- Participation costs the donor nothing and can make such a difference to others.
  （捐贈者不花分文就能改變他人一生。）
  ⇨ participation 指的是「參與」這個行為，動詞用 costs。
- My cousin spent all his savings on that sports car.
  （我表哥花了全部的存款買下那部跑車。）

2. 不定詞可置於句首當主詞，也可移到句尾，並用虛主詞 it 代替主詞的位置。

- To marry a guy whom I don't love cost me my happiness.
  = It cost me my happiness to marry a guy whom I don't love.
  （我嫁給我不愛的人，賠上我的幸福。）

1. 我花了鉅資從台灣飛來西班牙，只是為了看你。

中翻英：____________________________________

2. He didn't want to ________ much money on clothes.
(A) take (B) cost (C) spend (D) get

3. SMS and emails ________ less time and money than the traditional letter-writing style.
(A) take (B) cost (C) spend (D) get

4. It ________ students in U.K. so much effort to go to college but later they found out it ________ them too much money to acquire the degree. Therefore, they organized a protest, forcing the Government to take an action.
(A) took ; took (B) took ; spent
(C) spent ; cost (D) took ; cost

5. Utah's immigration law has already ________ taxpayers in excess of $85,000 ________ in federal court.
(A) cost ; to defend (B) took ; defending
(C) spent ; defending (D) cost ; spending

答案

1. It cost me a fortune to fly (all the way) from Taiwan to Spain just to see you.

2. (C) spend
他不要花很多錢在衣服上。

解析 cost 對應的主詞為事物或虛主詞 it；spend 則表示個人對某事物的花費，主詞是人。由於本題主詞為 he，因此答案為(C) spend。

3. (B) cost

簡訊和電子郵件比傳統寫信的方式省時省金錢。

解析 cost 可用來表示金錢、時間（非明確時間長度）、精力及生命的消耗或代價，主詞須為事物或虛主詞 it；spend 則表示人在某事物上的花費。由於主詞為 SMS and emails，因此動詞選 cost。

4. (D) took ; cost

英國大學生費盡千辛萬苦進大學，但他們發現取得學位所費不貲，因此他們發動抗議，迫使政府採取行動。

解析 表達花費時間或精力的動詞為 take 或 spend，當主詞為 it 時，動詞則應選擇 take；若表達花費金錢，主詞又為 it 時，動詞用 cost，因此答案為(D) took ; cost。

5. (A) cost ; to defend

猶他州移民法已經在聯邦法庭多花了納稅人 8 萬 5 千美元。

解析 若表達花費金錢，而主詞又為 it 時，動詞則為 cost（主詞為人時用 spend），後面可接不定詞延續語意，答案為(A) cost ; to defend。

MEMO

DAY 03 比較句型 I

像……一樣……

as + adj. / adv. + as...

- Finding a soul mate is not as easy as you imagined.
  找到靈魂伴侶不如你想像般簡單。
- Rebecca is not as kind as her brother (is).
  瑞貝佳不像她哥哥這麼好心。

觀念透析

1. 此句型第一個 as 為副詞，第二個 as 為連接詞，引導一個副詞子句，一般省略與主要子句相同的部分。兩個 as 中間依需要，使用形容詞、副詞或數量詞 many 及 much。「as...as」用以表示二者程度相同。例如：

- The secretary isn't as competent as you thought (she is competent).
  （這祕書並沒有你所想的這麼能幹。）
- She plays the piano as elegantly as she does (= plays) the violin.
  （她彈鋼琴和拉小提琴一樣優美。）

2. 延伸句型：

S + V + { as + adj. / adv. + as possible / as + adj. / adv. + as sb. can }　盡可能；盡量

此句型意思為「盡可能……」。「as...as sb. can」等於「as...as possible」。can 可隨時態變化替換成 could，但不能用其他助動詞。此延伸句型中 possible 前面省略了「it is」。

- Please come as early as you can.
  = Please come as early as (it is) possible.
  （請盡可能早來。）

Day 01
Day 02
Day 03
Day 04
Day 05
Day 06
Day 07

1. ________ four girls and three boys of the Hindu community forcibly converted to Islam in 2011.
(A) So many as (B) As much as
(C) So much as (D) As many as

2. I'm sorry, sir, but your wife is ________ a jay bird.【學測】
(A) so crazily as (B) as crazily as
(C) as crazy as (D) so crazily as

3. His technical skills were ________ perfect ________ his signature has obscured the names of the Brothers Grimm and Hans Christian Andersen.
(A) the same ; as (B) as ; as
(C) so ; that (D) such ; that

4. Their job was to secretly learn ________ .
(A) as many possible as about the enemy can
(B) as much possible as the enemy can
(C) as much as possible about the enemy
(D) so many as possible about the enemy

5. You guys can eat ________ .
(A) so many rice as you want
(B) as much rice as you want
(C) as many rice as you want
(D) so much rice that you want

答案

1. (D) As many as
印度教社區多達4位女孩和3位男孩在2011年被逼皈依伊斯蘭教。
解析「so...as」通常用於否定句，而 girls 和 boys 為可數名詞，應用 many 修飾，因此應選擇(D) As many as。

2. (C) as crazy as
對不起，先生，但你的妻子和松鴉一樣瘋狂。

解析 本句「as...as」中間填入形容詞 crazy 作主詞補語，「so...as」通常用於否定句，答案為(C) as crazy as。

3. (C) so ; that
他的技巧如此完美，以致於他的名望使格林兄弟和安徒生黯然失色。

解析 本題前後兩個子句為因果關係，且因為 perfect 為形容詞，必須用 so 而不是 such 修飾，因此答案選「so...that」。

4. (C) as much as possible about the enemy
他們的工作是盡可能地祕密了解敵人。

解析 本題應選擇 much 來修飾 learn；同時應使用「as...as possible」的句型來表達「盡可能」的意思，答案為(C) as much as possible about the enemy。

5. (B) as much rice as you wants
你們想吃多少飯都可以。

解析 rice 為不可數名詞，應與 much 搭配。「so...that」句型後方應接完整子句，「so much rice that you want」少了受詞，因此答案選(B) as much rice as you want。

①A較B優秀；②A較B差

①A + be superior to + B

②A + be inferior to + B

- The products of our company are superior to those of yours.
  我們公司的產品比你們公司（的產品）好。
- Synthetic fabric is inferior to cotton fabric.
  化學纖維布料不如棉質布料好。

本句型為比較級句型的變化型，「-ior」為拉丁文的比較級，後面不加連接詞 than，而搭配介系詞 to。

S + be + superior / inferior / junior / senior + to + 受格
= S + be + better / worse / younger / older + than + 主格

- He is two years senior to me.
  = He is two years older than I.
  （他比我大兩歲。）

junior 年輕的	senior 年長的	prior to （順序上）較……優先的
exterior 外部的	interior 內部的	anterior 以前的
superior 較好的	inferior 較差的	posterior 後面的

- Always be particularly respectful to those older than you even if they are junior to you in position.
  （對於年紀比你大的人一定要特別尊敬，即使他們在職位上比你資淺。）
- Prior to the invention of the electric bulb, he had made numerous experiments.
  （在發明電燈泡之前，他已經進行過許多次實驗。）

1. 萊恩比我老五歲，但看起來跟我年紀一樣大。（使用 senior to）

____

2. LED bulbs are considered ________ incandescent and compact fluorescent lamps, due to their excellent energy efficiency and long life.

(A) inferior to　　(B) superior to
(C) superior than　　(D) better to

3. You are neither superior ________ your younger brother.
(A) or inferior than (B) nor interior to
(C) or worse to (D) nor inferior to

4. I would be very cautious about giving feedback to someone who is very much ________ me.
(A) senior to (B) old than
(C) senior than (D) older to

答案

1. Ryan is senior to me by five years but looks as old as I am.

2. (B) superior to
LED 燈泡比白熾燈和省電螢光燈來得好，因為他們優越的節能功能和使用壽命。
解析 本題應選形容詞作為 LED 燈泡的補語，語意為 LED 燈泡較後面的其他燈泡為佳，所以選 superior（較好的）並搭配介系詞 to。

3. (D) nor inferior to
你和弟弟沒有誰好誰壞。
解析 「既不……也不……」為「neither...nor...」，因此(A) or inferior than 及(C) or worse to 為錯誤選項，(B) interior 意思為「內部的」，與語意不合，答案為(D) nor inferior to。

4. (A) senior to
當我提供意見給比我年長很多的人時，我會非常小心。
解析 若要表示「年長」，可以用 senior to 或是 older than。

……幾倍於……；……是……的幾倍

倍數 + as + adj. + as…

倍數 + 比較級 + than…

倍數 + as + { many + Ns + as… / much + N + as… }

倍數 + the + N + of…

- Based on the number of monthly visits, Facebook is four times bigger than Twitter and five times bigger than YouTube.
  根據每月造訪量，臉書是推特的四倍大，以及 Youtube 的五倍大。

1. 表倍數關係的基本句型是在「as...as」之前放上倍數如：half、one and a half times、twice、three times 等，兩個 as 之間則放入形容詞或副詞。另外還可以用「倍數 + 比較級 + than」的方式表達。

- The window is three times as large as that one.
  = The window is three times larger than that one.
  （這扇窗戶是那扇窗戶的三倍大。）

2. 當遇到名詞時，可將「many + N（複數）」或「much + N」置於「as...as」之間，或是用「倍數 + the + 計量單位名詞 + of」來表示。

- He spent half as much money as I did.
  = He spent half the amount of money as I did.
  （他花的錢是我（花）的一半。）
- This box is twice the size of that one.
  （這個盒子是那個的兩倍大。）

DAY 03

實力養成

1. Your room is ________ mine.
(A) as twice large as
(B) larger half than
(C) twice as large as
(D) half as large than

2. We could have our computer storage devices hold ________ current devices.
(A) 100 times as dense as
(B) 100 times as the density as
(C) the density of 100 times of
(D) denser 100 times than

3. Psychologists say that if children go through a disturbing event before the age of ten, they are ________ likely to suffer psychological problems ________ so teenagers.
(A) three times as ; as
(B) as three times ; as
(C) three times so ; as
(D) as three times ; than

4. Women in this rich Asian country are five ________ now getting advanced degrees ________ in 1995.
(A) as many times ; as
(B) times as many ; as
(C) as much time ; as
(D) the same time ; as

5. Alaska is estimated approximately ________ Texas.
(A) as twice as the size of
(B) twice the size than
(C) twice the size as
(D) twice the size of

答案

1. (C) twice as large as
你的房間是我的兩倍大。

解析 (A) as twice large as 應該改成「twice as large as」；(B) larger half than 應改為「twice larger than」；(D) half as large than 應改為「twice as large as」或「twice larger than」。

2. (A) 100 times as dense as

我們可以讓電腦儲存裝置的裝載量比現在大上100倍。

解析 討論倍數時，倍數後面接「as...as」，中間應為形容詞或副詞，也可以說「100 times the density of」。

3. (A) three times as ; as

心理學家說若小孩在10歲前有不愉快的經歷，他們發生心理問題的機率，是青少年的三倍。

解析 討論倍數時，可以使用「倍數 + as + adj. / adv. + as」，答案為(A) three times as ; as。likely 在此為形容詞，表示「很可能的」。

4. (B) times as many ; as

現在富裕亞洲國家的女性，正在取得高學歷的人數是1995年的五倍之多。

解析 討論倍數時，可以使用「倍數 + as + adj. / adv. + as」，答案為(B) times as many ; as。

5. (D) twice the size of

阿拉斯加的面積估計大約有德州的兩倍大。

解析 討論倍數時，可以使用「倍數 + the + 計量單位名詞 + of」或「倍數 + as + adj. / adv. + as」的用法，因此答案為(D) twice the size of。

DAY 04 比較句型 II

句型速記 1 較喜歡……而較不喜歡……；寧可……而不願……

prefer + N / V-ing + to + N / V-ing
prefer + to VR + rather than + VR
S + would rather + VR + than + VR
S + would + VR + rather than + VR

- I prefer sleeping to watching TV.
  = I prefer to sleep rather than watch TV.
  = I would rather sleep than watch TV.
  = I would sleep rather than watch TV.
  我寧願睡覺而不願看電視。

在表達偏好時，可以使用四種基本句型：

1. 第一種句型「prefer + N / V-ing + to + N / V-ing」用來比較兩個名詞或動名詞：

- Why do people prefer fast-food restaurants to more comfortable ones?
  （為何大家喜歡速食餐廳勝過更舒適的餐廳呢？）
- I prefer sitting in front of the computer and typing to riding the scooter outside on a raining day.
  （我寧願坐在電腦前打字，也不要下雨天在外面騎機車。）

2. 第二種句型「prefer + to VR + rather than + VR」用來比較兩個動詞。

- I prefer to travel independently rather than join a packaged tour.
  （我偏好單獨旅遊勝過跟團。）

3. 第三種句型為「S + would rather VR + than + VR」等於「S + would + VR + rather than + VR」：
   - He would rather not do anything at all than not do it well.
     = He would not do anything at all rather than not do it well.
     （他寧願什麼事都不做，而不願做不好。）
   - My grandparents would live in the countryside rather than live in the big city.
     （我的祖父母寧願住在鄉下也不要住在大城市裡。）

4. would rather 和 prefer (to) 可以單獨使用。
   - James would rather not go to Disneyland.
     （詹姆士寧可不要去迪士尼樂園。）
   - I prefer the red dress (than the white one).
     （我比較喜歡這件紅色的洋裝）。

1. 他們寧願把錢捐給孤兒院，而不是花在衣服上。

   中翻英：______________________________

2. I really ________ rushing home and eating with my family to eating out.
   (A) prefer　　(B) would like
   (C) would rather　　(D) appreciate

3. "Did you critisize him for his mistakes?" "Yes, but ________ it."
   (A) I'd rather not have done　　(B) I'd not rather
   (C) I'd better not do　　(D) I'd rather not doing

4. It is so much easier to go home after a long day at school and turn on the television ________ sit down and do our homework.
   (A) instead of　　(B) than
   (C) rather than　　(D) but not

1. They (would) rather give the money to the orphanage than spend it on clothes.

= They would give the money to the orphanage rather than spend it on clothes.

= They prefer to give the money to the orphanage rather than spend it on clothes.

2. (A) prefer

我寧願趕回家和家人一起吃飯也不要在外頭吃。

解析 比較兩個事物時，可使用「prefer A to B」、「would rather A than B」、「A instead of B」等句型。本句句尾為 to 加動名詞 eating，判斷應選(A) prefer。

3. (A) I'd rather not have done

「你因為他的錯誤而批評他嗎？」「是的，但我寧願沒有那麼做。」

解析 此句為與過去事實相反的假設，rather 後方接完成式否定句表示對所做的事感到後悔。

4. (C) rather than

在學校度過漫長的一天後，回家打開電視比坐下寫功課來得輕鬆多了。

解析 若要表達「不是……而是……」，可以使用 instead of 或 rather than。instead of 必須接名詞或動名詞，因此本題答案為(C) rather than。

越……，越……

The + 比較級 + S + V, the + 比較級 + S + V

- **The more** you practice, **the better** your English will be.
  你越練習，你的英文就會越好。

觀念透析

1. 本句型為「越……，（就）越……」的意思，前一句為表示「程度」的關係副詞子句，兼有連接詞的作用，後一句為主要子句。比較級可以是形容詞或副詞。

- The worse I sing, the more I practice.
  （我唱得越糟，就越努力練習。）
- The more you perform, the greater your self-confidence (is).
  （越常表演，信心越強。）

2. 有時為了縮短語氣，可以將後面的 be 動詞省略。

- The more, the merrier.
  （越多越好。）
- The sooner, the better.
  （越快越好。）

1. 我們越意識到時間管理的重要，我們就越快能達成目標。

中翻英：____

2. The more educated a man is, the ________ is the expectation for dowry（嫁妝）at the time of marriage.【指考】
(A) lower (B) higher (C) better (D) worse

3. ________ our task, the higher level of performance we will exhibit.
(A) We devote to the more time
(B) The more time do we devote to
(C) The more time we devote to
(D) The more time we are devoted to

4. The more medicine we take, ________ .
(A) our disease would be cured faster
(B) the faster our disease would be cured
(C) the faster cured our disease would be
(D) would our disease be cured faster.

5. ________ , the more depressed you are .
(A) The more you work (B) The more work you are
(C) The more your work (D) The more do you work

答案

1. The more aware we are of the importance of time management, the sooner we will reach our goal.

2. (B) higher
男人教育程度越高，結婚時對嫁妝期望越高。
解析 本題為「the + 比較級……, the + 比較級……」的句型。expectation（期望）應該用 high 或是 low 來修飾，根據語意，答案為(B) higher。

3. (C) The more time we devote to
我們花越多時間完成任務，展現出的成果就越好。
解析 在使用「the + 比較級..., the + 比較級...」的句型時，須把句中的「形容詞 + 名詞或副詞」往前放，同時 devote 在此應使用主動語氣（we devote time to our task）。

4. (B) the faster our disease would be cured
藥吃越多，病越快好。
解析 在使用「the + 比較級..., the + 比較級...」的句型時，須把句中副詞的比較級放在句子前面，其他的部分則維持不變，答案為(B) the faster our disease would be cured。

5. (A) The more you work
工作越多，會越沮喪。
解析 在使用「the + 比較級..., the + 比較級...」的句型時，須把副詞改成比較級放在句子前面，其他的部分則維持不變（主詞為 you、動詞為 work），答案為(A) The more you work。

正如……，……也一樣……

$$\text{as } S_1 + V_1, \begin{cases} \text{so} + S_2 + V_2 \\ \text{so + be 動詞 / 助動詞} + S_2 \end{cases}$$

- Just as a perfect lover never exists, so a perfect job can never be found.
  就如同完美情人不存在一樣，完美的工作也不可能找得到。
- As wealth ruins your life, so does poverty.
  如同財富會毀滅人生，貧窮也會。

在本句型中，連接詞 as 帶領附屬子句，so 為副詞帶領主要子句，說明兩個類似的狀況。so 後方的句子若有 be 動詞或助動詞，常置於主詞前作倒裝。

- As your father works industriously, so should you guys study hard.
  （就像你父親努力工作一樣，你們也該認真念書。）
- As water is to the plant, so is exercise to me.
  （運動和我的關係正如同水和植物的關係。）

陷阱題直擊

1. As wealth ruins your life, ________ cautious.
（由於財富毀滅人生，你應該要謹慎。）
(A) so you should be
(B) so should you be
(C) you should be
(D) should you be

1. as 在本句為連接詞，意思是「由於」，而非「如同」，因此主要子句前不可有 so，也不可用倒裝句。
答案：(C) you should be

1. 正如太多油脂戕害健康，過多貪欲則有損心靈。

中翻英：____

2. ________ always needs a captain, so a company cannot survive without a president.

(A) A ship (B) Because a ship
(C) As soon as a ship (D) As a ship

3. He flew higher and higher. As his pride soared, so ________ his height.

(A) did (B) is (C) was (D) does

答案

1. As excessive grease damages your health, so too much greed hurts your soul.

2. (D) As a ship

如同船需要船長，公司也不能沒有總裁。

解析 本題用「As + S_1 + V_1, so + S_2 + V_2」的句型來表達「正如⋯⋯；同樣地⋯⋯」 的意思，as 需要與 so 搭配，故答案為(D) As a ship。

3. (A) did

他飛地越來越高，當他正得意飛揚時，他的高度也升高了。

解析 本題為「as..., so...」的句型，so 後方的助動詞代替 soared，所以要選過去式 did，答案為(A)。

MEMO

DAY 05 表目的、結果、原因句型

句型速記 1 為了……；以便……

S + V + { in order that / so that } + 子句

S + V + { in order to / so as to } + VR

- We prayed that the storm could let up soon so that we could start out.
  我們祈禱，暴風雨盡快停歇，這樣我們才能出發。
- I came in order to say goodbye to him.
  我來是為了和他說再見。

觀念透析

1. 連接詞片語如「in order that / so that」後方接子句，為表達目的、結果之副詞子句。子句中可使用 can、could、may、might、will、would 等助動詞。要注意 in order that 可以放在句首，但 so that 不行。

- I got up early in order that I can see the sunrise.
  = I got up early so that I can see the sunrise.
  （我早起以便能看到日出。）

2. 除了接子句外，也可用「in order to / so as to」接不定詞。in order to VR 可放在句首以加強語氣，so as to 則不行。此時不定詞的意義主詞，須和主要子句的主詞一致。

- In order to enter a good college, I put my nose at the grindstone.
  （為了上一所好大學，我孜孜不倦地用功。）
- Men eat so as to live.
  （人吃東西是為了活命。）

1. Eric晚下班，這樣客戶才能聯絡得到他。

中翻英：____

2. They found that the ants sacrifice themselves ________ preempt a threat.【學測】
(A) so that (B) in order that (C) in order (D) in order to

3. The death of the diva was kept secret ________ shock the public as little as possible.
(A) in order that (B) that (C) so that (D) so as to

4. ________ stay healthy and fit, John exercises regularly. He works out twice a week in a gym.【學測】
(A) So that (B) In order that (C) In order (D) In order to

5. The memory capacity of the new computer has been increased ________ more information can be stored.【學測】
(A) so as to (B) so that (C) as often as (D) in order to

答案

1. Eric left work late in order that his client could reach him.

2. (D) in order to
他們發現螞蟻犧牲自己以先行避免威脅。
解析 依語意判斷，可知動詞詞組「preempt a threat」為目的，因此前面應接 in order to。

3. (D) so as to
隱瞞天后的死訊是為了盡量不震驚大眾。
解析 由於「shock public as little as possible」為動詞詞組，所以應選 so as to 來引導，表示目的。

4. (D) in order to

為了保持健康和身形，約翰固定運動。他每周到健身房健身兩次。

解析 由於「stay healthy and fit」為動詞詞組，而「so as to」不可放在句首，所以應選「In order to」來引導，表示目的。

5. (B) so that

新電腦的記憶體容量已增加，可以儲存更多資料。

解析 「more information can be stored」為表目的之子句，須由 that 來引導。在時態上，主要子句為現在完成式，時間上早於後面的副詞子句。本題應選擇(B) so that 來帶領表目的的子句。

2 句型速記 為了……

to VR..., S + V...

- To avoid misunderstanding, he gave her a clear explanation.
  為了避免誤解，他給她做了清楚的解釋。
- To develop financial responsibility, children should learn to manage their own money at a young age.
  為了養成財務責任心，小孩應該在年幼時學習管理自己的金錢。

觀念透析

本句型為「in order to VR」的省略。用來表示目的（為了……），修飾主要子句，置於句首時語氣比較強烈。

- The CEO devised a thorough business plan to revitalize the company.
  （為了活化公司，總裁訂了全面的企業計畫。）
- To keep your children healthy, please drink water instead of sweetened beverage.
  （為了維持小孩健康，請喝水，勿喝甜飲料。）

1. ________ this wedding party is as romantic as it can be, the wedding planner has been working overtime every day for three weeks.
(A) To have ensured (B) Ensured
(C) To ensure (D) Having ensured

2. ________ , the Government decreased its domestic shopping.
(A) For trade balance (B) For balancing
(C) To trade balance (D) Trading balance

3. ________ our own land, we will fight until all of us die.
(A) Safeguard (B) Safeguarding
(C) Safeguarded (D) To safeguard

4. ________ for her son's education, the mother finally felt relieved.
(A) Having paid (B) To have paid
(C) Paid (D) To pay

5. ________ employee's productivity, the company should encourage employees to travel or engage in leisure activities.
(A) To maintain (B) maintained
(C) Having been maintained (D) maintain

答案

1. (C) To ensure
為了要辦出浪漫的婚禮，婚禮祕書已經每天加班三週了。
解析 由句意可判斷「辦出浪漫的婚禮」為「加班三天」的「目的」，應使用 to 引導。

2. (A) For trade balance
為了貿易平衡，政府減少國內採購。
解析 「trade balance」應為名詞詞組（貿易平衡），而非動詞詞組，因此應使用介系詞來引導，答案應選(A) For trade balance。

3. (D) To safeguard
為了保衛家園，我們會戰鬥到死亡為止。

解析 由於「our own land」為名詞，因此得知 safeguard 為動詞，意思是「保衛」；依句意判斷，「safeguard our own land」為表示「目的」的語氣，應由 to 引導。

4. (A) Having paid
付了小孩的教育費後，母親終於鬆了一口氣。

解析 由語意判斷前後兩個子句為因果關係，而非表目的，因此應選由「Because she had paid for her son's education」轉成的分詞構句「Having paid for her son's education」。

5. (A) To maintain
為了維持員工生產力，公司應該鼓勵員工旅行或從事休閒活動。

解析 由下一句判斷，「maintain employee's productivity」為「目的」，因此應使用 to 來引導動詞詞組。

以免、唯恐……

S + V + { lest / for fear (that) / in case (that) } + S + (should) + VR

- You must work hard lest you (should) fail.
  = You must work hard for fear (that) you (should) fail.
  = You must work hard in case (that) you (should) fail.
  你一定要努力工作以免失敗。

1. lest 意思為「以免……」，表示「為了預防某件事情發生」，其意義和 in case 和 for fear 類似。在詞性上，lest 為副詞連接詞，引導副詞子句，在該子句中，只能用助動詞 should，但 should 可省略，直接接原形動詞：

- You may want to handle your leg injury as soon as possible lest <u>you miss your game next week</u>.
（你該盡快處理腿傷，以免下周無法參賽。）
- The famous movie star always disguised himself as a homeless person for fear that <u>he be spotted by his fans and the paparazzi</u>.
（這位知名影星總是扮成街友，害怕被影迷和狗仔隊逮到。）
⇨ 本句 for fear that 接的子句中，省略了 should，主詞 he 後方直接接原形動詞 be。

2. in case 置於句首時，可當 If 使用，有「如果、萬一」的意思。

- In case he is here, tell me.
（如果他來找我的話，就告訴我。）

1. 他仔細檢查所有手邊的文件以免錯過任何重要線索。(使用 lest)

中翻英：______________________________

2. The tour guide warned us not to go too far ________ that we might get lost.
(A) for fear (B) lest (C) so (D) in order

3. I crept into the elementary school and quickly dropped a bundle of basic reading books into a bag ________ anyone see me with something from "little kids" school.
(A) so that (B) for fear of (C) until (D) lest

4. It is also claimed that it was used to make the women look unattractive ________ other tribes would not capture them and sell as slaves.
(A) because (B) in that (C) for fear that (D) so that

5. It got to the point ________ I was afflicted by anorexia（厭食症）, which in turn caused me to nearly have a heart attack.
(A) what (B) lest (C) unless (D) where

1. He carefully examined all his documents in hand lest he miss any critical clue.

2. (A) for fear
導遊警告我們不要走遠，以免迷路。
解析 由句意可知子句「we might get lost」為表達否定目的（以免……）的子句；該子句可以用「lest / for fear (that) / in case (that)」來引導。因此答案為(A) for fear。

3. (D) lest
我躡手躡足地溜進國小，很快地把一捆基礎讀本丟進袋子裡，怕有人看到我帶著「小朋友學校」的東西。
解析 表達否定目的的子句可以用「lest / for fear (that) / in case (that)」來引導。(A) so that 表示肯定目的，與語意相反；(B) for fear of 應該接名詞而非子句；若選擇(C) until，則表示直到某人看見才停止偷偷摸摸，與語意不合。句中的「anyone see」使用原形動詞，因此可判斷本句使用(D) lest 並且省略了 should。

4. (D) so that
也有說法指出，它的作用是讓婦女看起來不吸引人，如此其他部落才不會抓她們去當奴隸賣掉。
解析 (B) in that 意思是「因為」，若選擇(C) for fear that，則語意正好相反，故答案為(D) so that。

5. (D) where
後來我被厭食症困擾，反而造成我幾乎心臟病要發作。
解析 「I was afflicted by anorexia」在此為關係子句，修飾 the point，就該關係子句的句型架構來判斷，該子句需要關係副詞來引導。

4 句型速記 因為、由於（表原因）

① because of + N / because + S + V

② since / as + S + V

③ due to / owing to / on account of / thanks to + N

- The ambassador could not be arrested for his drunk driving **because he enjoyed** diplomatic privilege. 【學測】
  大使不會因酒後駕車而被逮捕，因為他享有外交特權
- **Owing to** the typhoon, the game was cancelled.
  由於颱風，比賽取消了。

觀念透析

1. 本句型用以表達原因，because / as / since 表示「因為」，屬於連接詞。它所引導的子句，稱為從屬子句或副詞子句。該子句可放在主要子句後，若要強調語氣，則可放在主要子句前。

- Julia put on 10 kilograms of weight within two months **because** she consumed too much fat and took no exercise at all. 【學測】
  （茱莉亞在兩個月內重了10公斤，因為她攝取太多脂肪卻一點都沒有運動。）
- He must have stolen your laptop **since** he was the only one here at that moment.
  （他一定是把你的筆電偷走了，因為當時只有他一個人在這。）

2. 表達原因時，也可用 because of / due to / owing to / on account of / thanks to 接名詞構成副詞片語：

(1) because of 較為口語，後面可接名詞、代名詞、動名詞或 what 引導的名詞子句，可置於句首、句中以及句尾。

- He spent 24 years in prison because of his fight for equal rights for all races.【學測】
  （他因為爭取種族平等而坐牢24年。）
- I can't sleep well because of what you said.
  （我因為你說的話而睡不好。）

(2) due to 可以作修飾語以及置於 be 動詞之後作主詞補語，**後方接名詞**。

- We were late to the meeting due to traffic jams.
  （因為塞車，我們在會議上遲到了。）
- The deletion of both names was due to the severe damage caused by the typhoons bearing the names.【學測】
  （兩個名字都因為該名字的颱風造成重大損害而遭刪除。）

(3) owing to 後方接名詞，to 在此為**介系詞**。多用逗號和句子其他部分隔開，可放在句首、句中或句尾。

- Owing to the torrential rain, landslides occurred in some mountainous areas.
  （由於豪雨的關係，有些山區發生山崩。）
- They decided to postpone the trip, owing to the change of the weather.
  （由於天氣變化，他們決定將旅行延後。）

(4) on account of 可作修飾語和主詞補語，後方接名詞。

- The diva cannot sing as she used to on account of her cancer.
  （這位女歌手的癌症讓她無法像以前一樣高歌。）
- It is on account of all his hard work that he passed the exam.
  （由於他的努力，因此才通過考試。）

(5) thanks to 比較正式，通常帶有感謝含義，但有時翻成「多虧」時，帶有諷刺意味。

- It was thanks to your kind assistance that we paid off our debt in time.
  （幸虧你好心幫忙，我們才能及時將債務還清。）

• Thanks to <u>your arrogance</u>, we lost our game.
（都是因為你的自負，我們才輸掉了比賽。）

1. The General Motor Company was in severe financial difficulty mostly ________ the business of car manufacturing was no longer profitable.【學測】
(A) so that (B) due to
(C) because (D) although

2. He was absent from school ________ illness.
(A) on account of (B) since
(C) on account for (D) because

3. People enjoy attempting to say the nonsensical phrases ________ sex and age.【指考】
(A) as a consequence of (B) regardless of
(C) In terms of (D) on account of

4. ________ the witness's accurate description, the police were able to find the robber in a short time.【學測】
(A) Were it not for (B) With regard to
(C) In addition to (D) Thanks to

5. Experts believe our personality has something to do with our order of birth in the family. ________ them, children in every family are treated differently and thus develop different personalities.
(A) According to (B) Because of
(C) Thanks to (D) In addition to

答案

1. (C) because
通用汽車公司身陷嚴重財政泥淖，主因是汽車製造業務不再有利可圖。

解析 由語意可判斷前後兩個子句為因果關係。(A) so that 表示目的；(B) due to 必須接名詞，不可接子句；(D) although（雖然）與語意不合。

2. (A) on account of

他因病沒來上學。

解析 (B) since 和(D) because 必須接子句，(C)為錯誤寫法，只有(A)選項可接名詞 illness 作為表原因的副詞片語。

3. (B) regardless of

不論性別和年齡，大家喜歡嘗試說些無意義的詞彙。

解析 (A) as a consequence of（由於）；(B) regardless of（無論）；(C) in terms of（就……而言）；(D) on account of（由於）。就語意判斷，答案應為(B) regardless of。

4. (D) Thanks to

多虧了證人的準確描述，警方才能在短時間內找到搶匪。

解析 (A) Were it not for（要不是……）句型為假設語氣，主要子句須有助動詞 should、could、might 或 would；(B) With regard to（關於）；(C) In addition to（除了……之外）；(D) Thanks to（多虧了）。根據語意判斷，本題應選(D)。

5. (A) According to

專家相信我們的個性和家中排行有關。根據他們所言，每個家庭中的兒童所受的待遇也因此不同，進而發展出不同的個性。

解析 (A) According to（根據）；(B) Because of（因為）；(C) Thanks to（多虧了）；(D) In addition to（除……之外）。根據語意判斷，本題應選(A)。them 指前方提過的 Experts。

MEMO

DAY 06 表讓步句型

句型速記 1 儘管、雖然……

though
although
even though
} + S_1 + V_1, S_2 + V_2

- Although my computer is very old, it still runs very well.
  雖然我的電腦很舊，但仍運作得很好。
- He will come over for dinner even though it rains.
  即使下雨，他還是會過來吃晚餐。

1. though / although / even though 意思是「雖然……但是……」，皆可當作連接詞，引導**副詞片語**或**副詞子句**，修飾主要子句。它們可放在主要子句的前或後。

- Though in her 70's, she continues with her labor of love.
  雖然她70多歲，她仍繼續從事熱愛的工作。
- I will try it, though I may fail.
  （即使我可能失敗，我也要試一下。）

2. though / although / even though 帶領的子句為副詞子句，用來和主要子句搭配，此時主要子句就**不能再有 but**，以避免有兩個連接詞。

- Although these words come from the Internet, they are often said to be from a "Martian language" of outer space.
  （雖然這些話來自網路，卻經常被說成外太空的「火星文」。）
- Though he did take Troy in the end, the victory he gained was not so glorious.
  （雖然他最終攻下特洛伊，但他贏得並不光采。）

3. though 也可當作副詞，置於句尾，表「然而」的意思；although 和 even though 則只能當作連接詞。
   - It is a physically and mentally demanding course ; he took it though.
     （這門課在體能和心理上都很要求，但他還是選了。）

1. Helen showed deep remorse for her wrong accusation of her son. _________ she did not apologize to him directly, she tried to do something to make up for the mistake.
   (A) Though (B) Even if (C) So long as (D) In case

2. _________ he entered the room, he rushed into the toilet.
   (A) Even though (B) Even if (C) As soon as (D) As long as

3. _________ , he could only crawl on the floor fumbling for his broken glasses.
   (A) He didn't know what to do
   (B) Although he felt helpless
   (C) Not knowing what to do
   (D) Knowing not what to do

4. The flowers and bushes along the roadside became browned _________ .
   (A) as though burned
   (B) if they had been swept by fire
   (C) even though sweeping fire
   (D) even if they were swept by fire

1. (A) Though
   海倫因錯誤指責她兒子而深深自責，雖然她並沒有直接向他道歉，但她試圖彌補錯誤。

解析 由前後子句語意判斷，此為讓步句型，因此(A) Though（雖然）為正確答案。so long as 意思為「只要」；in case 指「萬一」。

2. (C) As soon as
他一進門就衝進廁所。

解析 由前後語意判斷，此為表時間的副詞子句，因此(C) As soon as 為正確答案，意思是「只要」。

3. (C) Not knowing what to do
他不知道該怎麼辦，只能在地板上爬，摸索尋找他破掉的眼鏡。

解析 由前後語意判斷，兩句為因果關係；因此(A) He didn't know what to do 及(B) Although he felt helpless 為錯誤選項；(D) Knowing not what to do 的否定詞 not 要移到 knowing 之前；答案(C) 為「Because he did not know what to do」簡化而來的分詞構句。

4. (A) as though burned
路邊的鮮花和灌木叢變得烈燄肆虐過般的焦黃

解析 as if 和 as though 意思都是「好像、似乎」，一般多用於口語，常與 look、seem 連用，主詞多是 it，引導一個假設或比喻子句。as if 比 as though 更常用。

無論如何、不管……

No matter + 疑問詞 + S + V, S + V

- **No matter how** well we do at school, most of us will feel inadequate when we go into the adult world.
  無論我們在學校表現多好，大多數人在進入成人世界後，都會覺得不夠。
- **No matter where** you go, I'll go with you.
  不論你去哪裡，我都與你同行。

1. 「No matter + 疑問詞」的句型為表讓步的附屬子句，引導副詞子句，可置於主要子句之前或之後。疑問詞包括：who、whom、what、when、where 以及 how。

- No matter what he says, don't believe him.
  = Don't believe him no matter what he says.
  （不管他說什麼，不要相信他。）

2. 此句型也可改寫成：whoever、whomever、whatever、whenever、wherever 和 however。whoever、whomever、whatever 可引導名詞子句，在子句中當主詞或受詞；whenever、wherever 和 however 則具有副詞性質，引導副詞子句。

- No matter who you are, you can't do whatever you want in your life.
  = Whoever you are, you can't do whatever you want in your life.
  （不管你是誰，都無法任意做自己想做的事。）
- Whoever wants it can have it.
  （任何想要的人都可以擁有它。）
- He travels whenever the opportunity offers.
  （他一有機會便去旅遊。）

1. ________ he is rich or poor, she will stay with him for the rest of her life.
(A) Whether (B) No matter (C) As if (D) Even though

2. ________ how many packages of this product I purchased, I could only use one coupon.
(A) Whether (B) No matter (C) As if (D) Even though

3. ________ my teacher was turning enraged, his voice stayed level.
(A) Because (B) No matter (C) Now that (D) Even though

4. Kevin is a resolute person and seldom gives up ________ what difficulty he faces.
(A) because (B) no matter (C) now that (D) even though

5. ________ they take place in the cities or in the mountains, they cause a large number of deaths and a vast amount of destruction, including disrupted water supply, transport and telecommunications services.
(A) If (B) Whatever
(C) Whether (D) No matter where

答案

1. (A) Whether
無論他有錢沒錢，她都要與他共度此生。
解析 本句使用讓步句型，根據「rich or poor」，判斷應選擇 Whether。No matter 後方必須接疑問詞再接子句。

2. (B) No matter
不管本產品我買幾包，我都只能使用一張折價券。
解析 本句使用讓步句型，根據「how many packages」，判斷應選擇 No matter。

3. (D) Even though
即使我的老師非常憤怒，他的聲音仍保持冷靜。
解析 憤怒（enraged）聲音卻能保持冷靜（level），兩者為相反的情緒，因此應選擇(D) Even though（即使）。

4. (B) no matter
凱文是很果決的人。不管面對什麼困難，他都很少放棄。
解析 依照語意以及「what difficulty he faces」來判斷，應選擇 no matter 來帶領讓步子句。

5. (C) Whether
不管是發生在城市或是山區，它們都造成大量的死亡和破壞，其中包括供水、運輸和電信中斷。
解析 根據語意，可知本題為讓步子句，同時根據連接詞 or，判斷應選 Whether 來帶領子句。

3 句型速記 儘管……，還是……

名詞 / 形容詞 / 副詞 + as / though + S + V, S + V

- Icy as the road was, he drove very fast.
  儘管路面結冰，他開車依然飛快。
- Fast though the taxi runs, sometimes you arrive at the destination faster by MRT.
  儘管計程車跑得快，有時搭捷運還比較快到達目的地。

本句型將原本讓步句型中的名詞、形容詞或副詞放到句首，以加以強調。要特別注意的是，**把名詞置於句首加以強調時，不可以加冠詞**。再者，although 不能用在本句型，只能放在句首。

- Native Chinese speaker (N) though I am, I don't know what this word means.
  （儘管我母語是中文，我也不知道這個詞是什麼意思。）
- Sincere (adj.) as the female artist looks, people don't believe she really feels guilty.
  （儘管這位女藝人看起來很真誠，大家還是不信她真的感到愧疚。）
- Much (adv.) as I hope that another world lies beyond this life, I believe that our presence on earth is a mission.
  （儘管我希望此生後還有另一個世界，我仍相信我們存在於世上是一項使命。）

DAY 06

1. 儘管很高，這位超級名模體重卻只有38公斤。

中翻英：____

2. _________ Germany is affected by the financial tsunami, its unemployment rate remains high.
(A) Few though (B) Little though
(C) Little although (D) As few

3. _________ last season, the real estate market remained strong.
(A) Despite the economy grew slowly
(B) In spite of the economy grew slowly
(C) As the economy grew slowly
(D) Slowly as the economy grew

4. _________ Facebook seems, many fear the penetration of privacy.
(A) Convenience though (B) As convenient
(C) Conveniently as (D) Convenient though

5. _________ Guanshan is, it is where I dream to live.
(A) As a small town (B) Though a small town
(C) Small town as (D) Despite a small town

答案

1. Tall though she is, this supermodel weighs as little as 38 kilograms.

2. (B) Little though
德國受金融海嘯影響雖小，失業率卻居高不下。
解析 本句以副詞 little 修飾 affected，並放在句首加以強調，因此答案為(B) Little though。

3. (D) Slowly as the economy grew
儘管上季經濟成長緩慢，房市卻依然強勁。
解析 despite 及 in spite of 為介系詞，不可接子句；由於兩個子句為對比的概念，as（當、因為）在此與語意不合，故答案為(D) Slowly as the economy grew。

4. (D) Convenient though
雖然臉書似乎很方便，許多人擔心隱私遭到侵犯。
解析 由於本題為倒裝句型，句首應為 seem 的補語，因此選(D) Convenient though。

5. (C) Small town as
關山雖是小鎮，卻是我夢想生活的地方。
解析 由於本題為倒裝句型，因此句首應為主詞補語 small town，答案為(C) Small town as。

縱使、即使

even if
even though

- He promised to come even if it rains.
  他保證即使下雨他還是會來。
- My father attended my wedding on time even though the rain poured.
  即使下了傾盆大雨，我爸爸還是準時參加我的婚禮。

1. even if / even though 的句型意思是「即使、雖然」，兩者皆為連接詞，用來引導副詞子句，用法與 though、although 相同，但語氣更為強烈。

- The ants sacrifice their lives every evening even if the colony isn't under attack by predators.【學測】
（即使群聚沒有掠食者攻擊，螞蟻每晚還是犧牲自己的生命。）
- Many elementary and junior high school teachers around the age of 50 are anxious to retire, even though they can teach for many years if they want to.
（許多50歲左右的中小學教師急於退休，儘管如果他們想要的話還可以教許多年。）

2. even if 所帶領的子句，既可以是事實，也可以是預想或假設。

- Even if you were rich, she wouldn't marry you.
（即使你有錢，她也不願意跟你結婚。）
⇨ be 動詞使用 were，表示與現在事實相反，事實上你並不有錢。

1. It is not pleasant to be arrested in front of one's children, ________ one knows that what one is doing is right.【學測】
(A) even although (B) even though
(C) notwithstanding (D) regardless

2. ________ she seldom left her house and never married, she wrote some wonderful poems about nature, love, life, and death.
(A) Even though (B) Since
(C) When (D) If

3. ________ Pam's mother didn't ask her to, she volunteered to help her do the washing.
(A) However (B) Despite (C) Nevertheless (D) Even though

4. They treated her ________ she were a patient suffering from a contagion.
(A) if (B) although (C) as if (D) even though

5. This ghost showed him how happily his employee's family is celebrating Christmas, ________ they were very poor.
(A) as if (B) now that (C) even though (D) in case

1. (B) even though
儘管行得直、做得正，在小孩面前被逮捕仍令人不快。
解析 notwithstanding（儘管）通常作副詞；regardless 亦為副詞，兩者皆不能引導子句；even although 為錯誤寫法。

2. (A) Even though
即使她很少離家，也從未結婚，她仍寫了些關於自然、愛、生命和死亡的美妙詩文。
解析 根據語意（很少離家卻能寫出不同主題的詩），前後兩個子句為矛盾的事實，應使用讓步句型，故答案為(A) Even though。

3. (D) Even though
潘姆的母親雖然沒有要求，她仍主動幫忙清洗。
解析 (A) However、(B) Despite 以及(C) Nevertheless 為副詞，不可連接子句。

4. (D) even though
即使她是個傳染病病患，他們還是加以治療。
解析 根據語意，應使用讓步句型，although 不可放在句中，故答案為(D)。

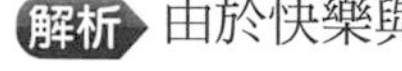

5. (C) even though
這隻鬼讓他看到他員工的家庭雖窮，但仍開心地慶祝聖誕節。
解析 由於快樂與貧窮為衝突概念，故應選擇(C) even though。

無論是否……

Whether (or not) + S + V, S + V

- I'll go on with my project, whether I can get enough support or not.
  不論是否能得到足夠的支持，我都會繼續我的計畫。

1. whether 多與 or not 連用，用來引導副詞子句，意思為「無論是否……」。「whether...or...」也可以連接兩個選項，表示「無論是 A 還是 B」。
   - The economy is improving whether conservatives like it or not.
     （經濟在復甦，不管保守派喜不喜歡。）
   - Whether we are rich or poor, we are all equal.
     = Rich or poor, we are all equal.
     （人不分貧富一律平等。）

2. 引導名詞子句作間接問句時，則譯為「是否……」。
   - I don't know whether he could find a way out of his depression.
     （我不知道他是否能找到走出沮喪的方法。）
     ⇨ 此句中 whether 帶領的子句作為 know 的受詞，為名詞子句，也是間接問句。

1. 不論喜歡與否，我們都必須在星期三前完成它。

   中翻英：____

2. __________ you agree with my decision to move abroad or not, I am going to do it.
   (A) If　(B) Which
   (C) Weather　(D) Whether

3. Facing a variety of food choices every day, we have to consider __________ the food damages our health or not.
   (A) how　(B) whether
   (C) when　(D) where

4. __________ she went to the prom with, her father would not agree.
   (A) Whoever　(B) Whether
   (C) Whatever　(D) If

5. Checking ________ the students understand, teachers will ask them to do experiments, presentations, etc.
(A) whether (B) weather
(C) wither (D) wether

1. Whether we like it or not, we have to finish it before Wednesday.

2. (D) Whether
不管你同不同意我移居國外的決定，我都會做。
解析 if 不能當作「無論……」解釋，且本句並不需要 which 作為主詞或受詞使用。weather 指天氣，須注意與 whether 混淆。

3. (B) whether
每天面對各種食物的選擇，我們必須考慮該食物是否會危害健康。
解析 當句尾有 or not 時可知本題應選 whether 來帶領名詞子句。whether 在此作「是否」解釋。

4. (A) Whoever
不管她和誰去畢業舞會，她老爸都不會同意。
解析 由句型判斷，本題應選擇 Whoever 當作 with 的受詞。

5. (A) whether
為了確認學生是否了解，老師們會要求他們做實驗、報告等。
解析 (A) 為「是否」；(B) 為「天氣」；(C) 為「枯萎」；(D) 指「閹羊」。

DAY 07 表條件句型

除非……，否則……

Unless S + V..., S + V...

- We cannot achieve true friendships unless we are true to ourselves.
  除非我們對自己誠實，否則我們無法實現真正的友誼。
- Your mind tends to grow dull unless you exercise it with new stuff on and off.
  你腦子會變遲鈍，除非你不時用新事物鍛鍊它。

unless 用來表達「若非」、「除非」，unless 引導出否定的條件句，語氣比「if...not...」強烈。unless 表未來條件時，要用現在式代替未來式。

- Unless you study, you will fail the exam.
  （除非你念書，否則你考試不會過。）

比較：If you don't study, you will fail the exam.
（如果你不唸書，你考試不會過。）

- In Samoa, a woman is not considered attractive unless she weighs more than 200 pounds.
  （在薩摩亞，除非女人的體重超過200磅，否則她不被認為具有吸引力。）

1. Reynolds runs workshops ________ owners can be involved in building their own factories.
(A) in order that (B) unless (C) though (D) in spite of

2. ________ Ben kept asking and begging, Tom finally agreed to his request.
(A) As (B) Though (C) Unless (D) For

3. No hunting is allowed in spring, ________ it is the reproductive season for the animals and bear hunting can only be done in the winter.【指考】
(A) because (B) as if (C) whether (D) unless

4. Reformers think that legal prohibition and raising the drinking age will have little effect ________ accompanied by educational programs to help young people develop responsible attitudes towards drinking.
(A) besides (B) without (C) when (D) unless

答案

1. (A) in order that
雷諾辦研討會，好讓業主可以參與建造自己的工廠。
解析 (A) in order that（為了）；(B) unless（除非）；(C) though（儘管）；(D) in spite of（儘管）。本題應選 in order that 表示目的。

2. (A) As
因為班恩不停要求拜託，湯姆終於同意了他的請求。
解析 由句義判斷兩句為因果關係，故應選擇(A) As。

3. (A) because
春天禁止狩獵，因為是動物繁殖季，而獵熊只能在冬天進行。
解析 由句義判斷「the reproductive season」和「No hunting is allowed」為因果關係，故應選擇(A) because。

4. (D) unless
改革者認為，除非搭配教育方案，否則立法禁止同時提高合法飲酒年齡，以幫助青少年建立飲酒負責任的態度，成效不大。
解析 由句意判斷本題應選擇(D) unless 來帶領否定條件句，指除非搭配教育方案，否則不會有效果。accompanied by（伴隨、隨同）。

句型速記 2 如果……就……

If + S + V, S + (will) + V

- If you follow the directions closely, you will find it easy to operate the new machine.【學測】
  如果你仔細地遵照指示，你會發現新機器很容易操縱。
- If it rains tomorrow, I will not go to the party.
  如果明天下雨，我將不會去舞會。

觀念透析

1. if 句型可用來描述「可能發生的事情」或「真實條件」。表未來條件時，條件句使用現在簡單式「If + S + V」代替未來式，結果句則使用未來式「S + will + V」。

- If the sun comes out, this room will get hot.
  （如果太陽出來，這間房間就會變熱。）
- If I have enough time, I will cook tonight.
  （今晚如果我有時間，我會煮飯。）

2. 當描述一般情況或習慣時，結果句可以直接用現在簡單式「S + V」。當描述定律時，未來式或現在簡單式皆可。

- If I have enough time, I cook every evening.
  （只要有時間，我每晚都會煮飯。）
- If I go to a friend's house for dinner, I usually bring a bottle of wine or some flowers.
  （如果我去到一個朋友家吃飯，我通常帶一瓶酒或鮮花。）
- If metal gets hot it will expand / expands.
  （金屬受熱會膨脹。）

1. Water ________ if the temperature ________ 0℃.
(A) freezed ; reached (B) freeze ; reach
(C) will freeze ; reaches (D) will freeze ; will reach

2. You'll need the store receipt to show proof of purchase if you ________ to return any items you bought.【指考】
(A) want (B) wanted
(C) have wanted (D) had wanted

3. ________ Victoria violates the school rule again, ________ end up getting kicked out of school.【學測】
(A) When ; she's (B) If ; she'll
(C) If ; she would (D) As ; she shall

4. If the plan ________, it ________ counter droughts. But in reality, cloud forming technology is still experimental.【學測】
(A) worked ; will help (B) works ; helps
(C) worked ; would help (D) works ; will help

5. Sometimes Jerry ________ me with my homework if he has time.
(A) will help (B) help
(C) helps (D) will be helping

答案

1. (C) will freeze ; reaches
當氣溫達到至攝氏零度，水便會凝結。
解析 此為自然定律，條件句「當氣溫達到攝氏零度」必須使用現在簡單式，結果句「水便會凝結」可用現在簡單式或未來式。water 和 temperature 為單數名詞，因此(B) 選項應該改為 freezes 和 reaches。答案選(C) will freeze ; reaches。

2. (A) want
如果你想退還已購買的物品，你會需要收據證明購買行為。

解析 本題為一般條件句，並不是與事實相反的假設句，if 領導的子句使用現在簡單式，答案為(A) want。

3. (B) If ; she'll
如果維多利亞再次違反學校規則，她最終將被退學。

解析 由句意以及第一個子句的時態判斷，此為表未來條件的句型，故答案應選(B) If ; she'll。

4. (D) works ; will help
若計畫成功的話，就有助於對付乾旱。但實際上，造雲技術還在實驗階段。

解析 由句意可知道計畫尚未成功，因此應選擇表未來條件的句型，答案為(D) works ; will help。

5. (C) helps
有時傑瑞有空時就會幫我做功課。

解析 由 sometimes 得知本句講述一般事實、習慣，故時態應為(C) helps。

只要……的話……

as / so long as + S + V...

- As long as the taxpayers want the school, we build a school.
只要納稅人希望有學校，我們就蓋學校。
- Paris is a wonderful place to stay as long as it's within your budget.
只要預算許可，巴黎絕對是值得停留的美妙城市。

1. 此句型用來表示「只要……就……」。「as / so long as」後接副詞子句，表條件，功能和 only if、on condition that、provided that 相同。

- You may borrow my laptop computer so long as <u>you keep it intact and return it on time</u>.
（只要你能不損傷它並及時歸還，你就可以借我的筆電。）

2. 表未來條件時，副詞子句用現在式代替未來式。
- So long as you stay optimistic, you will find a solution to your current predicament.
（只要保持樂觀，一定會找到方式解決當下的困境。）

3. as long as 還可以表示尺寸、距離、時間的長度。
- This river is twice as long as that one in your hometown.
（這條河是你家鄉那條河的兩倍長。）

1. 只要你持續練習，任何困難都可以克服。

中翻英：____

2. War is avoidable ________ people use their heads and are willing to talk things out.
(A) though (B) but (C) as long as (D) nevertheless

3. ________ the discovery of DNA, scientists think that they may have the power to clone life itself.
(A) On (B) With (C) As long as (D) Not until

4. ________ the casualties continue to occur daily, some Americans are even beginning to suggest a national prohibition of alcohol.
(A) As (B) Although (C) So long as (D) In spite of

5. ________ I have read the novel, I understand why Ann Lee was desperate to shoot the movie *Brokeback Mountain*.
(A) Now that (B) In that (C) So long as (D) Not until

1. So / As long as you keep practicing, you can overcome any difficulty.

2. (C) as long as
戰爭是可以避免的，只要人們用智慧且願意談個清楚。

解析 (A) 雖然；(B) 但是；(C) 只要；(D) 儘管。依照語意，應選(C) as long as 引導條件句。

3. (B) With
隨著**DNA**的發現，科學家們認為他們可能有複製生命的力量。

解析 本題空格後方為名詞詞組，判斷須選介系詞。(A) 指「在……上」或「在……的時候」；(C)為連接詞，表示「只要……的話」；使用(D) Not until 時，主要子句須倒裝。答案為(B) With。

4. (A) As
由於每天持續出現意外事故，有些美國人甚至開始建議國家禁止飲酒。

解析 由句意判斷兩句應為因果關係，所以答案為(A) As（由於）。in spite of / despite 意思為「儘管」，皆為介系詞，後面不可以接子句。

5. (A) Now that
現在看了小說之後，我才明白為什麼李安要義無反顧地拍攝電影《斷背山》。

解析 由句義判斷，兩個子句為因果關係，故可選表原因的 now that （既然）或是 in that（因為）。in that 表示「因為」，只能放在句子中間；now that 表示「既然、因為」，在口語中可省去 that，一般放在句首。句首若為否定詞 not until，主要子句需倒裝。

Level Four

進階篇

The English Patterns You Got to Know

Day 1 假設語氣句型 I

Day 2 假設語氣句型 II

Day 3 對過去事實的推斷

Day 4 否定句型

Day 5 倒裝句型

Day 6 祈使句 & 感嘆句

Day 7 疑問句型

DAY 01 假設語氣句型 I

1 句型速記 如果……（與現在事實相反）

If + S + { were / V-ed } …, S + { should / would / could / might } + VR

- If we were in Barcelona today, we would be able to see Gaudi's buildings.
  如果我們今天在巴塞隆那，我們就能看到高第的建築。
- If I had a million dollars, I might donate some fund to some charities.
  如果我有一百萬美元，我會捐出一些錢給慈善機構。

此句型為假設語氣，表示與現在事實相反的假設；if 所帶領的條件子句若用 be 動詞，**不論第幾人稱都用 were**，一般動詞則用過去式；主要子句則使用助動詞的過去式 should、would、could、might 加原形動詞。

- If I were a millionaire, I would travel all over the world.
  （假如我是百萬富翁，我要環遊世界。）⇨ 但是我不是百萬富翁。
- If everyone had clean water to drink, we would suffer from a lot fewer diseases.
  （如果大家有乾淨的飲用水，我們就會少受很多病痛之苦。）
  ⇨ 不是大家都有乾淨的飲用水。

1. Maybe if they realized the problems it causes, they ________ drinking from a glass at home or carrying water in a refillable steel container instead of plastic.【指考】

(A) will try　　(B) will be trying
(C) would have tried　　(D) would try

2. If she _________ with her job, she shouldn't be pondering over jumping ship.
(A) were contented (B) contented
(C) contents (D) is contented

3. If I lived in Japan, I _________ sushi every day.
(A) might have eaten (B) might eat
(C) will eat (D) eatr

4. If I _________ you, I would find a new place to live.
(A) was (B) am (C) were to (D) were

5. If he were you, he _________ the resources of the family and start his own business.
(A) could be utilized (B) can utilize
(C) could utilized (D) can be utilized

答案

1. (D) would try
也許如果他們明白它導致的問題，就會嘗試在家用玻璃杯喝水，或用可重複使用的鋼杯裝水喝，而非塑膠容器。

解析 由於 if 子句為過去簡單式，可判斷此句型為與現在事實相反的假設（實際上他們不明白它導致的問題），因此主要子句應使用「would / should / might / could + VR」的句型，答案選(D) would try。

2. (A) were contented
如果她滿意她的工作，就不該思索跳槽這件事。

解析 content 除了本身作形容詞，也可以以被動式表示「滿意的」。又由於主要子句為「should + VR」的句型，判斷該句與現在事實相反（其實她不滿意她的工作），if 子句應為過去簡單式，答案為(A) were contented。

3. (B) might eat
如果我住在日本，我就能每天吃壽司。

解析 由於 if 子句為過去簡單式，可判斷此句型為與現在事實相反的假設，因此主要子句應該為「would / should / might / could + VR」的句型，答案選(B) might eat。

4. (D) were

如果我是你，我會找新的地方住。

解析 由於主要子句為「would + VR」的句型，可判斷此句型為現在事實相反的假設，if 子句應使用過去式動詞或 were，答案為(D) were。

5. (C) could utilize

如果他是你，他就能利用家裡的資源創業。

解析 「if I were you」表示與現在事實相反，主要子句應該為「would / should / might / could + VR」的句型；同時，由於 realize 後面接有受詞，可知主要子句應為主動語氣，答案選(C) could utilize。

如果……（與過去事實相反）

If + S + had Vp.p., S + {should / would / could / might} + have + Vp.p.

- If I had studied harder, I might have passed the bar.
  若我當初念書認真點，我也許就能取得律師執照。
- If you had driven more cautiously, this accident might have been avoided.
  若你當初更加小心開車，這起事故可能就可以避免的。

此句型為與過去事實相反的假設法，此時 if 條件子句用過去完成式，主要子句則用「should / would / could / might + have + 過去分詞」來表示。

- If we had rehearsed a little more, our debut could have been more satisfactory.
  （如果我們當時更常排練，我們的首演應該可以更令人滿意。）
  ➪ 當時沒有更常排練。
- Samson might never have been defeated if he had kept the secret to himself.【指考】
  （如果參孫有保守祕密，他便可能永遠不會被打敗了。）
  ➪ 當時沒有保守祕密。

1. If you ________ some money for your pension, you ________ a more financially stable life after retirement.
(A) saved ; can enjoy
(B) save ; could enjoyed
(C) had saved ; could enjoy
(D) had saved ; could have enjoyed

2. If ________ a snowstorm, we would not have been stuck in the airport.
(A) there was not (B) there has not been
(C) there had not been (D) there had had

3. If I had gone to England for the business, I ________ Sandra's visit.
(A) had missed (B) would have missed
(C) miss (D) missed

4. I would have bought a convertible（敞篷車）if I ________ it.
(A) had been able to afford (B) would have been able to afford
(C) am be able to afford (D) was able to afford

5. If you ________ me of your willingness, I can spare you a ticket for the concert in this coming month.
(A) had informed (B) would have informed
(C) inform (D) informed

1. (D) had saved ; could have enjoyed

如果你有存一些退休金，你就能享受經濟更穩定的退休生活。

解析 若是與現在事實相反的假設，則副詞子句為過去簡單式，主要子句為「should / could / might / would + VR」；若是與過去事實相反的假設，則副詞子句為過去完成式，主要子句為「should / could / might / would + have Vp.p.」，正確答案為(D) had saved ; could have enjoyed。

2. (C) there had not been

要不是有暴風雪，我們也不會被困在機場。

解析 由於主要子句為「would + 現在完成式」，所以 if 子句應為過去完成式，以表示與過去事實相反的假設，答案為(C) there had not been。

3. (B) would have missed

如果我去英國出差，我就錯過珊卓的拜訪了。

解析 由於 if 子句為過去完成式，所以主要子句應為「should / could / might / would + have Vp.p.」，以表示與過去事實相反的假設。正確答案為(B) would have missed。

4. (A) had been able to afford

如果我當初負擔得起，我會買敞篷車。

解析 由於主要子句為「would + 現在完成式」，所以 if 子句應為過去完成式，以表示與過去事實相反的假設。

5. (C) inform

如果你告知我你的意願，我可以留一張下個月音樂會的票給你。

解析 由於主要子句使用 can 當助動詞，而非 could，因此可知本句表未來條件，if 子句則應使用現在簡單式。

MEMO

1 句型速記 要不是……

①與現在事實相反

Were it not for + N, / If it were not for + N, / If there were not for + N, + S + would / should / could / might + VR

②與過去事實相反

Had it not been for + N, / If it had not been for + N, / If there had been no + N, + S + would / should / could / might + have Vp.p.

- Were it not for the heat of the sun, nothing could live.
  若無陽光，萬物便不能生存。
- Had it not been for her, I would have got lost this morning.
  今早要不是她，我就迷路了。

「were it not for + N」為「if it were not for + N」的倒裝句，意思是「若非、要不是」，用在與現在事實相反的條件子句，主要子句則是「過去式助動詞 + 原形動詞」；與過去事實相反的條件子句則是「had it not been for + N」，主要子句是「過去式助動詞 + have + Vp.p.」。

- No machine would work for long if it were not properly lubricated.
  （機器若沒有適當的潤滑劑，就不能長期運作。）
- Were it not for (= If it were not for) that annoying habit of his, Jerry would be an attractive man.
  （要不是他那個令人厭惡的習慣，傑里會是一位很迷人的男性。）
- If it had not been for his help, my plan would have failed last year.
  （要不是他的幫助，我去年的計畫可能就會失敗了。）

Day 01
Day 02
Day 03
Day 04
Day 05
Day 06
Day 07

陷阱題直擊

1. If ______ an endangered species, I would take it home and raise it.
（如果牠不是瀕臨絕種的動物，我就會帶牠回家養牠了。）
(A) it is not
(B) it is not for
(C) it were not for
(D) it were not

1. 「If it were not for...」的意思是「要不是有……的話」，容易與「If + S + were...」（如果……）混淆。若選擇(C) it were not for，意思會是「要不是有這些瀕臨絕種的動物」，與語意不合。

答案：(D) it were not

1. 要不是有作業，我今天晚上就去聽音樂會了。

中翻英：______________________________

2. _________ your encouragement, I would have failed in the examination.
（請選出錯誤的選項）
(A) If it had not been for　　(B) Without
(C) If it were not for　　(D) But for

3. Frankly speaking, _________ your kind help, I couldn't have conquered this difficulty successfully.
(A) if it were not for　　(B) if there were not for
(C) if it had not been for　　(D) were it not for

4. _________ people dropping out of the labor force, the unemployment rate would be over 11 percent.
(A) Were it not for　　(B) If there was not for
(C) If it was not for　　(D) Was it not for

1. If it were not for / But for / Without / Were it not for my homework, I could go to the concert tonight.

2. (C) If it were not for
要不是你的參與，我考試不會過。

解析 因為「參與」是過去的事情，本題應使用與過去事實相反的用法，因此可選(A) If it had not been for、(B) Without 及(D) But for 的句型來表示。不可使用與現在事實相反的句型(C) If it were not for。

3. (C) If it had not been for
老實說，要不是您的幫助，我沒辦法成功解決這個難題。

解析 本題為與過去事實相反的否定用法，因此使用「If it had not been for」的句型來表示，(A)、(B)、(D) 皆為與現在事實相反的句型。

4. (A) Were it not for
要不是有退出勞動力的人，失業率會超過11%。

解析 由主要子句的 would be 可判斷此為與現在事實相反假設語氣，因此 if 子句應為過去式動詞或 were。要表示「若非……」的意思，可使用「if it were not for / were if not for / but for / without + N」的句型，因此答案為(A) Were it not for。

但願……

S + wish (that) + { S + were / V-ed（與現在事實相反）; S + had + Vp.p.（與過去事實相反）

- I wish I had a brother to accompany me.
  真希望我有一個哥哥陪我。
- I wish that I had gone to the movies with you last weekend.
  我真希望上週末有和你一起去看電影。

wish 有兩種用法，一是祝福或是期望，例如：I wish you a happy new year.（祝你新年快樂。）以及 How I wish to visit Paris next year!（真希望明年能去巴黎！）；一是表示「但願」的意思，指不會實現的願望，若是與現在事實相反，動詞用 were 或過去簡單式；若是與過去事實相反，則動詞用過去完成式。

- I wish (that) today were a holiday.
  （要是今天放假就好了。）
- I wish I had known the answer then.
  （但願我當時知道答案。）

1. I wish that the whole world ________ how little humanity needs in life.
(A) knows (B) has known (C) knew (D) is known

2. I wish I ________ twenty years ago. You just never listen!
(A) were not choose to marry you
(B) do not choose to marry you
(C) hadn't chosen to marry you
(D) didn't choose to marry you

3. If Paris could foresee the occurrence of this war, he would wish he ________ in love with Helen in the first place.
(A) will not fall (B) didn't fall
(C) had never fallen (D) falls

4. Oh, my! Thirty books are needed for the new semester! I wish I ________ only half of them!
(A) have (B) will have (C) had (D) to have

5. Americans wish ________ individuals rather than ________ members of a large social unit, their family.
(A) they can be considered ; ✗ (B) they could be seen ; ✗
(C) to be thought as ; as (D) to be regarded as ; as

1. (C) knew

我希望全世界都知道人類生活的需要有多低。

解析 當 wish 表示與現在事實相反的希望時，應使用過去式動詞 knew；此外，由於本句有間接問句當作受詞，因此應使用主動語氣。答案為(C) knew。

2. (C) hadn't chosen to marry you

我希望我20年前沒有選擇嫁給你。你從不聽我說話！

解析 當 wish 表示與過去事實相反的希望時（選擇嫁給你是過去發生的事實），應使用過去完成式，故答案為(C) hadn't chosen to marry you。

3. (C) had never fallen

如果巴利可以預見這場戰爭的暴發，他會希望一開始便從未愛上海倫。

解析 本題表示與過去事實相反的希望（「戰爭」和「愛上海倫」都是過去已經發生的事實），所以接在 wish 後面的子句應使用過去完成式，答案為(C) had never fallen。

4. (C) had

天啊！新學期需要30本書！我希望我有一半就好了！

解析 當 wish 表示與現在事實相反的希望時，應使用過去式 had。

5. (D) to be regarded as ; as

美國人希望被看成個體，而不是家庭這個大型社會單位的一份子。

解析 wish 除了接子句外，也可接不定詞表達希望。to be regarded as（被視為……）。

但願……就好了（表示強烈的希望）

If only + 假設語氣子句

= How I wish + 假設語氣子句

- If only I knew how to use a computer.
  = (How) I wish (that) I knew how to use a computer.
  要是我知道怎麼用電腦就好了。

「If only + 假設語氣子句」的意思是「要是……就好了」。若是與現在事實相反，則子句用過去式或be動詞 were；若與過去事實相反，則使用過去完成式「had + Vp.p.」。

- If only I were a paparazzo. In that case, I would have spled on them.
  （真希望我是狗仔，這樣我就能監視他們了。）
- The accidental suffocation could have been avoided if only the mother had known about a side-bed crib.
  （要是這位母親知道有側邊嬰兒床可用，意外窒息就可以避免了。）

1. It's late now. I still haven't found a place to stay. If only the hotels ______________ !

(A) are booked up (B) are booking up
(C) were not booking up (D) were not booked up

2. Matilda was pretty and charming. However, _________ by mistake, she was born into an average family.

(A) as if (B) if only
(C) what if (D) as for

3. If only he ________ his own land, things would be completely different.
(A) have (B) has (C) had (D) had had

4. Why didn't you show up last night? If only you ________ !
(A) came (B) have come (C) had come (D) would come

5. ________ you have grown up, you should learn to be responsible for the things you do.
(A) Now that (B) If only
(C) The next time (D) In some cases

答案

1. (D) were not booked up
很晚了，我還沒有找到住宿的地方。要是旅館沒有被訂滿就好了。
解析 If only 的句型若表示與現在事實相反的假設，則該子句用過去簡單式；而「飯店被訂滿」應用被動句表示，答案為(D) were not booked up。

2. (A) as if
馬莉妲又漂亮又迷人。然而，彷彿是個錯誤一樣，她生在一個普通家庭。
解析 (A) as if（彷彿）；(B) if only（但願）；(C) what if（假使……呢？）；(D) as for（至於、 說到）。

3. (C) had
如果他擁有自己的土地，情況就截然不同了。
解析 由主要子句的「would + VR」可得知，本題使用 if only 來表示與現在事實相反的假設，所以答案為(C) had。

4. (C) had come
你昨晚為什麼不出現？要是你來就好了！
解析 由句意可知本題為與過去事實相反的句型，時態應為過去完成式。

5. (A) Now that
既然你已經長大了，你應該學會為你做的事情負責。
解析 由句意可知兩句為因果關係，因此應選擇 Now that（既然）來引導附屬子句表達原因。

MEMO

DAY 03 對過去事實的推斷

表對過去肯定／可能／否定的推測

S + must / may / can't + have + Vp.p.

- He must have forgotten my name.
  他一定忘了我的名字。
- It must have rained, for the ground was very wet this morning.
  今早地面濕濕的，一定是下過雨了。
- You can't have seen him last week ; he was in New York then.
  你上個禮拜不可能看到他，他當時在紐約。

must / may / can 皆為語態助動詞（modal auxiliary），表達「推測、可能」的意思，後面如果接原形動詞，則表示對現在事實的推測；如果接完成式，則表示對過去事實的推測。can 表對過去的推測時，多用在疑問句或否定句。

1. 對現在事實的推測：

- I am not sure, but I think Sam may be seeing someone.
  （我不確定，但我想山姆應該有約會的對象。）
- This must be Cliff's room. Look how messy it is.
  （這一定是克里夫的房間，你看有多亂。）

2. 對過去事實的推測：

- Christianity may have first held the view of transmigration of souls.
  【指考】
  （最先抱持靈魂輪迴觀點的也許是基督教。）
- I suspected Sedric could have been killed, judging from a long scream.
  （從一聲漫長的尖叫來判斷，我懷疑西追可能已經被殺死了。）

1. I'm not sure, but if I remember it correctly, I ________ Tom in America last year.
(A) can see (B) must have seen
(C) may have seen (D) may as well see

2. I couldn't find my purse. It ________ on my way home.
(A) must steal (B) had to be stolen
(C) must have been stolen (D) had to have stolen

3. The pyramids in Egypt ________ by aliens.
(A) may be built (B) may have been built
(C) may build (D) may have built

4. It ________ a century before the doctor finally came out of the ICU and explained to us that my father had had a stroke.
(A) must take (B) must have taken
(C) had to have taken (D) may be taking

5. The golden age of synthetic perfumes ________ with the introduction of Chanel No. 5.【指考】
(A) may have come (B) may come
(C) may be coming (D) have come

答案

1. (B) must have seen
我不知道，但如果我沒有記錯的話，我去年在美國一定看過湯姆。
解析 表達對過去事實的推測應使用「語態助動詞 + have Vp.p.」；再者，由於已提到「if I remember it correctly」，因此(B) must have seen 較(C) may have seen 更為適合。

2. (C) must have been stolen
我找不到我的錢包。一定是在回家的路上被偷了。
解析 表示對過去事實肯定的推測，應使用「must have Vp.p.」，因此答案為(C) must have been stolen。

3. (B) may have been built
埃及金字塔也許是外星人蓋的。
解析 對於過去可能的推測，應使用「may have Vp.p.」；此外，本句使用被動語態表示金字塔是被外星人蓋的，答案為(B) may have been built。

4. (B) must have taken
感覺應該有一世紀之久，醫生才走出加護病房，向我們說明我父親得了中風。
解析 表示對過去事實肯定的推測，應使用「must have Vp.p.」。

5. (A) may have come
香精的黃金時代可能是隨著香奈兒 5 號的問世而開啟。
解析 此句表示對過去可能的推測，應使用「may have Vp.p.」，因此答案為(A) may have come。

本來應該……（與過去事實相反）

S + ought to / should + have + Vp.p.

- Judith ought to have practiced more then so she would be better prepared for this chance.
茱蒂絲當時應該多練習，對於這個機會才能更有所準備。

should / ought to 同屬語態助動詞，有表達義務之意，後方接原形動詞時表示現在或未來該做的事情；若是接完成式，則表示「過去該做卻沒有做」的行為、狀態，帶有責難或遺憾的意味。

- He should have inspected the equipment before switching it on.
（在打開開關前，他應該檢查儀器才對。）
- My secretary ought to have warned me earlier that my wife was coming.
（我的祕書應該早點警告我，我妻子要過來。）

1. 你昨天應該去看醫生。

中翻英：＿＿＿＿＿＿＿＿＿＿＿＿＿＿＿＿＿＿＿＿＿＿＿＿＿＿＿＿＿＿

2. But for humor, the world ________ be lifeless.
(A) couldn't (B) would (C) need (D) ought

3. I ________ to my parents last week, but I was too busy working on my thesis to remember.
(A) ought to write (B) ought to be writing
(C) ought to have written (D) should write

4. The rebels ________ the capital and caught the ruler by now.
(A) should have occupied (B) should occupy
(C) should be occupied (D) ought to occupy

1. You ought to have seen the doctor yesterday.

2. (B) would
沒有幽默，世界就沒有生命了。
解析 But for 意思是「要不是……」，為假設句型的一種，當描述的事為對目前事實的假設時，主要子句為「S + could / should / would / might + VR」，答案為(B) would。

3. (C) ought to have written
我上週該寫信給我父母，但我忙著寫論文忙到忘了。
解析 「should / ought to + have Vp.p.」可用來表示「過去該做卻未做」的句型，因此本題答案為(C) ought to have witten。

4. (A) should have occupied
反叛軍現在應該已經佔領首都並已逮捕統治者。
解析 「should / ought to + have Vp.p.」可用來表示「應該已經完成某事」，且本題應採用主動語氣表示叛軍為佔領的動作者，答案應選(A) should have occupied。

最不可能、最不適合、最不願意

the last + N + { to VR / (that) + S + V }

- He is the last person to steal your money.
  他絕非是偷你錢的人。
- The last thing he wants to do is to offend you.
  他最不願意做的事就是觸怒你。

the last 直譯為「最後的」，指最後順位的選擇或可能性，接不定詞或形容詞句表示「最不可能」、「最不願意」或「最不適合」的意思。

- English is the last thing <u>that I have interest in</u>.
  = The last thing <u>that I have interest in</u> is English.
  （我對英文最不感興趣。）
- The last star sign <u>to have a successful long distance relationship with</u> is Leo.
  （最不能與之談遠距離戀愛的星座是獅子座。）
- The last thing <u>that this driver-beating artist should have done</u> was to have lied in the press conference.
  （這位毆打駕駛的藝人最不應該做的就是在記者會上撒謊。）

1. Hope is ________ so you should always stay optimistic for your future, especially when you are suffering.
(A) the latest thing to lose　　(B) the last thing for loss
(C) the least thing to lose　　(D) the last thing to lose

2. _________ is to try to please everyone.
(A) The last thing one should be done
(B) The last thing one should do
(C) The late thing one should do it
(D) The late thing one should do

3. The last investment tool _________ is bonds.
(A) I am chosen (B) to choose me
(C) I will choose (D) I will be chosen

4. The last job that an impatient person _________ a teacher.
(A) happy with is (B) is happy is
(C) is happy with is (D) is happy with

5. The _________ person I should have gone to the beach _________ my wife.
(A) late ; with was (B) last ; with was
(C) last ; was (D) late ; with

答案

1. (D) the last thing to lose
最不該失去的就是希望，所以你永遠應該對未來保持樂觀態度，尤其是當你痛苦的時候。

解析 latest 意思是「最近的、最新的」；the least 是 little 的最高級，指「最少的、最不重要的」。本題應選 the last（最後的）以表示「最不該」，後面接不定詞或形容詞子句進行修飾，故答案為(D) the last thing to lose。

2. (B) The last thing one should do
最不該做的事情之一就是試圖取悅每個人。

解析 本題使用「the last + N + 子句」的句型來表示「最不該……」。此外，由於形容詞子句的主詞為 one，是動作 do 的執行者，應採用主動語態，答案為(B) The last thing one should do。

3. (C) I will choose
我絕不會選擇的投資工具是債券。

解析 由於 I 是 choose 的執行者，因此「the last + N + 子句」後面接的子句應採用主動語態。

4. (C) is happy with is
沒耐性的人最不樂於從事的工作就是當老師。

解析 由於 the last job 後面的形容詞子句必須有動詞，主要子句本身也必須有動詞，因此本句應該有兩個動詞。第一個 is 為形容詞子句的主詞，第二個 is 為主要子句的主詞。「sb. is happy with sth.」指「某人滿意某事」。

5. (B) last ; with was
我絕不該和我的妻子一起去海灘。

解析 由於本題有「最不該……」的意思，因此應選擇「the last + N + 子句」的句型。因為是「跟」某人去海灘，所以記得加上介系詞 with。

沒有……不……；每當……必定……

can't / never / no... + without + V-ing / N

- They never discuss without quarreling.
  他們討論一定吵架。
- I can't do anything without consulting you.
  我做事不能不問你。

「never...without + V-ing / N」為雙重否定句型，意思「沒有……不……」、「每一次……都……」，除 never 外，也可代換成 no、not、hardly 等否定詞。

- She never goes to a bookstore without buying some books.
  （她每次進書店，一定會買一些書。）
- No account of the solar system would be complete without mention of comets.
  （沒有提到彗星，對太陽系的敘述就不夠完整。）

- No one learns English without making mistakes.
  （大家學英文都會犯錯。）

1. There is ________ hardships.
(A) no success without (B) no success but
(C) not successful but (D) not successful without

2. Not a student has access to the library ________ his student card.
(A) without showing (B) but showing
(C) without being shown (D) but to show

3. This shy boy can ________ look at the girl he admires ________ blushing.
(A) not ; but (B) never ; without
(C) no ; without (D) never ; but

4. No alternation of the contract ________ prior mutual agreement.
(A) shall not be made without (B) shall be made but
(C) shall be made without (D) shall not be made but

5. My husband ________ watches TV news without ________ .
(A) not ; angry (B) never ; angry
(C) not ; to get angry (D) never ; getting angry

答案

1. (A) no success without
沒有困難就不會成功。

解析 本題使用「no...without + V-ing / N」的雙重否定句型，表示「沒有……便不……」，「not...but...」是指「不是……而是……」，因此(B) no success but 以及(C) not successful but 為錯誤選項。再者，there is 後面接的是名詞，選項(D)的 successful 為形容詞，故不合。答案為(A) no success without。

Day 01 Day 02 Day 03 Day 04 Day 05 Day 06 Day 07

2. (A) without showing
所有學生進入圖書館都要出示學生證。

解析 由句意判斷本句為「not...without + V-ing / N」的雙重否定句型，表示「沒有……便不……」；同時，「學生出示學生證」為主動語氣，應選擇 showing，本題答案為(A)。

3. (B) never ; without
這位害羞的男生每次看著愛慕的女生都會臉紅。

解析 本句使用「never...without + V-ing / N」的句型來表示「每次……必會……」，答案為(B) never ; without。

4. (C) shall be made without
若無雙方事先同意，該合約不得更動。

解析 「not...but...」的意思是「不是……而是……」，與本文語意不合，應使用「no...without...」的雙重否定句型。

5. (D) never ; getting angry
我丈夫每次看電視新聞都會發脾氣。

解析 當一般動詞為否定時，需搭配助動詞，因此(A) not ; angry 及(C) not ; to get angry 為錯誤答案。而介系詞 without 後面須接名詞或動名詞當受詞，故答案為(D) never ; getting angry。

未必、不一定

not necessarily

- A happy man does not necessarily have a fortune.
  幸福的人未必富有。
- Inventions do not necessarily refer to those big in size. They can be as small as the safety pin or the safety razor.
  發明不一定指體積大的物品，也可以小如別針或安全刮鬍刀。

not necessarily 為副詞，可以修飾動詞或形容詞，意思為「未必是……」；not necessary 意思則是「不必要的」，為形容詞，兩者容易混淆，須特別注意。

- Bankruptcy does not necessarily result in the disappearance of a company.
  （破產不一定會造成一家公司的消失。）
- It is not necessary to buy an expensive car.
  （沒有必要買一輛很貴的車。）

1. ________ I have a good ear for music, it ________ that I can always sing a song in tune.
   （儘管我音感很好，但這未必意味著我唱歌不會走音。）

2. People living in these tall buildings ________ willing to climb so far just to get home.
   (A) necessary (B) are not necessary
   (C) are not necessarily (D) necessarily

3. Stress ________ bad. Sometimes work is done better under pressure.
   (A) is not necessary (B) is not necessarily
   (C) does not necessarily (D) does not necessary

4. The rich ________ happy.
   (A) are not necessarily always (B) are always not necessary
   (C) is not always necessary (D) is not always necessarily

答案

1. Despite the fact that / In spite of the fact that ;
   doesn't necessarily mean / doesn't always mean

2. (B) are not necessary
住在這些高樓大廈裡的人不一定願意只為了回家而爬這麼遠。
解析 主詞是 people，須選 are 作動詞；同時，willing 為形容詞，所以必須用副詞 necessarily 來修飾，答案為(B) are not necessary。

3. (B) is not necessarily
壓力不見得不好。有時候，有壓力會把工作做得更好。
解析 stress 為不可數名詞，故 be 動詞應選擇 is。而 bad 為形容詞，應該以副詞 necessarily 加以修飾。

4. (A) are not necessarily always
富人不見得開心。
解析 「the + 形容詞」代表具有某種特性的一群人，須搭配複數動詞；另外，happy 須以副詞 always 修飾，再以 not necessarily 修飾 always happy，表示「不全然都很開心」的意思。

句型速記 4 太……而不能……

too + adj. / adv. + to VR

- One is never too old to learn.
  活到老學到老。
- It is never too late to mend.
  亡羊補牢，為時未晚。

觀念透析

1. 「too...to VR」中間放入形容詞或副詞，表示「太……而不能……」，後方的不定詞用來修飾副詞 too，表否定的結果。

- The water is too hot to drink.
  = The water is so hot that it can't be drunk.
  = The water is too hot for drinking
  （這水太熱了，不能喝。）

2. 「too...not to VR」為雙重否定，表示「很……以致於能……」，相當於「so...that...」。
   • She is too wise not to know it.
   （她太聰明了，所以不會不知道這件事。）

1. 天氣沒冷到無法游泳的地步。

   中翻英：____

2. Mr. Jones was ________ angry to say anything at all.
   (A) too much (B) so much (C) so (D) too

3. The car ran too ________ to stop before it hit the wall.
   (A) quick (B) hurry (C) fast (D) haste

答案

1. It is not too cold to swim.
2. (D) too
   瓊斯先生憤怒到說不出話來。
   解析 too much 和 so much 須接名詞表示「太多的……」。「too + adj. / adv. + to V」句型表示「太……而不能……」，答案選(D)。「so ...that...」是指「太……以致於……」。
3. (C) fast
   車子開得太快而來不及在撞上牆之前停下來。
   解析 本題需選副詞來修飾動詞 run，(A)為形容詞，(B)只能作名詞和動詞，(D)也只能作名詞和動詞，只有(C) fast 可當形容詞和副詞。

DAY 05 倒裝句型

1 句型速記 只有……才能……

only + { 副詞片語 / 副詞子句 } + be動詞 / 助動詞 + S + V

- Only in Taiwan can you enjoy a wide variety of cuisine at low prices.
  只有在台灣，你才能以低價品嚐各式各樣的美食。
- Only when one is away from home does he realize how sweet home is.
  只有當一個人離家時，才知道家的甜蜜。

此為倒裝句型，把 only 和強調的部分（副詞片語或副詞子句）放在句首，並將 be 動詞或助動詞放在主詞之前，若兩者皆無時，則要加上do、does 或 did。

- Only <u>in the leading museums</u> can the objects be fully appreciated by the world.
  （只有在大博物館，物品才能全球共賞。）
  原句：The object can be fully appreciated by the world only in the leading museums.
- Only by enjoying English can a student excel in English.
  （只有透過享受英語，學生才能在英語上脫穎而出。）
  原句：A student can excel in English only by enjoying English.

1. Only through sacrifice and perseverance ________ able to complete their " mission impossible."
(A) were they (B) they were (C) they did (D) did they

2. Only ________ using earplugs ________ protect his ears.
(A) with ; can he (B) by ; he can
(C) with ; he can (D) by ; can he

3. Only in human beings ________ the adipose gene（脂肪基因）________.

(A) ✗ ; can be found　　(B) can ; be found
(C) ✗ ; be found　　(D) can ; find

4. Only when he got to the office ________ this company ________ bankruptcy.

(A) he learned ; go　　(B) did he learn ; go
(C) he learned ; to go　　(D) did he learn ; went

1. (A) were they
只有通過犧牲和毅力，他們才得以完成他們「不可能的任務」。
解析 able 是形容詞，表示「能夠的」。本題使用「only + 副詞片語 + 倒裝句」的句型，強調「through sacrifice and perseverance」，因此必須把動詞 were 往前放，故答案為(A) were they。

2. (D) by ; can he
只有透過使用耳塞，他才能保護自己的耳朵。
解析 由於表達「進行某種動作的方式」需用 by，同時本題使用「only + 副詞片語 + 倒裝句」的句型，強調「by using earplugs」，因此須把助動詞 can 往前放，答案為(D) by ; can he。

3. (B) can ; be found
脂肪基因只有在人類身上被發現。
解析 本題用 only 的倒裝句型，強調「in human beings」；由於主詞為「the adipose gene」，因此須用被動語氣 be found（被發現），同時以助動詞 can 進行倒裝。

4. (D) did he learn ; went
當他抵達辦公室，才得知公司破產了。
解析 由句意判斷，主要動詞 learn（得知）後面接名詞子句當受詞，同時必須使用過去式助動詞 did 來進行倒裝。再者，破產為過去發生的事，因此選 went 作為子句的動詞。

2 句型速記 否定詞置於句首

否定副詞 否定副詞片語 副詞子句	+ be動詞 / 助動詞 + S + V

- Not a word did he say.
  他不發一語。
- Little did I think we would meet 30 years later.
  我想不到我們30年後會重逢。
- Not until I saw him did I feel relieved.
  我看到他才感到放心。

1. 常用的否定副詞有：Not、Never、Hardly、Little、Few 等。
2. 常用的否定副詞片語有：In no way、By no means、Under no circumstances 等。
3. 常用的副詞子句有：「Only when + S + V」、「Not until + S + V」等。
4. 為了強調句中的否定部分，將否定詞放在句首，並把助動詞或 be 動詞放在主詞之前，形成倒裝。要注意的是，助動詞往前移，後方的動詞仍須配合助動詞。
   - Neither did I witness the robbery.
     = I did not witness the robbery, either.
     （我也沒有目擊到搶案。）
   - Rarely have I seen such a beautiful skyscraper.
     = I have rarely seen such a beautiful skyscraper.
     （我很少見過這麼漂亮的摩天大樓。）

1. Little ________ this football player ________ that 24 days after Super Bowl, his team would release him.
(A) is ; realized (B) is ; realize
(C) did ; realize (D) was ; realized

2. Little ________ that life as she knew it was about to change forever after her debut.
(A) she knew (B) she did knew
(C) was she known (D) did she know

3. ________ he told me so ________ he had intended to commit suicide.
(A) It is not until ; I do not know (B) Not until ; I did not know
(C) Not until ; didn't I know (D) It's not until ; didn't I know

4. Little ________ about making a difference in our co-worker's life so far.
(A) we think (B) we have thought
(C) were we thought (D) have we thought

5. ________ we start to live simply can we go inward to find out the power inside us.
(A) It is until (B) It is not until
(C) Not until (D) Not until does

答案

1. (C) did ; realize
這位足球球員，想都沒想到在超級盃 24 天後，他的球隊會將他釋出。
解析 本題使用否定倒裝句型來強調否定詞 little。realize 為一般動詞，且得知被釋出的事實發生在過去，須用助動詞 did 來搭配進行倒裝，原句為「He did not realize...」。

2. (D) did she know
她想不到她的人生在首演後會就此改變。

解析 本題使用否定倒裝句型來強調否定詞 little，並且使用助動詞 did 配合 know 進行倒裝。

3. (C) Not until ; didn't I know
他告訴我後，我才知道他曾打算自殺。

解析 本題使用 not until 否定倒裝句型來強調「he told me so」這個時間點。由於動詞為 know，且該敘述發生在過去，因此須使用助動詞 did 來進行倒裝。

4. (D) have we thought
我們也沒想過改變同事的人生。

解析 本題使用否定倒裝句型來強調否定詞 little。由句尾 so far（到目前為止）可知時態為現在完成式，因此須將 have 前移來進行倒裝。

5. (C) Not until
直到我們開始過簡單生活，才能往內心找出蘊含的力量。

解析 本題使用 not until 否定倒裝句型來強調「we start to live simply」這個條件。若本句句首為「It is not until」，則後方子句不需倒裝。

句型速記 3 直到……才……

S + be動詞 / 助動詞 + not + V + until...
= It is not until… + that + S + V
= Not until... + 助動詞 + S + V

- We do not realize the true value of health until we lose it.
  = It is not until we lose it that we realize the true value of health.
  = Not until we lose it do we realize the true value of health.
  直到失去健康我們才知道它真正的價值。

1. 「not...until...」可用來表示「某種狀態的改變」，not 通常會與 be 動詞或助動詞配合使用。until 後面接某時間或條件。

- John Forbes Nash did not recover from his mental illness until <u>2002</u>.【學測】
（約翰・納許的精神病到 2002 年才恢復。）

2. 「It was not until」後面接某時間或條件，再接 that 子句。

- It was not until <u>the arrival of the Industrial Revolution</u> that these mills were put to bigger use.【學測】
（直到工業革命時，這些工廠才被廣泛使用。）

3. 若將「not until」放在句首，則須把助動詞或 be 動詞往前移，形成倒裝句。

- Not until <u>children finish their homework</u> are they allowed to watch TV.
（孩子們要完成他們的功課才能看電視。）

1. The burden on my heart won't be relieved ________ back what I have owed him.
(A) until did I pay (B) until I paid
(C) until do I pay (D) until I pay

2. ________ George became famous ________ about George's endeavor.
(A) It's not until ; did we learn (B) Not until ; we learned
(C) Until ; we don't learn (D) Not until ; did we learn

3. ________ the pioneering scientific work of Louis Pasteur in the late 1860's ________ identified as a living organism.
(A) Not until ; that yeast
(B) It was not until ; was yeast
(C) It was not until ; that yeasts was
(D) Not until ; did yeast

4. ________ Tracy flew to New York to study art, ________ the culture shock repeatedly mentioned by her teacher.
(A) Not until ; she realized
(B) It was not until ; did she realize
(C) Not until ; that she realized
(D) Not until ; did she realize

答案

1. (D) until I pay
直到我償還我對他的虧欠，我心中負擔才會得到寬慰。
解析 只有當 not until 置於句首時，才需倒裝。根據主要子句的 won't，可知 until 應接現在簡單式表示時間條件。

2. (D) Not until ; did we learn
直到成名，喬治的努力才為我們所知。
解析 本題使用 not until 倒裝句型來強調「George became famous」。由於動詞時態為過去式，因此須使用助動詞 did 來進行倒裝。

3. (C) It was not until ; that yeasts was
直到路易・巴斯德在 1860 年代後期的開創性研究，酵母才被確定是一個活性有機體。
解析 本句句首為「It was not until」，後面接子句，不需倒裝，答案為(C) It was not until ; that yeasts was。

4. (D) Not until ; did she realize
直到崔西飛往紐約學習藝術，才明瞭老師不斷提及的文化衝擊。
解析 本題使用 until 倒裝句型來強調「Tracy flew to New York to study art」。由於動詞時態為過去式，因此須使用助動詞 did 來進行倒裝。

MEMO

DAY 06 祈使句 & 感嘆句

句型速記 1 如果……，那麼……

祈使句 + { , and / , or } + S + V

- Take a look of these photos, and you will know how lovely it is.
  看看這些照片，就會知道它有多麼可愛。
- Give me liberty, or give me death.
  不自由，毋寧死。

1. 祈使句後接「and + 子句」時，有條件句「if + S + V」（如果）的特性。
   - Stand up, and you will see farther.
     = If you stand up, you will see farther.
     （站起來，你就可以看遠一點。）
2. 祈使句後接「or + 子句」時，有條件句「if not...」（否則、要不然）的特性。
   - Spit that chewing gum out of your mouth, or I will get my hand into your mouth and get it out for you.
     = If you don't spit that chewing gum out of your mouth, I will get my hand into your mouth and get it out for you.
     （把口香糖吐出來，不然我就把手伸進去幫你拿出來。）

1. Take two tablets every day, ________ you will feel much better after several days.
   (A) or (B) when (C) if (D) and
2. Dress warmly, ________ get a cold.
   (A) and you (B) if you will (C) or you will (D) you will

3. Constantly save your file while you are writing the report, ________ need to rewrite them if the computer crashes down.
(A) or you will (B) and you will (C) which you will (D) or will you

答案

1. (D) and
每天吃兩片藥，幾天後你會感覺好多了。
解析 依照句意，本題的意思為「如果……那麼……」，為肯定語氣的祈使句，應使用連接詞 and。

2. (C) or you will
穿暖活點，不然你會感冒。
解析 「穿暖活點」和「你會感冒」為相反的關係，因此應選連接詞 or，表示「若不……則……」。

3. (A) or you will
寫報告時要一直儲存文件，不然電腦當機了，你就必須重寫。
解析 由於前後兩個子句為相反的關係，應使用連接詞 or 表示「若你不……則……」。

務必……、確定……

be / make + sure + { **of + N** / **to + VR** / **that + S + V** / **wh-疑問詞 + S + V** }

- Make sure you eat right when you are expecting a baby!
當你在懷孕時，務必要確保飲食正確。
- Be sure you're right, then go ahead.
確定你是對的，便勇往直前。

DAY 06

「make sure / be sure」表示「確認、把……弄清楚」，常作祈使句，可以接「of + 名詞 / 動名詞」、不定詞、that 和 what 等引導的名詞子句。

- You'd better make sure <u>of a window seat</u> when you book a ticket online.
（在網路上訂票時最好能確認訂的是靠窗的位子。）
- They should be sure <u>to eat</u> a good balance of protein, carbohydrate, and fat.
（他們一定要平衡攝取蛋白質、碳水化合物和脂肪。）
- I really enjoy the food in this restaurant. I'm sure <u>(that) I will come again</u>.
（我真的很喜歡這家餐廳的食物，我肯定我會再來。）

1. We will make sure ________ and legality of the work environment.
(A) to constantly improve
(B) of constantly improve
(C) of constant improvement
(D) constant improvement

2. ________ that you put down every word the teacher says.
(A) Make sure　(B) Make sure of
(C) To make sure　(D) To make sure of

3. The pet owners should always make sure ________ they feed their puppies is easy to swallow.
(A) what　(B) which
(C) that　(D) of

4. Can you make sure ________ the wording of my thesis lest it should be returned by my professor?
(A) of　(B) that
(C) to　(D) which

5. They should make sure ________ the sanitation（環境衛生）of the restaurant.
(A) of inspect (B) to inspect
(C) of inspection (D) that inspects

1. (C) of constant improvement
我們會確保工作環境持續改善及合法性。
解析 make sure 後面可以接「of + N」或是不定詞，然而若接不定詞，則(A) to constantly improve 後面還需要受詞，因此答案為(C) of constant improvement。

2. (A) Make sure
務必要將老師所說的每一個字寫下來。
解析 本句為祈使句，句首使用原形動詞而非不定詞。(B) Make sure of 後方只能接名詞或動名詞，不能接子句，故答案為(A) Make sure。

3. (A) what
寵物飼主應永遠確保餵食寵物的食物容易吞嚥。
解析 由於 feed 為授與動詞，後面接直接受詞和間接受詞。本題應選不需先行詞的複合關係代名詞 what 當作 feed 的直接受詞。

4. (A) of
你可不可以確認我的論文用字，免得被教授退回？
解析 由於 make sure 後面必須要用 of 連接後面的名詞 the wording of my thesis，答案為(A)。

5. (B) to inspect
他們務必要檢查餐廳環境衛生。
解析 本題應選擇不定詞「to inspect」連接句尾的受詞「the sanitation of the restaurant」。

句型速記 3 多麼……（感嘆句）

① How + adj. / adv. + S + V

② What + { a(n) + adj. + N / adj. + N(s) } + S + V

- How beautiful this little village is!
  這個小村莊真漂亮！
- What a cute little baby he is!
  他真是個可愛的嬰兒！

1. 感嘆句有 what 和 how 兩種開頭，主詞和動詞放在句尾，同時加上驚嘆號，用來表示強烈情感。若是「how + adj. / adv. + S + V」的句型，意思是「多麼……呀！」，強調 how 後面所接的**形容詞或副詞**。

- How seriously (adv.) they played the football match!
  （他們打足球賽打得好認真！）

2. 以 what 開頭的感嘆句強調的重點在於 what 後面所接的**名詞**。若為單數可數名詞，前面須加不定冠詞 a / an；後面的主詞和動詞可以省略。

- What a big mistake (N) he had made!
  （他犯下一個很大的錯誤！）
- We spent half hour in the traffic jam. What a waste of time (N) (it was)!
  （我們在車陣中等了半小時。真是浪費時間！）

1. ________ to believe that he would apologize to me!
(A) How idiot was I (B) How idiot I was
(C) What an idiot was I (D) What an idiot I was

2. What ________ !

(A) are you a liar (B) you are a liar

(C) a liar are you (D) a liar you are

3. What ________ to pay for such a stupid mistake!

(A) a high price is it (B) it is a high price

(C) a high price it is (D) is it a high price

4. How ________ dances!

(A) does the ballerina beautifully (B) the ballerina does beautiful

(C) beautifully the ballerina (D) beautiful the ballerina

答案

1. (D) What an idiot I was

我好白痴，以為他會道歉！

解析 本題考名詞感嘆句，其句型架構為「What + (adj.) + N + S + V」，因此答案為(D) What an idiot I was。

2. (D) a liar you are

你這個大騙子！

解析 本題考名詞感嘆句，其句型架構為「What + (adj.) + N + S + V」，因此答案為(D) a liar you are。

3. (C) a high price it is

為這樣一個愚蠢的錯誤付出的代價好高昂！

解析 本題考名詞感嘆句，其句型架構為「What + adj. + N」，因此答案為(C) a high price it is。

4. (C) beautifully the ballerina

那位女芭蕾舞者跳得多麼漂亮！

解析 本題應選副詞以修飾動詞 dances，感嘆句句型為「How + adj. / adv. + S + V」，答案為(C) beautifully the ballerina。

DAY 07 疑問句型

1 句型速記 間接問句

直述句
祈使句 } + 疑問詞 + S + V
一般問句

- I don't know why she is upset.
  我不知道她為什麼生氣。
- Try to remember who opens the door.
  試著記住是誰打開這扇門。
- Do you know where she lives?
  你知道她住在哪裡嗎？

觀念透析

1. 獨立使用的問句為直接問句；若將一個問句併入另一個句子中，擔任主詞或受詞者，則稱為間接問句。間接問句的句型，是把疑問詞放在句首，然後直接接「主詞 + 動詞」而成。助動詞如 will、should、would、must、may、can 等，須保留，但如果是 do、does、did 等助動詞，則必須去掉。

- The instructor questioned the class what he had said earlier.
  （老師問全班他剛才說什麼。）
- My mother knows how I spend my allowance.
  （我母親知道我怎麼花零用錢。）

2. 間接問句的疑問詞也可接不定詞。

- I am not sure what I should do next.
  = I am not sure what to do next.
  （我不確定接下來該怎麼做。）

1. My father asked me to tell him ________ .
(A) who was my dream girl (B) who my dream girl be
(C) who to be my dream girl (D) who my dream girl was

2. She asked me ________
(A) where is the clinic (B) where the clinic was
(C) the clinic is where (D) where to the clinic

3. He asked me ________ arrive.
(A) when the plane (B) when would the plane
(C) when the plane would (D) when the plane does

4. His coach told him ________ for the national game.
(A) why he was not picked (B) why was he not picked
(C) why wasn't he picked (D) for what wasn't he picked

1. (D) who my dream girl was
父親叫我告訴他，我夢中情人是誰。
解析 本題考間接問句句型，也就是「wh-疑問詞 + S + V」，答案為(D) who my dream girl was。

2. (B) where the clinic was
她問我診所在哪裡。
解析 本題考間接問句句型，其架構為「wh-疑問詞 + S + V」，答案為(B) where the clinic was。

3. (C) when the plane would
他問我班機抵達時間。
解析 本題考間接問句句型，故答案為(C) when the plane would。

4. (A) why he was not picked
他的教練告訴他沒有被選入去打全國賽的原因。
解析 本題考間接問句句型，答案為(A) why he was not picked。

2 句型速記 是否……

S + V + if / whether + S + V

- I don't know whether he's coming.
  我不知道他是否會來。
- When I asked if she was angry about what she had lost, she admitted to being frustrated occasionally.【學測】
  當我問她是否對於失去的感到憤怒，她承認偶爾覺得很挫折。

觀念透析

1. 當助動詞開頭的 Yes / No 問句（以 yes 或 no 來回答的問句）改間接問句時，須由 whether 或是 if 來引導。如果子句中出現 or not，則只能用 whether；間接問句當主詞、介系詞的受詞或是作為 be 動詞的補語時，也只能用 whether。

- Whether he will come (or not) doesn't concern me.
  （他來不來我才不管。）⇨ 作主詞。
- Her parents concerned about whether she can pass the exam.
  （她的父母關心她是否能通過考試。）⇨ 作介系詞的受詞。
- The question is whether she can keep the secret.
  （問題在於她是否能保密。）⇨ 作 be 動詞的補語。

2. whether 和 if 帶領的間接問句和 wh-疑問詞帶領的間接問句一樣，後方直接接「主詞 + 動詞」。

- Whether you can complete the project in time is another matter.
  （你能否在時間內完成企劃案是另一回事。）
- A young blind American wrote to Mrs. Eustis to ask if there was such a dog to help him.
  （一位年輕的美國盲人寫信詢問悠提斯女士，是否有這樣的狗可以幫助他。）

1. When American hosts ask ________ hungry, you should give a direct answer instead of just being polite.
(A) whether are you (B) are you
(C) if are you (D) if you are

2. The general manager wondered ________ come of the new system.
(A) whether or not good anything would
(B) if anything good would
(C) if or not good anything would
(D) if would anything good

3. I was wondering ________ we should take a break or not.
(A) that (B) if (C) whether (D) since

1. (D) if you are
當美國的主人問你餓了沒，你應該給直接的答案，而非客氣。
解析 本題考「是否」的間接問句，其句型為「if / whether + S + V」，本題應選(D) if you are。

2. (B) if anything good would
總經理不知道新系統會不會有成效。
解析 本題考「是否」的間接問句，其架構為「if / whether + S + V」，此外修飾 anything 的形容詞 good 應採後位修飾，故答案為(B) if anything good would。

3. (C) whether
我不知道我們是否應該休息一下
解析 間接問句有 or not 時，應選 whether。

句型速記 3 附加問句

S + V, 助動詞 / be動詞 + S?

• Many European countries have run into their own economic problem, haven't they?
許多歐洲國家已經遇到了自身的經濟問題，不是嗎？

觀念透析

1. 附加問句是配合直述句的簡短問句。直述句若為肯定句，附加問句則為否定句；直述句為否定句時，附加問句則用肯定句。時態必須與前方直述句一致。附加問句的主詞要用代名詞代替：it 代替 this、that、不定詞或動名詞等；they 代替 these、those、people 等。

• Lady Gaga's new song is a big hit, isn't it?
（女神卡卡的新歌是暢銷曲，是吧？）

• Mother told you not to bully your sister, didn't she?
（媽媽說過不要欺負你妹妹，不是嗎？）

2. 若為祈使句，則附加問句為「will you?」，表客氣的語氣時用「would you?」。

• Be quiet, will you?
（安靜點好嗎?）

3. 若是祈使句「Let's + V」，則附加問句使用「shall we?」

• Let's leave here, shall we?
（我們離開這裡好嗎？）

4. 直述句若是 there 引導的存在句（有……），附加問句用「be動詞 + there?」。

• There are many Thai restaurants on the Sunset Boulevard, aren't there?
（日落大道上有許多泰國餐廳，對嗎？）

1. Steven seldom visits his parents, ________ ?
（史蒂芬很少探訪他的父母，對不對？）
(A) doesn't he (B) does Steven
(C) does he (D) is he

1. 附加問句的主詞須為代名詞，因此不能選(B)。又主要子句因為有否定副詞seldom，所以附加問句應為肯定句。

答案：(C) does he

1. I guess he never goes to church, ________ ?
(A) doesn't he? (B) does he?
(C) don't I (D) do I?

2. She's got a heartwarming smile, ________ ?
(A) isn't she? (B) is she?
(C) has she? (D) hasn't she?

3. I suppose he was not your best schoolmate, ________ ?
(A) don't I? (B) do I?
(C) wasn't he? (D) was he?

4. No one betrayed you, ________ ?
(A) didn't he? (B) did they?
(C) didn't they? (D) did he?

5. Open the door for me, ________ ?
(A) will you? (B) don't you?
(C) shall you? (D) may you?

1. (B) does he?
我猜他從來沒有去教堂，對吧？
解析 本題考附加問句概念。由於主要子句有否定副詞 never，因此附加問句須使用肯定句。

2. (D) hasn't she?
她的微笑令人感到溫馨，對吧？
解析 本題考附加問句概念。主要子句為肯定句，動詞為現在完成式（口語用法），因此附加問句為否定句「hasn't she?」。

3. (D) was he?
我猜他不是你最好的同學，對吧？
解析 本題中尋求肯定的問題是「he was not your best schoolmate」，因此附加問句為「was he?」。

4. (B) did they?
沒有人背叛你，不是嗎？
解析 本題除了考附加問句之外，也考代名詞概念。No one 的代名詞為 they；同時，由於有否定詞 no one，因此附加問句為肯定句。

5. (A) will you?
幫我開門好嗎？
解析 祈使句的附加問句為「will you?」；若是「Let's VR」的句子，則用「shall we?」。

為什麼……呢？（加強疑問語氣）

Why + is / was + it + that + S + V?

- Why is it that the beauty always suffers from the toughest challenges in life?
  為何紅顏總是薄命？

本句型用以強調 why，it 是虛主詞，指後方 that 帶領的完整子句。此句型多用在當問句較長的時候。

- Why was it that he was absent?
  = Why was he absent?
  （他為什麼缺席呢？）
- Why is it that green olives come in glass jars but black olives come in cans?
  （為什麼裝綠橄欖的是玻璃罐，但裝黑橄欖的是鐵罐？）
- Why is it that on a phone or calculator the number five has a little dot on it?
  （為什麼電話或計算機的五號鍵上有個小點？）
- Why is it that no matter what color bubble bath you use the bubbles are always white?
  （為什麼不管使用什麼顏色的泡泡浴，泡沫始終是白色的？）

陷阱題直擊

1. ________ Joseph so hesitant to answer the cop's question?
（為什麼約瑟夫回答警察問題時如此猶豫？）
(A) Why was it that
(B) That is why
(C) Why did
(D) Why was

1. 由問號可知本題為問句，因此(B) That is why 為錯誤答案；「Joseph so hesitant to answer the cop's question」不是完整子句，少了 be 動詞，故(A)及(C)不能選。

答案：(D) Why was

1. 他為什麼很少提到他的兒童時代？(使用 Why is it... 句型)

中翻英：______________________________

2. ________ his gaze was tinged with darkness?

(A) Why was it that　　(B) That is why
(C) Why was　　(D) Was why

3. ________ steal bread? His parents have a bakery!

(A) Why was it that　　(B) That is why he
(C) Why did he　　(D) Why was he

1. Why is it that he rarely mentions his childhood?

2. (A) Why was it that
為何他的目光灰暗？

解析 由問號可知本題為問句，因此(B) That is why 為錯誤答案；再者「his gaze was tinged with darkness」是完整子句，故(C) Why was 以及(D) Was why 為錯誤問句結構，答案為(A) Why is it that。

3. (C) Why did he
為何他要偷麵包？他爸媽開麵包店耶！

解析 由問號可知本題為問句，(B) That is why he 全句應為直述句，故為錯誤答案。「steal bread」不是完整子句，無法接(A) Why was it that，(D) Why was he 應接 stealing bread，故答案為(C) Why did he。

附錄

Appendix

The English Patterns You Got to Know

高分寫作必備句型

善用轉折詞與妙用句型，有助於寫出漂亮的主題句、延伸文意並加強文章流暢度，讓您的英文作文如虎添翼！

Appendix 附錄 高分寫作必備句型

斷定

As far as + S + be + concerned, S + V	就……而言，……
Certainly, S + V	當然，……
For whatever reasons, S + V	無論如何，……
Granted that + S + V	假定……；就算……
Generally speaking, S + V	一般而言，……
I am convinced that...	我相信……
Indeed, S + V, but S + V	沒錯，……，但是……
It is generally agreed that...	一般認為，……
It is widely / generally believed that...	一般認為，……
It is (high) time for + 名詞 + to VR	該是……的時候
Naturally, S + V	當然，……
Needless to say, S + V	不需說，……
Of course, S + V	當然，……
There was no exception that...	毫無例外，……
名詞 + is no exception	……也不例外
There is no denying that...	不可否認，……
There is no doubt that...	無疑地，……
To be sure, S + V	誠然，……
Undoubtedly, S + V	無疑地，……

贊成&反對

I agree with + 人 / 想法	我同意某人／某想法
I agree that...	我同意……
I am a strong believer in + 名詞	我堅信……
I am a big fan of + 名詞	我絕對支持……
I couldn't agree more with + 人 / 想法	我非常同意……
I support the idea that...	我支持……的這種想法
I share the view that...	我持相同的看法
I disagree with + 人 / 想法	我不同意……
I don't like the view that...	我不贊同……這個意見

列舉&補充

S + contain / include / consist of + 名詞	包括……
For example, S + V	例如……
For instance, S + V	例如……
First(ly)... Second(ly)... Third(ly)... Finally...	第一……第二……第三……最後……
First... Next... Then... Finally...	第一……然後……接著……最後……
First of all, S + V	首先，……
In terms of + 名詞, S + V	在……方面，……

..., such as + 名詞 (A, B, and C)	像是……
One..., another..., last...	一個……另一個……最後……
There are A, B, and C.	有 A、B 和 C
To take + 名詞 + for example, S + V	以……為例，……
Also, S + V	而且，……
Again, S + V	再者，……
Beyond that, S + V	除此之外，……
Besides, S + V	此外，……
Equally important, S + V	同樣重要地，……
Furthermore, S + V	而且，……
For one thing, S + V. For another, S + V	一方面，……；另一方面，……
In addition, S + V	此外，……
In addition to + 名詞, S + V	除了……之外，……
Likewise, S + V	同樣的，……；而且，……
Meanwhile, S + V	在此同時，……
Moreover, S + V	再者，……
Namely, S + V	也就是說，……
Specifically, S + V	特別是，……
What's more, S + V	更甚者，……；而且，……

比較&對比

Also, S + V	同樣地，……
In the same way, S + V	同樣地，……
Likewise, S + V	同樣地，……
Similarly, S + V	同樣地，……
Although + S + V, S + V	雖然……，……
Conversely, S + V	相反地，……
Despite + 名詞, S + V	儘管……，……
Even though + S + V, S + V	即使……，……
However, S + V	然而，……
In comparison with + 名詞, S + V	和……相比，……
In contrast, S + V	相比之下，……
Instead, S + V	相反的，……
Instead of + 名詞, S + V	並非……，而是……
In spite of + 名詞, S + V	儘管……，……
Nevertheless, S + V	不過，……
Notwithstanding + 名詞 / S + V, S + V	儘管……，……
On the contrary, S + V	相反地，……
On the other hand, S + V	另一方面，……
Still, S + V	仍然，……
Whereas, S + V	反之，……
Yet, S + V	但是，……

原因&結果

因 + cause / result in / lead to / contribute to / be responsible for + 果	A 造成 B
果 + result from / be a result of / be a consequence of / be due to + 因	B 起因於 A
As a result of + 名詞, S + V	因為……的關係，……
Because of this, S + V	因為如此，……
Because of + 名詞, S + V	因為……，……
Due to + 名詞, S + V	由於……，……；因為，……
Since S + V, S + V	既然……，……
Thanks to + 名詞, S + V	幸虧……，……
The reason why... is that (because)...	（某事的）原因是……
Accordingly, S + V	於是，……
As a result, S + V	結果，……
As a consequence, S + V	因此，……
Consequently, S + V	結果，……
For this reason, S + V	因此，……
Hence, S + V	因此，……
It follows that...	由此可見……
Therefore, S + V	因此，……
Thus, S + V	因此，……

時間&地方

At the same time, S + V	同時，……
Afterward, S + V	後來，……
At last, S + V	最後，……
At present, S + V	目前，……
Currently, S + V	目前，……
During..., S + V	在……期間，……
Eventually, S + V	最後，……
Finally, S + V	最後，……
Gradually, S + V	漸漸地，……
Immediately, S + V	立即地，……
In the future, S + V	在未來，……
In the meantime, S + V	在此時，……
Later, S + V	後來，……
Meanwhile, S + V	同時，……
Once, S + V	曾經，……
Previously, S + V	以前，……
Recently, S + V	最近，……
Simultaneously, S + V	同時，……
Soon, S + V	很快地，……
Suddenly, S + V	突然間，……

Then, S + V	然後，……
At the front, S + V	在前方，……
At the rear, S + V	在後方，……
Beside..., S + V	在……旁邊，……
Behind..., S + V	在……後面，……
Beneath..., S + V	在……下面，……
Beyond..., S + V	越過……，……
In the distance, S + V	在遠處，……
Within sight / Out of sight, S + V	在視線之內 / 之外，……

強 調

Above all, S + V	最重要地，……
Especially, S + V	特別是，……
Indeed, S + V	的確，……
In fact, S + V	其實，……
In particular, S + V	尤其是，……
Most important, S + V	最重要的是，……
Of course, S + V	當然，……
Surely, S + V	沒錯，……
S + be + truly...	……真的……
To tell the truth, S + V	說實話，……

總 結

All in all, S + V	總的來說，……
Above all, S + V	總之，……
As might be expected, S + V	正如所料，……
Finally, S + V	最後，……
In any case, S + should + VR	無論如何，……都應該……
In this case, S + V	既然這樣，……
In such a context, S + V	在這種情況下，……
In a word, S + V	簡言之，……
In short, S + V	簡言之，……
In brief, S + V	簡言之，……
In conclusion, S + V	總而言之，……
In other words, S + V	換句話說，……
Lastly, S + V	最後，……
Last but not least, S + V	最後也最重要的是……
On the whole, S + V	整體而言，……
To conclude, S + V	總而言之，……
To sum up, S + V	總而言之，……
To summarize, S + V	總而言之，……

國家圖書館出版品預行編目資料

4週破解英文常考句型／張翔、易敬能著
新北市：鴻漸文化，2012.08

面； 公分

ISBN 978-986-6187-76-6（平裝）

1.英語 2.句法

805.169 101008285

4週破解 英文常考句型

編著者●張翔、易敬能
出版總監●歐綾纖
出版者●鴻漸文化
副總編輯●陳雅貞
發行人●Jack
責任編輯●羅麗如
美術設計●吳吉昌
排版●王鴻立
編輯中心●新北市中和區中山路二段366巷10號10樓
電話●(02)2248-7896 傳真●(02)2248-7758

總經銷●采舍國際有限公司
發行中心●235新北市中和區中山路二段366巷10號3樓
電話●(02)8245-8786 傳真●(02)8245-8718
退貨中心●235新北市中和區中山路三段120-10號（青年廣場）B1
電話●(02)2226-7768 傳真●(02)8226-7496
郵政劃撥戶名●采舍國際有限公司
郵政劃撥帳號●50017206（劃撥請另付一成郵資）
新絲路網路書店●www.silkbook.com
華文網網路書店●www.book4u.com.tw
PChome商店街●store.pchome.com.tw/readclub
出版日期●2012年8月

本書係透過華文聯合出版平台（www.book4u.com.tw）自資出版印行，並委由采舍國際有限公司（www.silk.com）總經銷。

全系列展示中心 新北市中和區中山路二段366巷10號10樓（新絲路書店）

本書採減碳印製流程並使用優質中性紙（Acid & Alkali Free）與環保油墨印製。

Smart Cards 句型背誦卡

the + 單數名詞

表全體或抽象概念

- The polar bear is a bear native largely within the Arctic Circle and its surrounding seas and land masses.
  北極熊是遍布於北極圈及周圍海域和土地的本土熊類。
- The average visitor to the Middle East finds camels fascinating.
  一般前往中東的遊客都深深地為駱駝著迷。

1

the + adj.

形容詞作名詞（集合用法）

- The rich are not always happier than the poor.
  富人未必都比窮人幸福。
- The homeless are a diverse group facing many difficulties.
  街友是一群面臨著許多困境的多元化族群。

2

①名詞 + 現在分詞 / 過去分詞
②形容詞 + 現在分詞 / 過去分詞
③副詞 + 現在分詞 / 過去分詞
④形容詞 + 單數名詞-ed
⑤數量 + 單數名詞

複合形容詞

- Wedding planning is very time-consuming.
  籌備婚禮非常耗時。
- Smart phones are now in widespread use.
  智慧型手機目前被廣泛使用。
- He is a kind-hearted old man.
  他是一個好心的老人。

3

so + adj. / adv. + as to + VR
so + adj. / adv. + that + 子句
such + a + (adj.) + N + that + 子句

如此……以致於……

- Sam was so lazy as to enrage his supervisor.
  山姆懶散到使他上司發怒了。
- Jason ran so fast that no one could catch up with him.
  傑森跑得很快，以致於沒有人可以追得上他。
- He is such an honest man that everybody trusts him.
  他很誠實，以致於（所以）大家都相信他。

4

adj. / adv. + enough + to VR

足夠去……

- It is warm enough to swim.
  天氣夠溫暖可以去游泳了。
- Does he sing well enough to attend the *American Idol* show?
  他唱歌有好到可以參加《美國偶像》嗎？

5

to one's + 心理名詞

令某人……的是

- To no one's surprise, it has enjoyed similar popularity.【學測】
  毫不令人意外的是，它受到同樣的歡迎。
- I ordered a dress online, but, much to my disappointment, it was not as beautiful as it looked on the website.
  我網購了一件洋裝，但令我非常失望的是，它並沒有網站上看起來這麼漂亮。

6

for / of / with / through + N

表原因、理由的介系詞

- She trembled for fear.
  她因害怕而發抖。
- Nobody ever died of laughter.
  一笑治百病。
- With John away, we've got more room.
  約翰不在，我們的空間寬敞了一些。
- He made a serious mistake through carelessness.
  他由於粗心大意而犯下嚴重的錯。

7

with + the V-ing of + 名詞

隨著……

- With the approaching of Easter, winter departs and spring is near.
  隨著復活節的逼近，冬天遠去，春天翩然而至。
- Glass bottles became more and more popular in France with the opening of the Baccarat Factory.
  隨著巴卡拉工廠的開張，玻璃瓶在法國越來越炙手可熱。
- With the returning of the king, the Middle Earth reverted to its original peace.
  隨著王者再臨，中土回復原來的和平。

8

①besides + N
②except + N

①除了……還有……；②除了……以外

- I have a few friends besides you.
  除了你，我還有一些朋友。
  （我的朋友也包括你）
- Everyone will go except you.
  除了你之外，每個人都去。
  （去的人之中沒有你）

9

both A and B
A as well as B

A 和 B 都……

- Both Jeremy and Henry are engineers.
  傑洛米和亨利都是工程師。
- Jeremy as well as Henry is an engineer.
  傑洛米和亨利都是工程師。

10

①not A but B
②not only A but (also) B

①不是 A 而是 B；②不但 A 而且 B

- She is not my sister but my niece.
  她不是我妹妹，而是我姪女。
- Not only Jeremy but also Henry is an engineer.
  不只是傑洛米，亨利也是工程師。

11

①either A or B
②neither A nor B

①不是 A 就是 B
②既不是 A 也不是 B

- Now you have two choices. Either you give up your property or you go to jail.
  現在你有兩個選擇，不是放棄財產，就是去坐牢。（兩者擇一）
- Neither Jason nor Hulk is coming to the party.
  傑森和浩克都不會出席派對。（兩者皆非）

12

the former...the latter...
= that...this...
= the one...the other...

前者……，後者……

- The generation gap between parents and their teenage children occurs when the former have different values from the latter.
  父母和青少年之間的代溝發生在前者的價值觀與後者不同的時候。

13

①one...the other...
②one...another...the other...

①一個…，另一個…；②一個…，一個…，另一個…

- I have two brothers; one is in Taipei and the other is in Tainan.
  我有兩個兄弟，一個在台北，一個在台南。
- I possess three cars. One is a pick-up truck, another is a sedan and the other is a sports car.
  我有三輛車：一輛是小貨車，一輛是轎車，另一輛是跑車。

14

some...others...

有些……，另有些……

- Some are for the project, and others are against it.
  有一些人支持這項計畫，另有一些人反對。
- Some like skiing, while others like skating.
  有些人喜歡滑雪，也有些人喜歡溜冰。

15

some...others...still others...

有些……，有些……，另有些……

- At the swimming pool, some are swimming, others (= some) are sunbathing, and still others are drinking cocktails.
  游泳池畔，有些人在游泳，有些人在做日光浴，還有些人在喝著雞尾酒。

16

that of
those of

的……（代替前述名詞）

- The price of wheat is lower than that of rice.
  小麥的價錢比米還要低。
- The igloo's walls were solid and airtight whereas those of the tepee permitted a great deal of air to enter.
  雪屋的牆壁堅硬密閉，而圓錐帳篷的（牆壁）可讓空氣大量流通。

17

may / might as well + VR

大可、不妨

- We may as well build reservoirs where water can be stored in case of drought.
  我們不妨建水庫來儲水，以防範乾旱。
- Being such a successful pianist, he may as well be proud of himself, but Pletnev is not satisfied with that.
  身為成功鋼琴家，普雷特涅夫大可以自己為傲，但他不以此自滿。

18

can't (help) but + VR = can't help + V-ing

忍不住、不得不

- He cannot help but walk out of his house to check the abnormal noise from the bushes.
  他忍不住走出房子，查看灌木叢傳來的異常噪音。
- I can't help bursting out laughing every time I see him.
  我每次看到他都忍不住笑出來。

19

can not be too + adj. / adv.

再……也不為過

- Winnie thinks that she cannot be too full in an all-you-can-eat restaurant.
  薇妮認為在吃到飽的餐廳，吃再飽也不為過。
- One cannot be too cautious while driving at night.
  夜間開車盡量小心。

20

those who + are / V
people who + are / V

凡是……的人

- Christmas is a time for us to send Christmas cards to those who live far away.
  聖誕節是讓我們寄聖誕卡給遠方的人們的時節。
- People who have to make a living on their own may envy those who can succeed in the business of their family's.
  必須自立更生的人，也許會羨慕能叱吒於家庭事業的人。

21

...when + S +V

……之時

- No one knows exactly when our history began.
  沒有人確實知道我們的歷史從什麼時候開始。
- What can the police in one country do when criminals escape to another nation?
  罪犯逃到外國時，警方能怎麼辦？

22

the way + { that / in which } + 形容詞子句

……的方法、方式

- The way (that) they look at the world is different.
  = The way in which they look at the world is different.
  他們看這個世界的方式不同。

23

, which + V
, who + V

補述用法（非限定子句）

- I live in New York, which is on the east coast of the United States.
  我住在紐約，它位於美國的東岸。
- All of the beautiful scenes were made up by John, who was a blind man.
  所有的美景都是身為盲人的約翰編出來的。

24

what is + 比較級

更……的是

- He speaks English very well; what is more, he is good at English literature.
  他英語說得很好。此外，他精通英國文學。
- The forest turned dusky; what's worse, it began to bucket down.
  森林變陰暗了，更慘的是，開始要下大雨了。

25

S + go / enjoy + V-ing
S + do + (the) + V-ing

做／喜歡／從事某運動或活動

- Vivian went canoeing when she back-packed in California last year.
  薇薇安去年在加州自助旅行時，玩了獨木舟。
- Harry enjoys being a seeker in the match.
  哈利喜歡在比賽中當搜捕手。
- I do some jogging every morning.
  我每天早晨跑步。

26

There is no use + V-ing
= It is (of) no use + V-ing / to VR
= It is useless + to VR

做……是沒有用的

- There is no use crying over spilt milk.
  = It is no use crying over spilt milk.
  = It is no use to cry over spilt milk.
  = It is useless to cry over spilt milk.
  覆水難收。

27

have + { no / little / much } + trouble + (in) + V-ing

在……方面沒有／沒什麼／有很大的困難

- With a boy leading the way, we had little trouble in finding the old castle.
  有小男孩帶路，我們輕鬆地就找到了古城堡。
- They had much trouble tracing the footprint of the beast because of the heavy rain.
  大雨讓他們很難追蹤野獸的足跡。

28

① S + be + worth + V-ing
② S + be + worthy + { of N / of V-ing / to VR }
③ It is worthwhile + { V-ing / to VR }

值得……

- This book is worth reading.
  = This book is worthy of being read.
  = This book is worthy to be read.
  = It is worthwhile to read this book.
  這本書值得一讀。

29

{ stop / prevent / protect } + O + from + V-ing

阻止、防止……做某事；保護……不被……

- It is a matter of urgency to prevent endangered animals from becoming extinct.
  防止動物瀕臨絕種是很緊急的事，我們不能再拖了。

30

S + {ask / allow / (would) like / tell / persuade} + sb. + to VR

要求（允許、想要、吩咐、說服）某人做某事

- The class was not allowed to leave until the bell rang.
  直到鐘響了班上的學生才獲准離開。

31

S + be likely + to VR
It is likely + that + S + V

有可能、似乎

- People without confidence are likely to be influenced by others.
  沒有信心的人很有可能會被他人影響。
- It is not likely that he should have written it.
  他不可能會寫那樣的東西。

32

S + be + adj. + to VR

某人對某事的情緒

- I am glad to hear that you have been admitted to a university.
  我很高興聽到你進入大學。
- The teacher was enraged to see that the whole class was brawling.
  看到全班在吵鬧，老師很生氣。

33

V-ing / Vp.p. ..., S + V

分詞構句（主詞相同）

- He went out of the secret chamber, holding Tim Riddle's diary in his hand.
  他走出密室，手上拿著提姆瑞斗的日記。
- Written in simple English, the book is suitable for beginners.
  由於用簡單的英語寫成，本書適合初學者。

34

S_1 + V-ing / Vp.p., S_2 + V

獨立分詞構句（主詞不同）

- When night came on, we started on our way home.
  = Night coming on, we started on our way home.
  夜晚來臨，我們踏上歸程。
- If weather permits, we will have a picnic tomorrow.
  = Weather permitting, we will have a picnic tomorrow.
  如果天氣許可，我們明天會去野餐。

35

There is / are + S + V-ing（表主動）
There is / are + S + Vp.p.（表被動）

有……（there 句型）

- There are long lines of people waiting to get into Sodagreen's concert.
  大排長龍的人們等著進去看蘇打綠的演唱會。
- There are many wild animals killed in Africa.
  非洲有許多野生動物遭到殺害。

36

, including + 名詞 / 代名詞
= , 名詞 / 代名詞 + included
= , inclusive of + 名詞 / 代名詞

包括了……；……也被包括在內

- All on the plane were lost, including the pilot.
  = All on the plane were lost, the pilot included.
  = All on the plane were lost, inclusive of the pilot.
  機上的人全部罹難，包括機長在內。

37

S + V + with + N + { 現在分詞 / 過去分詞 / 形容詞 / 副詞 / 介系詞片語 }

帶有……；有……的（表附帶之狀態或動作）

- She sat reading, with her cat sleeping beside her.
  她坐著讀書，她的貓睡在旁邊。
- He went angrily away without a word spoken.
  他很生氣地走開，一句話都不說。

38

①物 + be used + { to + VR / for + V-ing / N }

②人 + { be used to / get used to } + V-ing / N

used 的用法① 被拿來作……之用
used 的用法② 習慣於……

- The Romans realized that glass could be used to make windows.
  羅馬人明白玻璃可以用來製作窗戶。
- I am used to having breakfast at home.
  我習慣在家吃早餐。

39

③人 / 物 + used to + VR

used 的用法③ 過去常……

- Bill used to arrive at school on time but now he is late for school almost every day; his behavior is quite abnormal.
  比爾以前都準時上學，現在他幾乎每天遲到，他的行為很異常。

40

S + { suggest / insist / recommend / demand / order } + that + S + (should) + VR

表建議、堅持、推薦、要求、命令

- He suggested that I share relevant personal stories to make my point.
  他建議我分享個人相關故事，好證明我的論點。
- When it was time for the bill, he told the manager he had no money and suggested that he have him arrested.【指考】
  結帳時，他告知經理他沒錢，並建議將其逮捕。

41

all (that) + S + { have to do / can do } + is + (to) VR

只需做／只能的事就是……

- All that we have to do for a happy life is be ourselves.
  為了快樂的人生，我們所要做的就是做自己。
- You are on your maternity leave. Now all you have to do is rest and take good care of your health.
  你正在放產假，現在你只要休息和照顧自己的健康就好了。

42

{see / watch / hear, feel / notice / ...} + O + {VR, V-ing}

感官動詞（看見／聽見／感覺／注意……）

- We saw the actor fall down.
  我們看見這個演員跌倒。
- I heard someone knocking loudly last night.
  我昨晚聽到有人大聲地敲門。

43

S + make / let / have + O + VR

使……；讓……（使役動詞）

- She makes her mother cry.
  她讓她母親哭了。
- My father would not let me take a taxi on my own.
  我爸爸不會讓我獨自搭計程車。
- That mother should have her children be quiet in public.
  那位母親應該讓她的小孩在公共場合安靜一點。

44

S + {keep, leave} + O + OC

使保持……的狀態

- They help to keep the tradition alive.
  他們協助讓傳統保存下來。
- People with mysophobia always keep their rooms tidy and spotless.
  有潔癖的人總是讓房間井然有序、一塵不染。

45

①By the time (when) S + V-ed, S + had Vp.p.
②By the time (when) S + V, S + will have Vp.p.

在……之前，已經……

- By the time the President gets here, we will have stood along the road to welcome him.
  總統到了的時候，我們會已經沿路站好迎接他。
- The restaurant had already been torn down by the time they met again.
  他們重逢時，餐廳已經被拆掉了。

46

It + is / has been + 時間 + since + S + 過去式

自從……已經有……

- It's a long time since I started my correspondence with Peter.
  我和彼得書信往來很久了。
- It has been a decade since Isabella dumped me.
  依莎貝拉甩了我已經10年了。

47

when / while / as + S + V

當……的時候

- When the sun sets, the ants seal up the entrance to their nest.【學測】
  日落時，螞蟻會封住巢穴的入口。
- As I dialed Andy's cell phone number, I don't know what I would say exactly.
  當我撥安迪的手機號碼時，我不知道我到底會說什麼。

48

once / as soon as + S + V
S + had no sooner + Vp.p. + than + S + V

一……就……

- Once you start doing Sudoku puzzles, it's hard to stop.
  一旦開始玩數獨，就停不了手。
- A person will grow out of allergy as soon as he or she reaches adulthood.【學測】
  人成年後就會擺脫過敏了。
- Yvonne had no sooner come than she was informed of discharged from her position.
  依梵剛到就被通知被免職了。

49

It is + adj. / N + { to VR / that + S + V }

對某事表達意見

- It is hard to break with a deep-rooted habit.
  積習難改。
- It is mean that you talked to Mom that way.
  你跟媽媽那樣說話很過分。
- It is a pity that you couldn't come.
  你不能來真可惜。

50

S + { think / consider / believe / find / take } + it + adj. / N + to VR

認為、覺得某事……

- Do you think it wise to interfere?
  你覺得干預是明智的嗎？
- I consider it bad table manners to open your mouth while eating.
  我認為進食的時候打開嘴巴是不好的餐桌禮儀。

51

S + seem + to VR
It seems + that + S + V

似乎……

Ann seems to be afraid of snakes.
= It seems that Ann is afraid of snakes.
安好像很怕蛇。

52

It is said that...
It is reported that...
It is believed that...

引述傳聞、報導、他人說法

- It is said that he is a millionaire.
  = People say that he is a millionaire.
  據說他是個百萬富翁。

53

It is + { 主詞 / 受詞 / 時間、地方副詞 / 副詞子句 } + that + S + V

正是……；就是……（強調句）

- It was about 600 years ago that the first clock with a face and an hour hand was made.
  就在六百年前，第一個有鐘面和時針的時鐘問世。
- It was with teamwork that we defeat the visiting team.
  正是靠著團隊合作，我們打敗了挑戰隊伍。

54

It takes + (人) + 時間 + to VR
事 take(s) + (人) + 時間
人 spend(s) + 時間 + (in) + V-ing

花費時間

- It took me three days to finish my homework.
  我花了三天完成我的作業。
- The flight will take eight hours.
  航程需要八個小時。
- She spends five hours studying every day.
  她每天花五個小時讀書。

55

It costs + (人) + 錢 / 代價 + to VR
物 cost(s) + (人) + 錢
人 spend(s) + 錢 + on + 物

花費金錢

- It cost me about $20,000 to buy the newest model of iPhone.
  最新型的 iPhone 花了我兩萬塊。
- The dress is going to cost her an arm and a leg.
  這件洋裝將會花她一大筆錢。
- My sister spent 5,000 dollars on her shoes.
  我姊姊花了五千元買下那雙鞋。

56

as + adj. / adv. + as...

像……一樣……

- Finding a soul mate is not as easy as you imagined.
  找到靈魂伴侶不如你想像般簡單。
- Rebecca is not as kind as her brother (is).
  瑞貝佳不像她哥哥這麼好心。

57

①A + be superior to + B
②A + be inferior to + B

①A較B優秀；②A較B差

- The products of our company are superior to those of yours.
  我們公司的產品比你們公司的（產品）好。
- Synthetic fabric is inferior to cotton fabric.
  化學纖維布料不如棉質布料好。

58

倍數 + as + adj. + as...
倍數 + 比較級 + than...
倍數 + as + { many + Ns + as... / much + N + as... }
倍數 + the + N + of...

……幾倍於……；……是……的幾倍

- The window is three times as large as that one.
  = The window is three times larger than that one.
  這扇窗戶是那扇窗戶的三倍大。
- This box is twice the size of that one.
  這個盒子是那個的兩倍大。

59

prefer + N / V-ing + to + N / V-ing
prefer + to VR + rather than + VR
S + would rather + VR + than + VR
S + would + VR + rather than + VR

較喜歡……而較不喜歡……；寧可……而不願……

- I prefer sleeping to watching TV.
  = I prefer to sleep rather than watch TV.
  = I would rather sleep than watch TV.
  = I would sleep rather than watch TV.
  我寧願睡覺而不願看電視。

60

The + 比較級 + S + V, the + 比較級 + S + V

越……，越……

- The more you practice, the better your English will be.
  你越練習，你的英文就會越好。
- The sooner, the better.
  越快越好。

61

as S_1 + V_1, { so + S_2 + V_2 / so + be動詞 / 助動詞 + S_2 }

正如……，……也一樣……

- Just as a perfect lover never exists, so a perfect job can never be found.
  就如同完美情人不存在一樣，完美的工作也不可能找得到。
- As wealth ruins your life, so does poverty.
  如同財富會毀滅人生，貧窮也會。

62

S + V + { in order that / so that } + 子句

S + V + { in order to / so as to } + VR

為了……；以便……

- We prayed that the storm could let up soon so that we could start out.
  我們祈禱，暴風雨盡快停歇，這樣我們才能出發。
- I came in order to say goodbye to him.
  我來是為了和他說再見。

63

to VR..., S + V...

為了……

- To avoid misunderstanding, he gave her a clear explanation.
  為了避免誤解，他給她做了清楚的解釋。
- To develop financial responsibility, children should learn to manage their own money at a young age.
  為了養成財務責任心，小孩應該在年幼時學習管理自己的金錢。

64

S + V + { lest / for fear (that) / in case (that) } + S + (should) + VR

以免、唯恐……

- You must work hard lest you (should) fail.
  = You must work hard for fear (that) you (should) fail.
  = You must work hard in case (that) you (should) fail.
  你一定要努力工作以免失敗。

65

① { because of + N / because + S + V }

② since / as + S + V

③ { due to / owing to / on account of / thanks to } + N

因為、由於（表原因）

- He spent 24 years in prison because of his fight for equal rights for all races. 【學測】
  他因為爭取種族平等而坐牢24年。
- Owing to the typhoon, the game was cancelled.
  由於颱風，比賽取消了。

66

though / although / even though } + $S_1 + V_1, S_2 + V_2$

儘管、雖然……

- Although my computer is very old, it still runs very well.
  雖然我的電腦很舊，但仍運作得很好。
- He will come over for dinner even though it rains.
  即使下雨，他還是會過來吃晚餐。

67

No matter + 疑問詞 + S + V, S + V

無論如何、不管……

- No matter how well we do at school, most of us will feel inadequate when we go into the adult world.
  無論我們在學校表現多好，大多數人在進入成人世界後，都會覺得不夠。
- No matter where you go, I'll go with you.
  不論你去哪裡，我都與你同行。

68

名詞 / 形容詞 / 副詞 } + as / though + S + V, S + V

儘管……，還是……

- Icy as the road was, he drove very fast.
  儘管路面結冰，他開車依然飛快。
- Fast though the taxi runs, sometimes you arrive at the destination faster by MRT.
  儘管計程車跑得快，有時搭捷運還比較快到達目的地。

69

even if / even though

縱使、即使

- He promised to come even if it rains.
  他保證即使下雨他還是會來。
- My father attended my wedding on time even though the rain poured.
  即使下了傾盆大雨，我爸爸還是準時參加我的婚禮。

70

Whether (or not) + S + V, S + V

無論是否……

- I'll go on with my project, whether I can get enough support or not.
  不論是否能得到足夠的支持，我都會繼續我的計畫。
- The economy is improving whether conservatives like it or not.
  經濟在復甦，不管保守派喜不喜歡。

71

Unless S + V..., S + V...

除非……，否則……

- We cannot achieve true friendships unless we are true to ourselves.
  除非我們對自己誠實，否則我們無法實現真正的友誼。
- Your mind tends to grow dull unless you exercise it with new stuff on and off.
  你腦子會變遲鈍，除非你不時用新事物鍛鍊它。

72

If + S + V, S + (will) + V

如果……就……

- If you follow the directions closely, you will find it easy to operate the new machine.【學測】
  如果你仔細地遵照指示，你會發現新機器很容易操縱。
- If it rains tomorrow, I will not go to the party.
  如果明天下雨，我將不會去舞會。

73

as / so long as + S + V...

只要……的話……

- As long as the taxpayers want the school, we build a school.
  只要納稅人希望有學校，我們就蓋學校。
- Paris is a wonderful place to stay as long as it's within your budget.
  只要預算許可，巴黎絕對是值得停留的美妙城市。

74

If + S + { were / V-ed }..., S + { should / would / could / might } + VR

如果……（與現在事實相反）

- If we were in Barcelona today, we would be able to see Gaudi's buildings.
  如果我們今天在巴塞隆那，我們就能看到高第的建築。
- If I had a million dollars, I might donate some fund to some charities.
  如果我有一百萬美元，我會捐出一些錢給慈善機構。

75

If + S + had Vp.p., S + { should / would / could / might } + have + Vp.p.

如果……（與過去事實相反）

- If I had studied harder, I might have passed the bar.
  若我當初念書認真點，我也許就能取得律師執照。
- If you had driven more cautiously, this accident might have been avoided.
  若你當初更加小心開車，這起事故可能就可以避免的。

76

{ Were it not for + N, / If it were not for + N, / If there were not for + N, } + S + { would / should / could / might } + VR

要不是……　（與現在事實相反）

- Were it not for the heat of the sun, nothing could live.
  若無陽光，萬物便不能生存。
- Were it not for (= If it were not for) that annoying habit of his, Jerry would be an attractive man.
  要不是他那個令人厭惡的習慣，傑里會是一位很迷人的男性。

77

{ Had it not been for + N, / If it had not been for + N, / If there had been no + N, } + S + { would / should / could / might } + have Vp.p.

要不是……　（與過去事實相反）

- Had it not been for her, I would have got lost this morning.
  今早要不是她，我就迷路了。
- If it had not been for his help, my plan would have failed last year.
  要不是他的幫助，我去年的計畫可能就會失敗了。

78

S + wish (that) + { S + were / V-ed（與現在事實相反）
S + had + Vp.p.（與過去事實相反）}

但願⋯⋯

- I wish I had a brother to accompany me.
  真希望我有一個哥哥陪我。
- I wish that I had gone to the movies with you last weekend.
  我真希望上週末有和你一起去看電影。

79

If only + 假設語氣子句
= How I wish + 假設語氣子句

但願⋯⋯就好了（表示強烈的希望）

- If only I knew how to use a computer.
  = (How) I wish (that) I knew how to use a computer.
  要是我知道怎麼用電腦就好了。

80

S + must / may / can't + have + Vp.p.

表對過去肯定／可能／否定的推測

- He must have forgotten my name.
  他一定忘了我的名字。
- It must have rained, for the ground was very wet this morning.
  今早地面濕濕的，一定是下過雨了。
- You can't have seen him last week ; he was in New York then.
  你上個禮拜不可能看到他，他當時在紐約。

81

S + ought to / should + have + Vp.p.

本來應該⋯⋯（與過去事實相反）

- Judith ought to have practiced more then so she would be better prepared for this chance.
  茱蒂絲當時應該多練習，對於這個機會才能更有所準備。

82

the last + N + { to VR
(that) + S + V }

最不可能、最不適合、最不願意

- He is the last person to steal your money.
  他絕非是偷你錢的人。
- The last thing he wants to do is to offend you.
  他最不願意做的事就是觸怒你。

83

can't / never / no... + without + V-ing / N

沒有⋯⋯不⋯⋯；每當⋯⋯必定⋯⋯

- They never discuss without quarreling.
  他們討論一定吵架。
- I can't do anything without consulting you.
  我做事不能不問你。

84

not necessarily

未必、不一定

- A happy man does not necessarily have a fortune.
  幸福的人未必富有。
- Inventions do not necessarily refer to those big in size. They can be as small as the safety pin or the safety razor.
  發明不一定指體積大的物品，也可以小如別針或安全刮鬍刀。

85

too + adj. / adv. + to VR

太……而不能……

- One is never too old to learn.
  活到老學到老。
- It is never too late to mend.
  亡羊補牢，為時未晚。

86

only + { 副詞片語 / 副詞子句 } + be動詞 / 助動詞 + S + V

只有……才能……

- Only in Taiwan can you enjoy a wide variety of cuisine at low prices.
  只有在台灣，你才能以低價品嚐各式各樣的美食。
- Only when one is away from home does he realize how sweet home is.
  只有當一個人離家時，才知道家的甜蜜。

87

{ 否定副詞 / 否定副詞片語 / 副詞子句 } + be動詞 / 助動詞 + S + V

否定詞置於句首

- Not a word did he say.
  他不發一語。
- Little did I think we would meet 30 years later.
  我想不到我們30年後會重逢。
- Not until I saw him did I feel relieved.
  我看到他才感到放心。

88

S + be動詞 / 助動詞 + not + V + until...
= It is not until... + that + S + V
= Not until... + 助動詞 + S + V

直到……才……

- We do not realize the true value of health until we lose it.
  = It is not until we lose it that we realize the true value of health.
  = Not until we lose it do we realize the true value of health.
  直到失去健康我們才知道它真正的價值。

89

祈使句 + { , and / , or } + S + V

如果……，那麼……

- Take a look of these photos, and you will know how lovely it is.
  看看這些照片，就會知道它有多麼可愛。
- Give me liberty, or give me death.
  不自由，毋寧死。

90

be / make + sure + { of + N / to + VR / that + S + V / wh-疑問詞 + S + V }

務必……、確定……

- Make sure you eat right when you are expecting a baby!
當你在懷孕時，務必要確保飲食正確。
- Be sure you're right, then go ahead.
確定你是對的，便勇往直前。

91

①How + adj. / adv. + S + V

②What + { a(n) + adj. + N / adj. + N(s) } + S + V

多麼……（感嘆句）

- How beautiful this little village is!
這個小村莊真漂亮！
- What a cute little baby he is!
他真是個可愛的嬰兒！

92

{ 直述句 / 祈使句 / 一般問句 } + 疑問詞 + S + V

間接問句

- I don't know why she is upset.
我不知道她為什麼生氣。
- Try to remember who opens the door.
試著記住是誰打開這扇門。
- Do you know where she lives?
你知道她住在哪裡嗎？

93

S + V + if / whether + S + V

是否……

- I don't know whether he's coming.
我不知道他是否會來。
- When I asked if she was angry about what she had lost, she admitted to being frustrated occasionally.【學測】
當我問她是否對於失去的感到憤怒，她承認偶爾覺得很挫折。

94

S + V, 助動詞 / be動詞 + S?

附加問句

- Many European countries have run into their own economic problem, haven't they?
許多歐洲國家已經遇到了自身的經濟問題，不是嗎？
- There are many Thai restaurants on the Sunset Boulevard, aren't there?
日落大道上有許多泰國餐廳，對嗎？

95

Why + is / was + it + that + S + V?

為什麼……呢？（加強疑問語氣）

- Why is it that the beauty always suffers from the toughest challenges in life?
為何紅顏總是薄命？
- Why was it that he was absent?
= Why was he absent?
他為什麼缺席呢？

96